PEACEMAKER

A DALÍ TAMAREIA MISSION
BOOK 2

E. M. HAMILL

STAR
BARD
BOOKS

DEDICATION

For Renee, Lori, and Ann
Love you three to the moon and back

ACKNOWLEDGMENTS

Once again, this book would not be the same if it weren't for the input of my fearless critique partners, who keep me on my toes and challenge me to become a better writer. Many thanks to LA Ashton, who alpha read this book, and to my betas Ashley Miller, Janean Dobos, and especially Katherine Henry Alexander for input on martial arts scenes.

Michael Mammay was invaluable for recon of plot holes, and critique of military, battle, and weapons scenes. Any remaining mistakes are entirely my own.

Jami Nord, my developmental editor, and partner in crime: thank you so much! You are my lens of clarity.

And thank you to the creative genius JCaleb Designs, who created the absolutely kick-ass cover for the second edition of *Peacemaker*.

A huge thank you to all the readers who took Dalí into their hearts and have been asking when more stories were coming. I will finally graduate from college at an advanced age just after this book goes to press, so I will be able to write things again that don't require APA citations!

My eternal love and thanks go out to my life partner Mark and my now adult children, Kylan and Gabriel, who tolerated this increasingly frustrated writer over the last two years as I tried to finish this novel and complete my BSN (firmly on my list of things NOT to do in the future).

Lastly, thank you to Ashley Kingsbury at NineStar Press for editing this book in its original form. I am forever grateful to you and Raevyn.

CHAPTER
ONE

I KEEP ENDING up in labyrinthine mazes. There's a psychological diagnosis in there, somewhere.

On the surface, Bariish displayed its harsh beauty, jagged mountains undulating in parti-colored heaves of red, yellow, and white. But beneath the planet's landscape lay a hostile, ugly environment. Valuable ore streaked the planet's crust in tight wires, a coveted material bringing astronomical prices in the open market. Danger lurked in the greed of fellow miners who would just as soon steal the ore someone else coaxed out of the rocky matrix to increase the weight of their own day's take, and thus the credits received at the end of their stint. Guards maintained a presence in the shaft, but the dark, noisy area contained warrens of tunnels which couldn't all be patrolled at once.

The heat in the mineshaft stifled me. Vibration from the pneumatic hammer pounded my bones as I chiseled out narrow fragments of rare metal and dropped them into a half-full bucket anchored between my boots. Sweat rolled off my back underneath the protective coveralls, burned my eyes behind the goggles I wore, and noise-canceling headgear formed a swamp around my ears. I didn't look forward to removing any of it.

Bitter dust rimed my mouth as I leaned the hammer against the stony wall and dug a water ration out of the deep thigh pocket of my coveralls. Heads-up informatics in my goggles displayed the depth from the surface, air quality, and the time remaining on my shift. Fifteen minutes, all conditions green. I was ready to get out. The claustrophobic awareness of two kilometers of rock overhead remained a constant companion and pressed as heavily as the still atmosphere in the tunnel. I finished the water and picked up my hammer again.

For more than two months, Ziggy and I had been undercover in this illegal mining operation. The first couple of weeks, I did little but register my take with the clerks, go back to our ship on the sandy apron where the rest of the itinerant miners camped, and pick blistered skin off my hands before collapsing into an exhausted coma. The hard physical labor on a planet where gravity was denser than my accustomed Gs proved a new conditioning challenge. My endurance increased each day, but there were limits on the number of hours we were allowed to scrape our take from the mine. The sound of the warning klaxon brought a sense of relief.

Many Nos, Cthash, and Tolkish drifters worked on the day shift: humanoid, oxygen-breathing species like mine, all drawn by the promise of galactic credits, having left their home systems for reasons of their own. I was the only human in the shaft, night or day. The only one in camp at the time. I kept a low profile, but oddities tend to draw attention.

I hate it when that happens.

A shove to the middle of my back sent me off balance. The powerful excavator danced in an uncontrolled frenzy across the rocks, and I spun, the container of ore threatening to spill. I managed to right it with one heel and shut off the hammer.

Two Nos stood behind me, sneering beneath steamed-up

goggles and safety helmets. Tracks of sweat traced pale lines against their grime-covered, glacial skin. The taller of the two thrust a quarter-full ore bucket at me and pantomimed I should empty my take into his.

I'd seen these assholes before. They'd performed the same act with other workers that week, beating the shit out of anyone who refused.

A quick glance around showed no guards close by—not that they would have heard anything over the din of mining activity. I leaned the equipment against the rock wall and capped my ore canister, leaving it inside the alcove where I worked. Empty-handed, I stepped out.

My specialized senses can't help me where the Nos are concerned. They're flat nulls, a blank broadcast muffling the spread of my empathic nets, but I've come to learn from close work with a Nos crewmate all I need to know is written in their body language.

Tall guy pointed to my bucket again and then to his. Tense, jerky. The smug, shorter Nos behind him stood in a relaxed, expectant slouch. So, he was the one in charge.

I shook my head and crossed my arms over my chest. *What are you going to do about it?* Excitement sang through my bloodstream, anticipating a fight. The pain of muscle beginning to shift in response to my changeling hormones remained invisible under my coveralls. The ache between my shoulder blades throbbed in a knot of eager, pent-up energy.

The taller Nos shoved his container at the short guy, who calmly took it and stepped back. I used the time to move into the center of the shaft, into the clear space between the magnetic tracks upon which the crew carrier rode.

He swung at me. *Here we go.*

I blocked the punch with my left hand and jabbed up with my right, striking the sensitive cartilage beneath his chin with the sharp angle of my thumb and fingers. His head jerked and he uttered a surprised grunt of pain. His other hand lashed out to sweep air as I ducked and drove both fists into his exposed left flank. He staggered back. I eased into a waiting stance, my fists raised as I circled and tried to keep both Nos in my line of sight. The little guy raised his goggles to his forehead and paced, trying to get behind me.

Rubbing his ribs, the tall one eyed me warily. His scrawny friend bounced on the balls of his feet and gestured impatiently for him to get in there and finish me.

The final klaxon signaling the end of the shift sounded as the tall one charged me again. Grabbing the wrist of his coveralls, I spun my body in three quick steps, crossing his arm over my back. I hooked my other arm around his knee and pulled him into a forward roll. He landed on his back with me on his stomach, and I struck his face before I rolled free. His nose crunched beneath the edge of my hand. I came up and scrambled to get some distance as he howled.

Other miners appeared at intervals down the shaft and headed toward the equipment racks near the platform. They noticed what was happening, and we started to draw a crowd.

It had to end quickly.

His smaller friend finally left the pail beside the tracks and came at me. He threw a punch, sloppy and inexperienced. No fighter there—I blocked his blow easily and reciprocated. My knuckles connected with the fragile bones and tender nerves around his eye and he stumbled back, cursing. The taller Nos, bright ichor streaming over his lips and chin, lurched in for more. I grabbed their bucket and swung it into his head. His goggles shattered. Nuggets of ore spilled to the ground as the cap dislodged. A side kick into his chest as he flailed sent him all the way back. He tripped over the rails and went down hard against the wall.

I tossed the bucket away and stood, panting, to see if the smaller guy wanted to come back. He looked like he was done, grimacing on the floor of the mine as he clutched the blood-streaked canister and scooped the ore back inside.

Movement out of the corner of my eye raised my hackles. I whirled into a defensive posture and found myself staring down the business end of an energy rifle.

The Nos guard behind the sights narrowed her eyes at me and glanced at the two on the ground. Her expression stayed cool, unreadable, but blue-dyed brows rose in approval behind her goggles. I massaged my bruised knuckles and didn't react. The rifle came down and she jerked her head for me to retrieve my equipment.

Other beings stared at me as I walked toward the platform to await our ride to the surface. By the time the crew car glided in, the guard managed to convince the smaller Nos to get off the tracks before he got dismembered, and the other sat groggily, but upright, against the wall of the tunnel.

I replaced the pneumatic hammer in the racks and stepped onto the magnetic-drawn transport. Once I clipped my safety harness to the hooks in the center of the platform, I sucked down my last water ration as the open-framed cars lurched into motion. We whooshed past the big limping Nos and his handler, and I waved at them in cheery farewell. They were not amused. I found the guard staring at me from the end of the car, and a grin flitted across her mouth before she looked away.

Outside the working areas, the shaft dropped into profound darkness. Only the heads-up readout inside my goggles provided light, luminescent numbers and script ticking off the dwindling number of meters to the surface ascent and the air quality. Fresh, cooler oxygen filled my lungs, temperatures plunging into a far more comfortable range when we neared the surface. The pale illumination of the entrance created a false dawn break against the sides of the uneven, machine-hewn cavern.

The oncoming shift waited to board the platform. I

glimpsed Ziggy among the crowd, clad in protective gear, and they greeted me with a nod. Via the implanted coms we both possessed, I heard their translated voice, though no one else could.

"Stay out of trouble."

I touched my chest innocently, hoping they could see the *Who, me?* expression through the dusty goggles. Zig couldn't know about the fight yet. My friend's wry amusement touched my empathic nets, so I gave them a tired thumbs-up.

The stream of dusty shift workers headed for the scales where the take for the day would be weighed and credited to our individual pay account. I fished the ID tag from around my neck for the surly Ferian clerk to scan and dumped my canister into the hopper.

He shoved my tag into the data slot, eyed the readout on the scale, and plugged numbers in with one furry digit. "Your share is—"

"Wait. This belongs with the load too." A voice speaking heavily accented Remoliad Standard interrupted the clerk. The Nos guard from the mine appeared behind the counter and tipped the contents of a familiar blood-streaked bucket into the hopper. She gave me a curt nod, and I returned the acknowledgment, veiling my surprise. She stared a little longer than even Nos politeness allowed, an enigmatic curve to her lips.

I was intrigued.

The Ferian cleared the numbers sourly, his lip curled back from lengthy canines, and re-entered a figure. The new total showed up in my goggles and I registered my agreement of the percentage. Best payday so far.

I headed for the hard-sided tent where the locker area and sonic cleansers were located, stowed my gear, and retrieved clean clothes. My unexpected bonus paid for an extra-long session in one of the cleansing booths where I reveled in the warmth and vibration for a full five minutes. With sweat and mineral dust gone from my skin and hair, I pulled on my clothes, dumped the coveralls in the locker, and went to find food.

Nothing changed hands for free in the mining camp, everything extortionate in price since the operation flew under the radar. With the off-going shift of miners paid, the temporary settlement teemed with activity. In the center of the tent city stood a canteen providing water rations and protein-packed, tasteless, obscenely expensive prepackaged meals from off world. On the edges of camp, dozens of enterprising beings had set up shop.

The best kind of food on any planet comes from the street vendors, and here was no exception. I avoided the meat when I purchased these offerings though. Bariish's arid landscape could not support any sort of animal large enough to butcher, and although what lay skewered on the smoking grills smelled good, I could not identify it. Many outlying worlds didn't hold the same dim views of sentient meat, banned by Remoliad-allied planets. I chose vegetables surrounded by a wrap of tough, sour flatbread baked in a stone oven and ate while pacing the sandy maze interweaving the fingers of rock.

The sun never fully set on the camp. Dusk stretched for twelve long hours in Bariish's northern hemisphere, and the slanted, carnelian light played capricious tricks on human eyes. Hard lines softened; pools of violet shadow formed between the metallic badlands of twisted ore poking up through the planet's crust. In the dry desert climate, temperatures plunged in the shadowed hours, daylight trapped in a memory of warmth within the rocks. The wind had the same tang of earth and copper the atmosphere my adopted home of Zereid carries but none of the moisture. Naturally circulated air of any humidity is still sweeter than the sterile, canned oxygen mix of a starship or space station.

On the fringes of the camp, drug dealers and peddlers

offered distractions from the tedium of shifts in the mine. Canopies out front of the deeper recesses in the badlands advertised the sale of pornography, and if holovids alone didn't scratch the itch, paid companionship. Even though they appeared to be independent sex workers, I couldn't bring myself to give them business. My first mission instilled an abiding hatred of sex trafficking.

But I was oh-so-fucking bored.

Boredom is my enemy. It gives me too much time to think, to twist the wedding bands on either hand against grooves worn into my skin and remember why I came.

Whose trust I betrayed to get this far.

The information I stole from the Shontavian Market pointed to this mining enterprise as a major funnel of income for several unsavory groups, including the one I believed responsible for the terrorist act that killed my husband, my wife, and our unborn child. We were supposed to identify the reclusive head of this operation, known only as the Overseer. So far, our target remained a faceless entity, and not one goddamned interesting thing had happened.

It didn't take long for my restlessness to build into the state where I dozed only a few hours at a time. While the rest of the day shift slept, I paced the silent camp in endless circles and looked for something stupid to do.

Ziggy, my partner in this mission, remained so incredibly focused on their undercover role as a miner they may as well have been a microscope. A Cthash, whose reptilian people lived mostly underground in their home system, Zig was in their element in the hot, stifling confines of the mineshaft. The small contingency of Cthash expatriates had welcomed them into the fold with open arms.

Like me, Zig is neither male nor female. Ziggy is an *ix*, a Cthash third gender. As luck would have it, their specialized gonads were in demand by one of the mated pairs, and while Zig might be getting laid in their off-hours, I was not.

Dangerous liaisons have been my downfall in the last year and a half. That cold, glinting edge of the unknown, the threat of violence, is my weakness. It allows me to feel something—a pulse-quickening semblance of passion—and reminds me I'm still alive: a situation in which I'm still not completely vested despite the efforts of beings much wiser and more compassionate than I am.

And on Bariish, just like anywhere else, there were opportunities to meet a willing stranger.

CHAPTER
TWO

SHE STOOD outside one of the tents where liquor was sold, watching me. I recognized her from the mine: the tall, female Nos guard. White hair lay close-cropped against her head. A single, brilliant shock of blue-dyed fringe matched her eyebrows and brushed above alabaster eyes.

There was heat in her gaze, and I paused.

We stared each other down for a minute until she jerked her head toward the dark crevice between two spires of rock. I hesitated. The scar under my sternum, marking a knife's passage and a brush with death, had been gained in a narrow space like that. Though the Zereid martial art of *zezjna* would always be my preferred defense, I now carried a twenty-five centimeters long blade of my own strapped to my thigh.

Caution probably read on my face. The corner of her mouth lifted in a wry twist, and she said in Remoliad Standard, "Afraid of me, human?" Her husky voice stirred the hair on the back of my neck in a not-unpleasant way. Expressive sapphire brows fired a challenge in her eyes and sparked a response in me. Anticipatory warmth spread in the tissues of my groin.

I should have known better than to risk liaison with a Nos.

Though they are our closest genetic cousins in the galaxy, nearly indistinguishable from a human in anatomical terms, my ability to feel the emotions of other beings comes up short against their null. Their lack of psychic talent negates the advantages I have with most other species. I knew nothing of her emotional state, sexual arousal, or intentions. She could want to fuck me, rob me, or kill me. Or all three.

So, naturally, I took the risk.

"Lead the way," I said in the same language, pitching my voice in a male timbre.

She gave no signal this surprised her. Though I masqueraded as a man, my features are decidedly ambiguous. My upper body and the secondary male characteristics I adapted had developed more muscle after the hard physical labor. Down under, I was still sexless. I would need to wait to discover what gender she anticipated without a way to capture the essence in my empathic nets.

Coarse sand crunched under our boots as I followed her into the passage. The long sleeves of her mining coveralls were tied around her hips. Glimpses of the small of her back tantalized me, moonlight-colored skin between the knotted material and the tight, sleeveless undershirt.

It didn't take long to learn her intentions.

She fell on me with a hunger I didn't need empathy to read. Hot, eager, and demanding, her mouth invaded mine. My work-roughened hands slid over the silky skin bared at her waist. She moaned and gripped my wrists, bringing my fingers up beneath the shirt to caress her breasts. The tissues of my mons rapidly engorged and rearranged to fulfill a male role. Her pheromones spoke to me in a silent, eloquent way, and her busy fingers working at the clasp of my pants left me no doubt. But I still needed time and pushed the front of her shirt up far enough to free her breasts, pale, blue-tinged nipples barely visible in the shadows. My tongue explored the pebbled ridges of her aureole, and she gave a hissing cry as I sucked a nipple into my mouth, my teeth grazing the sensitive flesh. She gripped the queue at the back of my head with her fist.

With my hands, I worked against the knotted sleeves of her coveralls. The jumpsuit slid down from her hips, and I found her naked beneath. A groan of desire rocked me, and I recaptured her mouth, our tongues meeting in a precursory advance. Her knees buckled as I slid my fingers between her legs in a gentle probe.

Nested folds of skin yielded to the touch. The innermost petal swelled against my hand. Warmth and wetness described her arousal to my fingertips as I stroked her. She hissed in pleasure, hips undulating forward in a rhythm as old as the galaxy. Her hand tightened on the hard flesh between my own legs, still concealed beneath my trousers.

"In me. Now," she demanded, kicking a foot free of her coveralls. She wrapped her leg around my thigh.

I undid the front of my pants one-handed and shoved them down. Cupping her buttocks, I supported her back against the still-warm spire of rock. Her legs encircled my waist as I slipped inside. She gasped at the sensation, her cockeyed smile of surprise and delight evident at the unfamiliar, smooth contours of my changeling genitalia. Equally speechless with pleasure, I found the rippled musculature of her internal flesh as unutterably exotic as my partner.

Her legs tightened around me; her guttural cries muffled in my shoulder as I thrust into her. Her excitement mounted and so did mine, even without the empathic feedback sex usually gave me. Her teeth fastened on my neck as she came, her spasm enveloping me and sending me over the edge. We spiraled down from the dizzy height of orgasm, panting, until she firmly pushed me away. I complied. A low, breathless laugh carried approval as she lowered one long leg to support her own weight, then the other.

"You are stronger than you look." She tugged the shirt down to cover her breasts.

"Thank you, I think." I fastened my pants.

"You are nothing like the males of my species." She slid the unzipped legs of her coveralls back over her boots, pulled them up, and retied the arms around her hips. "You cared for my pleasure."

"It adds to mine." The marks of her teeth stung, and my fingers came away streaked with red as I explored them. "You're a biter."

"Do humans fear pain in coupling?"

"Not all." I straightened my clothing and made certain the knife was still strapped at my thigh. "Least of all, me."

"No. I saw you in the shaft. You are a good fighter. Those fools in the tunnel were not prepared." Her crystalline eyes glinted in the ruddy light. "But you are too focused on what's in front of you and do not watch your back. I could have killed you."

"But you didn't."

"Fortunate for both of us." Her smirk transformed into a genuine grin. "What are you called?"

"Paul." My father might not approve of me taking his first name for this mission, but what he didn't know wouldn't catch me any grief. "Paul Urquhart."

"Urr-cut." Her tongue burred the R sound and gave the syllables an unfamiliar accent. "I have never been with a human male before."

"You still haven't. I'm a third-gender human."

Her brow furrowed between her blue-white eyes. "Like a Cthash?"

"Not quite. What's your name?"

"Kaisa." She ran her fingers through her spiky, pale hair with a sigh of satisfaction. "This was a pleasurable diversion, but it was not my primary reason to seek you out."

"You were looking for me?" I stiffened.

"Come, Paul Urr-cut. I wish to speak with you." She started to walk back the way we'd come and cast one diamond glance over her shoulder with her glittering eyes. "You will buy me liquor. I know you can afford it tonight."

The pavilion where libations were sold squatted near the edge of camp. I greeted the blue giant behind the bar with a nod, and she returned the gesture, cloudy silver eyes gleaming in the half-light of the shrouded tent. We had spoken verbally, the customary courtesy of Zereid telepaths uncertain in this rough sector. I kept my empathic nets furled for privacy when in her range, unwilling to risk an involuntary hint I gathered intelligence on this operation.

I inserted my tag into the slot of the dispenser. Kaisa plucked two shot tubes of an Ursetu distillation from the rack. The liquor she picked was expensive and had enough proof to knock the seven-foot-tall unblinking Zereid barkeeper on her ass with only a couple of sips. Her expression fired another challenge at me. I didn't react, returning Kaisa's even stare as I pulled the tag out of the reader after the sale was registered. Makeshift tables made of battered upturned cargo containers dotted the dark tent, and she led me to an isolated one at the back.

Kaisa dialed up the first shot. A measure of bronze liquid filled the cupped tip, and she thrust it at me. "You first."

The swirling metallic stuff reminded me of something. I took the proffered tube and slammed it back, never looking away from her.

Silky fluid warmed my throat. A comet's trail followed the alcohol down to my stomach where it burned with muted fire. My head spun momentarily, and I huffed an admiring laugh.

"Wow. That's something." I measured out another shot, and dark pearlescent stuff swirled into the glass. The color sparked a memory again. What was it? I handed Kaisa the tube. She downed it in one swallow, eyes closed as the liquor's effects made her sway on the box that constituted a seat in the classy establishment.

"This drink is called *agzi*. Only the Ursetu ruling caste is allowed to drink it, but they have no qualms about its export," she said. "They say it is the same color as the royal family's eyes."

The same bronze color as Rhix's eyes.

The erotic, charged dreams following my first mission were almost as frequent as my nightmares of Gresh and Rasida's deaths, the heart-pounding, sweaty lurch into wakefulness triggered by sexual frustration rather than pain and loss.

The guilt stayed the same.

Yeah, I am still one fucked-up human being.

"What do you want to talk about?" My voice rasped from the liquor.

"I will ask for your discretion, first." Kaisa sat back, studying me as she twirled the spent tube in her fingers. "There are few who know who I am."

"Aren't you a guard?"

"Too often, these days. I spend far more time in the mine than I should when I need to attend business matters. I am the Overseer. I want you to work for me as an enforcer."

A moment of blank comprehension, and then excitement streaked through me. I fought to keep a dispassionate expression.

"It could be quite lucrative for a being of your talent," Kaisa said. "Does that interest you?"

This could be the chance I was looking for. "It might. Tell me more."

"The presence of the vaping tent is damaging productivity. Intake has dropped by twenty percent since they arrived. Addicts unable to make enough to support their habits are stealing from others. The two you encountered are only the latest to crop up. I want you to convince the troublemakers to move on."

I narrowed my eyes. "I can't imagine they'll go quietly."

"No. But if you must make an example to discourage it … " She shrugged.

"I prefer not to kill, as a rule." I can't say I'll never kill again, not on my current path. But experiencing another being's death is something I will avoid whenever possible. "Won't that hurt your productivity too?"

"More miners will come. They always do." Kaisa dialed up the second tube of liquor and handed it to me. I threw it back, the delicious dizzy sense of vertigo no less acute this time.

"I have a counter proposal." My tongue got clumsier as the effect of the powerful distillation began to creep in. "I used to be pretty good at negotiating. Let me talk to them first to see if I can persuade them to leave."

"I do not see how talking would be useful."

"The threat of violence lends itself to persuasion. They already know I kicked their asses." I twisted the tube and watched the metallic stuff fill the glass. The swirl made me dizzy and raked up memories I had no business thinking about anymore—of sweat, sex, a whole lot of martial foreplay … and the first time I killed another living being. The shared terror of two gruesome deaths, forever recorded in my neurons. That horror liked to come to play in my nightmares too.

I gave her the last shot. She tipped it into her open mouth, her gaze locked with mine. Around the shiver of the alcohol's effect, she said thickly, "If you are squeamish, there are others interested in a chance to benefit financially from a little violence."

"So, I wasn't your first choice."

"No, but I have been watching you, Paul. You are thorough in whatever you do, whether it is mining, fighting … or fucking." Her scent drifted toward me in the confines of the tent. The combination of her pheromones and the warmth created by the Ursetu liquor began to reawaken other things in my anatomy. "If you persuade them to leave in less than twenty-four hours, you can work for me. I will pay you a percentage of the take on your shift to keep troublemakers in line. But if you convince the dealer to leave, you will receive a handsome bonus for taking care of that problem for me."

Emboldened by alcohol and drawn by the chemical lure of her sexual arousal, I leaned closer to Kaisa. "Is there anything else you would like me to do?"

Her slow smile sent a rush of change hormones into my bloodstream, ready for anything she wanted. "Oh, yes. But not against the rocks this time. My bed. You can give me pleasure, and then, I will focus on yours."

To quote one of the latest holovids my crewmates unearthed, she made me an offer I couldn't refuse.

CHAPTER
THREE

NEAR DAWN, I made my way outside the rocky spires to where personal ships lay arrayed in uneven clusters on the desert floor. I kept my senses extended to catch any hint of trouble lurking in the purple darkness between vessels. The nail marks sketched in stinging tracks across my back were an oddly satisfying reminder of what great sex can do. I was more relaxed than I'd been in weeks. The effects of the liquor had mostly worn off, and I had no sense of being watched as I threaded through the violet shadows. My mind already spun and calculated how I might further infiltrate the operation. A cold excitement built in my chest. One person closer to Skadi. I might not get another chance like this.

Old, battered, and barely spaceworthy, the short-hop vehicle Ziggy and I shared had only one bunk, the primary reason we worked opposing shifts. It made me wonder what Penumbra requisitions officer had a vendetta against our team. We had christened the ship *Owhra*, one of the twelve Ferian words for shit.

I tapped in a pattern of symbols with my fingers on the security pad, and the port creaked aside. Sensors tracked my movement and switched on the auxiliary power. The sickly yellow-green glow of the cabin lights flickered into life, and I turned automatically to the right to seal the door.

"You need to turn off your implant while you are rutting. I do not want to hear it."

The voice behind me caught me off guard, and I spun, hand on the hilt of my knife. Melos lounged on the bunk, his fingers clasped nonchalantly behind his yellow-haired head. Caked with dust, his boots left sulfurous drifts on the mattress beneath his crossed ankles.

"Get your feet off my bed," I shot back as my pulse stuttered back into a regular rhythm. "Sorry. Zig can't hear me in the mine."

"Lucky them." He sat up and pivoted his body, feet thudding to the deck. Another cloud of silt drifted and died. "How long before they come out of the tunnels?"

I checked the chronometer. "Two hours. Why are you planetside?"

"You are being recalled."

Stunned, I stared at him. "What?"

"Sumner wants you back on the *Thunder Child*. You have a rendezvous in twelve hours."

Anger snarled on the heels of disbelief. "No. No fucking way! I just got inside tonight."

"I do not want to know what you got inside tonight. Sumner says you go."

"Kaisa is the head of this operation. Didn't you hear anything we talked about?"

"Between her invoking the names of gods and screaming *Urr-cut* directly into your implant?"

"No, before that."

"Some. It did not sound like anything to do with Skadi or her whereabouts." Black-clad shoulders twitched in a shrug.

"Eight weeks, I've been looking for an opportunity to infiltrate the organization, and I finally got it." My fist slammed into the bulkhead. "Goddamn it, I can't go now!"

"Take it up with Sumner." Melos pulled a subspace cube out of his jacket and tossed it to me. Snatching the device out of the air, I stabbed my forefinger against the blinking recess with sullen resignation.

Sumner's visage appeared in holographic 3D above the unit. He was expecting my call. The flickering avatar said, "Yes, I'm recalling you. Take Melos's ship and meet me on board. He and Ziggy can follow later."

"I can't leave."

"Why?" Sumner's eyes narrowed, their peculiar blue-green color startling even in grainy holographic detail.

"The Overseer offered me a job. If I deliver on this, Kaisa will know I'm trustworthy. She could be my ticket into Skadi's organization." I straightened. "I want to stay."

Melos growled. "Why do you always argue?"

"I don't argue. I negotiate."

"Sounds like arguing to me," Sumner interjected dryly. "I'm sorry. I need you back here."

"This could be my only—"

"No." A warning crackle in his voice made me clamp my lips shut. "There will be other opportunities. I haven't forgotten what I promised."

Sumner pledged I would be involved when the Penumbra moved against the terrorist I believed carried out the bombing of Luna Terminal. Two years since my husband, my wife, and our unborn child were incinerated in the deadly blast. Two years since my soul got ripped screaming from my chest and I was sent straight into a personal hell, still trying to claw my way out.

One year and three missions since he made that promise. Not one step closer to finding Skadi until tonight. Now he ordered me to abandon the mission.

"Meet up with Ziggy at the end of the shift. Close your pay accounts and then head to the ship. I'll explain when you get here."

"Yes, Commander." The words dropped in blocks of icy courtesy. The call terminated in a fizz of static, and I tossed the cube back to Melos. He caught it in one black-gloved hand and tucked it back into his jacket as I slumped on the bunk, head in hands.

"You need to learn to trust him. He would not do this unless there was something more important." Melos's voice held its usual sharpness, but the edges were filed off. As always, his true feelings were a mystery my empathic senses couldn't filter. What he really thought remained unspoken, though my growing proficiency with the Nos language picked up a note of understanding. Even sympathy.

My breath came out in a harsh rasp as I conceded. "Do you know what's going on?"

"Not everything. He will inform us when the time is right. His superiors only tell him what he needs to know, as well."

"The Penumbra certainly likes its secrets."

"You are a spy now. If you do not keep secrets, you are in the wrong business."

I still had a few of my own.

And I had a couple of hours before I had to leave. I stood and punched the exit code on the door.

Melos frowned. "Where are you going?"

"Back to camp to get my gear together. I can sell it back or trade it. I'll turn in my tag as soon as the accountant's tent opens."

"I'll come with you."

"No. If I have to break things off with Kaisa, I don't want an audience."

"Call if you need backup." Melos stretched out on the bunk again.

He'd eventually follow me. My first errand would have to be quick.

I tapped the small bump behind my ear to turn off the communicator before I eased through the flap of the unmarked canopy.

Vaporous mist hung in the air and rapidly dissipated in the dry atmosphere, but the spicy scent marking the drug's presence lingered. My brain began to itch with the first inhalation.

The wizened Pilean sat at the back of the tent, flanked by two burly bodyguards. Pileans are difficult to tell apart; all four sexes have the same triangular facial features with sharp, unpleasant mandibles like an insect's, but their crests—the ridged area of the carapace between their triangular eyes—will tell you how old they are. This fellow's had a silver sheen, denoting mid-lifecycle for his species.

The shape of the crest is genetically unique to each family, though. This one had fluid heaves and whorls, a fingerprint cast in keratin. I had recognized the crest of the Pilean drug cartel the first time I saw it. This constituted an even bigger problem than Kaisa knew.

"Welcome back." He stood and spread his arms wide, a stick figure dressed in nanosilk robes. Remoliad Standard issued from a pendant translator, his mandibles clicking above the whispery sound of his own language. "I wondered when we'd be seeing you again."

"Did you?"

"You wander the camp at night. This is not the action of a being at peace with oneself. I offer respite from your troubled mind. I have some new things which bring peace at a reasonable price."

Something deep in my head said *yes*, and my hand twitched at my side. Out loud, I managed, "No. I'm here to settle my account. I'm leaving."

"Ah. I will be sorry to see you go."

The smell of the drug penetrated my senses as another waft

atomized into the tent. I saw and heard the delivery mechanism this time, suspended in the corner above the entryway. A thread-thin laser targeted movement in front of the door. Three slow steps took me out of the encroaching mist's range, but it was too late. The taste burned on my tongue.

The dealer took the offered tag from my hand. He inserted it into a reader and transferred credits from my account to his. I nodded curtly as the numbers were displayed, and he moved to complete the transaction.

Another hiss of the atomizer overpowered the receptors in my brain.

Fuck.

"Wait."

Sharp-tipped fingers hovered above the pad. "What will you have?"

"Two vials. I don't know how long it will be before ..."

"Is two enough?"

"Yes." My answer rang too sharply in the tent.

From the voluminous sleeves of his robe, he brought out two slender cylinders full of amber fluid, then, after a moment's pause, added another vial. "In appreciation of your patronage. Something new without the telltale scent. There will be no charge for the third."

I nodded, eyes averted. He corrected the transaction. I didn't bother to check the amount; I accepted the ampoules and my tag and left. Ducking into a jagged crevice, I removed the slim device from my pocket, inserted one of the amber vials into the receiving end of the vape with an unsteady hand, and thumbed the switch. One breath was all I needed. I still had control.

At least, that's the lie I told myself.

I should never have picked it back up. While I could recognize my habit, I figured I could still just walk away, but the damned atomizer in the tent was a nasty little trick on the

Pilean dealer's part. I slid back to a daily user before I knew it.

The mist-laden inhalation made its way into my lungs, warmth penetrating each bronchiole. Alveoli exchanged oxygen for the drug's molecules in a dizzy, euphoric rush. I held the breath as long as possible before I exhaled a slow curl of fragrant steam into the air. My body relaxed, my pulse dropped, and little by little, the tightness in my chest subsided. The warmth faded quickly, but I didn't need a second hit. Leaning against the rocks, I reveled in the chaos of contentment, the white noise of peace, and shut my eyes against reality.

CHAPTER
FOUR

I STOWED the device and chem vials in an inside pocket and left the rocky fissure behind.

The sun's first rays began to bathe the tips of the mountains; orange fire oozed down the peaks in a viscous wash of light as I made my way to the mine's entrance to meet Ziggy. For a few moments, I stared in stoned rapture, captivated by the rough splendor of the dawn landscape, my dark mood blunted by the effects of the vape's euphoria. Shaking myself out of the chemical reverie, I continued.

The platform emerged from the tunnel just as I arrived. Craning my neck, I searched for Zig among the osmosis of offloading and onloading miners, an opposing flow of anonymous coveralls and helmets. I finally spotted them in the middle of a cluster of Cthash headed for the ore scales and tapped my implant.

"Ziggy, it's me. We've been recalled."

They looked up, scanning the perimeter, and I raised a hand. "Melos is here. Sumner says cash in our tags and head out. Something's up."

Zig vanished into the stream of bodies, but from the center of the crowd an arm rose, a dark-scaled, three-taloned hand with the middle digit extended. I couldn't help but grin. It resembled an obscene gesture common in Sol Fed, but for a Cthash was a long-distance way of saying, "I heard you."

The squatty, hard-sided tent where credit tags were issued to miners occupied the opposite side of the weigh station. The accountant, a weathered, bald Nos with one arm, had heavily armed bodyguards bristling behind him in attentive menace as I turned in my tag. He converted the credits into a modest pile of high-denomination, mixed-origin currencies, untraceable and easily exchanged for galactic credit. The cash got tucked in an inside pocket of my jacket.

After collecting my gear, I had one more stop to make. An open market in the center of the camp served as a trading post for mining tools, gear, and the things others had pawned in exchange. The helmet and goggles were traded for a sealed flask of the Ursetu liquor Kaisa introduced me to the previous night, and then I returned to the ore ship. She stood at the bottom of the ramp as if she'd been expecting me.

"You recover quickly, Paul Urr-cut." Kaisa gave me a wicked grin. "I am due in the mine."

"I'm afraid I came to turn down the job. Something has come up. My ride leaves in an hour."

Her lips pressed together, a headshake of regret scattering her blue-dyed forelock. "I am sorry to hear it."

"I learned something else you won't like." Motioning for her to follow me away from the ramp, we moved closer to the noisy ore-sorting machinery. "The dealer is Pilean drug cartel. You might have a difficult time moving them on."

Kaisa made a sharp sound of disgust. "My employer and I expected the cartel would eventually try to move in. I had not realized they were already here. Thank you for the information. I am not unprepared."

"This is for you." I handed her the flask, and she grinned.

"Remember to savor life, like this drink," she said. "It can be shorter than we anticipate."

"I know that too well."

She saluted me with the flask, stashed it in the pocket of her coveralls, and slung her energy rifle over her shoulder. "There are things I must do at the mine. If you should return and I am still alive, make yourself known. The job will be open. Perhaps my bed as well."

She kissed me roughly, her hand tangled in my hair, and I returned it with all the attention it deserved. No one ever knows when they will experience the raw passion and promise of a kiss for the last time. She nipped my lip playfully as she drew away, and then Kaisa was gone, striding away into the dusty canyons toward the mine. I followed a short way and then veered off into the passage leading to the center of camp.

Melos's tall frame detached from a shadowed crack in the spires, and he fell into step beside me. "I see why you wanted another twenty-four hours."

"Shut up," I muttered. Tapping my implant, I inquired, "Ziggy, are you ready?"

"I'll meet you at our ship." Ziggy's translated voice came over the embedded device, and Melos nodded in acknowledgment.

"How long were you following me?" I asked Melos.

"I saw you buying the liquor in the marketplace and deduced it was for her. I needed to record a visual." He tapped his eye and widened the lids so I could see the fractal pattern of a microtech contact lens against the ice-colored iris. "If she's the Overseer, we need an image of her for the recognition software or Ka'pth and Ra'sho will poison us both for missing the opportunity. Besides, you've had a tail since you left the accountant's tent. I wanted to make sure you weren't robbed."

"Yeah?" I still wasn't clear if he'd seen me come out of the vape dealer's tent. I hated the fact I couldn't sense the emotions of the Nos species—not even Sumner, who was half human. After growing up on Zereid, a planet full of telepaths, and in Sol Fed, where everybody's feelings bled all over me when we came home, it was like being head-blind. "Do you see them now?"

"He's hard to miss. Tall. Lacerations and bruising to the left side of his face." As we emerged into the center of camp, Melos made a casual gesture to the fore. "Standing in front of the water tanks."

The unfriendly regard of the big Nos bully from the mine met my glance. Against his stark white skin, angry cuts and vivid purple bruises described an arc-shaped trauma which perfectly matched the end of an ore bucket. He sneered and took a few steps in our direction.

"Ah, yes."

"You know this one?" Melos snarked. "Another lover?"

"Hardly. He's a vape addict, according to Kaisa."

"He is not alone anymore." Melos's eyes darted to the opposite side, and I glimpsed the little prick who'd held Biggie's leash with two more rather large Nos. "Dalí, what did you do?"

"Nothing!" I protested, then shrugged. "He and the little guy tried to rob me yesterday. They were looking for a fight, so I gave them one. I was bored."

"You are a child." Melos blew out his breath, his mouth set in a grim line. We continued to walk an unhurried, arrow-straight path through the camp toward the passage which led out to the rocky plains and our parked ships. "Do you at least have a gun?"

"Only my knife."

"You need to start carrying more than a knife." He had a Sivad sidearm strapped to his hip, the gun attached to him so often I wouldn't have recognized Melos without it. He reached into his coat and pulled a smaller weapon from his shoulder rig. "You are fortunate I brought my spare."

"I don't usually need a gun." I tucked the weapon into my waistband under the jacket.

"*Zezjna* is not the answer to everything." He raised a pale eyebrow at me. "You cannot kick someone in the head if they are shooting at you."

The quartet was gaining on us. Almost a kilometer of desert broken by spiky fins of ore-laced stone lay between us and our ship.

"Run," Melos ordered as soon as we got outside. We sprinted for the nearest cover, an outcropping of mixed rock and metal jutting from the desert floor.

Projectiles whined and ripped sharp, jagged flakes from our shelter. One chip struck me in the face. Cursing, I put a hand to the stinging laceration and my fingers came away wet with blood.

"Exciting enough for you now?" Melos grunted. He scanned the terrain to the side for encroaching enemies. "Or will you still complain of being bored?"

"If we make it back to *Thunder Child*, I won't use the word 'bored' again." I flattened myself against the rock and rolled to return fire. The sidearm vomited four fiery barks, and one of my targets clutched at a lower limb before I jerked back. "Tedious. Mind numbing. But never bored."

Melos popped around the side of the ore spine and ripped a few well-placed volleys of his own into the cluster of boulders where our assailants took cover.

We both exhaled in relief as Ziggy's voice came over our implants. "Dalí, what did you do now?"

"Why does everybody assume it was me?" I yelped.

"Anybody hurt?"

"Dalí is bleeding," Melos said.

"Not much." I craned my neck to steal a look at the gang shooting at us and fired off another volley in their direction. A beam of concentrated light made a round smoky patch on the rock above my head. Shit. They'd gotten reinforcements. "Uh, what's your ETA? We're pinned down."

"Two minutes," Ziggy's translated voice informed us. "How many? What are they armed with?"

"About six of them. Small caliber projectiles. Low energy weapons."

"I'm in *Owhra*. Be prepared to move fast."

The ear-itching whine of *Owhra*'s engines gave a moment's warning before the battered, oval silhouette blocked out the sun. Ziggy spun the ship, and its engine wash blasted yellow sand and dust right into the rocks where our opponents lay hidden. Zig put the craft in a hover a meter and a half over the desert floor. The port slid open as Melos and I hauled ass out of our shelter in the outcropping.

"Go!" Melos grabbed my leg and boosted me upward. I crawled onto the deck and then turned around, extending my hands. He leaped.

I missed his hand, his fingers brushing the inside of my wrist.

He leaped again. This time I caught the sleeve of his jacket and pulled, my other hand finding his and locking my fingers around his forearm. He gripped my wrist as his other arm came up and searched for purchase.

A beam of light sliced through the dust and sand, swirling around us, striking Melos in the side.

He screamed in agony, burning flesh and smoking fabric heavy in my nostrils. For a heart-stopping moment he was dead weight, hanging one-armed from my hands as the ship lurched.

"We have to go! They're still shooting at us!" Ziggy shouted. "This piece of shit won't take a lot of damage."

Setting my teeth, I threw my weight backward, pulling Melos into the cabin with all my strength. Melos managed to find a foothold on the hull and raise his body enough to allow me to grab the waist of his pants and haul him inside.

"We're in!" I screamed at Ziggy. "Go, go!"

I hammered my palm against the release, and the port slammed home as Zig fired the engines up and away. Melos curled in a ball on the deck, his body trembling with pain.

"Everybody in one piece?" Ziggy called from the cockpit.

"Melos got shot with an energy weapon when I pulled him in." I seized the medical kit mounted on the cabin wall and used my knife to cut the still-smoking material away from his side. Melos shrieked, and I swallowed hard as the wound came into view. A raw, fist sized chunk of flesh between his left chest and armpit had been scorched and cauterized, deep enough that edges of bone glinted in an abstract painting of red, white, and char.

"Ziggy, we need to head for *Thunder Child* right away. This is bad. Way beyond my first aid skills."

"You are not leaving my ship behind," Melos countered. His already pale skin was without color, lips white and pressed tightly together.

"Once we are in orbit, Tommi can tell me what to do until we dock," Ziggy said. "Melos is right. You still need to rendezvous with Sumner. It's faster than *Owhra*. The two of you have a deadline."

Melos stifled a cry as I squirted a combination of antiseptic and numbing gel into the wound. His eyes streamed with tears of pain. As the anesthetic did its work, his body relaxed, and I cut away the rest of his upper clothing. The smell of burnt flesh made my stomach heave. I helped him sit on the bunk and held him steady as Ziggy brought *Owhra* in for a dust-off landing beside Melos's ship, grounded on the outer edge of the vessels arrayed on the desert apron.

"I hope your errand this morning was worth it." Melos glared at me from the corners of his glacial eyes as I collected my small bag of clothing and personal items from an overhead compartment. My hands fumbled the strap. Did he know?

Guilt ate away at my insides like acid, but I wasn't going to admit anything because of my own paranoia. I smirked at him instead. "Kissing Kaisa goodbye? Oh yeah, it was worth it."

"It better have been." His breath hissed between gritted teeth as he eased against the mattress. "Because when I see you again, I am going to kick your ass for getting high."

My smirk faltered, lips cold with shame.

His icy gaze met mine one last time. "If you wreck my ship, I will kill you."

CHAPTER
FIVE

MELOS HAD LEFT his two-passenger craft in standby power mode, ready to take off. This ship didn't have a name. The Nos don't believe in giving inanimate objects names, only designation numbers. He referred to the skiff as *Three* but with a deference that said the ship was more than a number to him—not the same kind of starry-eyed love affair Sumner had with *Thunder Child*, but it did make me wonder what happened to *One* and *Two*. The adrenaline rush had sobered me up a little, and I paid special attention to the pre-liftoff checks.

Only minutes passed between boarding and rising from the planet's surface, but my anxiety vibrated in high gear. I dislike traveling alone in a ship that's basically nothing but a cockpit. Without the distraction of talking to someone else, space is too big and too quiet with plenty of time for memories and bad habits to reassert themselves. Left to my own company, I am still in questionable companionship.

Outside the atmosphere, autopilot kicked in with preset rendezvous coordinates for a thirty-minute flight. It gave me time to slap a temporary synthetic skin over the laceration on my face before I donned the sensor glove and impatiently swept my hand to activate the heads-up display.

"Update on current events." Ka'pth and Ra'sho developed a personal retrieval system for me, a reorientation to the galactic climate for post-mission briefings I found especially helpful after being in isolated environments like Bariish for more than a month without news media updates. My Andari crewmates, the intelligence section of our team, also added any pertinent information they thought might interest me.

The first face to appear in my briefing file made me smile despite everything. It was my mother, Marina Urquhart, Sol Fed's Ambassador to the Remoliad. She had taken up the appointment I held on the day my life shattered and secured Sol Fed's future as a member of galactic society.

The clip came from one of the Allied networks which covered important proceedings and summits. Mom was listening to the speaker in front of the representative body, her expression set in a carefully neutral mask.

"I have yet to determine what benefit Sol Fed's membership provides to the Alliance," grunted the Burkani diplomat at the podium. "Their government refuses to send troops to participate in the joint fleet but expects our help. Not right. The number of humans spilling through the hub, seeking employment on Allied worlds, is increasing. Many of them are undesirables, even criminals in their home system, who cannot speak even the most common Remoliad language." He waved a thick, three-fingered hand. "Do not misunderstand me. Ambassador Urquhart herself is a credit to her species. An upstanding galactic citizen. Very nice. It is clear her time outside Sol Fed allowed her to become more civilized."

A mutter passed through the assemblage, and I read my mother's lips as she leaned over to speak to the lavender skinned Tolkish diplomat beside her: *Did he really just call me a credit to my species?*

The Tolkish male smiled ruefully and mouthed back, *Yes, I am afraid he did.*

The Remoliad Alliance held more than two hundred worlds in its membership, and not all were overly fond of the refugee status granted Sol Fed.

But the diplomat sitting next to Mom caught my eye. I paused the playback. The Tolkish representative was ridiculously beautiful like the rest of his humanoid species. Fine symmetrical features. Carmine eyes glowed with wicked mirth as he and my mother shared a private laugh at the Burkani's expense. He took my breath away, and I almost regretted I wasn't there. I didn't recognize him but had not followed Remoliad proceedings for more than two years, except for Mom's updates.

Focus, Dalí. The vape still affected my concentration, attention wandering down branching tunnels without end.

More Remoliad news followed. The Alliance expected to gain another new member, one I would not have predicted. Urset, the most stubborn of three small planets orbiting the star Yalo, had applied for expedited membership a few days ago. This surprised me. Joining the Remoliad meant the Ursetu would have to stop the manufacture and sale of bioengineered life forms like the deadly Shontavian mercenaries, something the Allied worlds opposed in no uncertain terms. Due to sanctions against trade with the Ursetu, Remoliad-affiliated consumers were forced to go through third and fourth parties to procure Urset's most lucrative export—high grade rubies used for technology and luxury items. I smelled the new trade agreements from here.

I scanned the rest of the thumbnail files for a hint of my new assignment. No top secret briefs. My resentment sprouted thorns. Other than the recent death of Urset's crown princess and the planet's subsequent decision to join the Remoliad—surprising, but hardly critical—nothing was happening in the galaxy which would require Sumner to pull me away from this mission.

A familiar ship grew larger in my view screen. Despite my poisonous mood, the sight of my home between worlds filled me with warmth and relief as much as my restlessness would allow.

Sumner christened the slender, needle-prowed blockade runner *Thunder Child* after the doomed frigate in *War of the Worlds*—he devoured ancient science fiction by writers like H.G. Wells and J.S. Fields as avidly as our out-system crewmates consumed old-Earth movies. The ship currently housed eight of us: the Andari, the three Cthash siblings, Sumner, Melos, and me.

Thanks to my skillful punch of the auto-docking sequence button, *Three* nestled into its cramped bay in *Thunder Child's* hull without crashing. Waiting for me in protective gear at the end of the first airlock, my crewmate Tommi's reptilian version of a sunny grin beamed through her face mask. I answered in kind, glad to see her even if it meant decontamination was about to begin. After prolonged contact with an undeveloped planet and its bacterial fauna, the process prevented my crewmates' exposure to any microbes hitching a ride from the surface. Nothing could convince me Tommi didn't take a certain sadistic pleasure in the process though.

"You know the drill. Clothes off."

"Remove clothing for decontamination," a mechanical voice droned in redundant insistence. I rolled my eyes.

"You two just can't wait to see me naked."

"Yeah, keep protesting. I might actually believe you're modest." Tommi's translated voice came over my implant, the susurrate Cthash language muffled into whispers behind the insulating helmet.

Tommi hissed and bared her sharp teeth in a grin as I shucked out of my jacket and shirt and exposed my back, still marked with Kaisa's nail tracks. "Oh, you have been a naughty human."

"Please. I already heard about it from Melos." A pang of guilt went through me as I dropped the garment into the waiting decon bin beside my gear bag. "How is he? How soon can they intercept?"

"He's stable, Dalí. Ziggy's got him comfortable. We'll rendezvous with them and head for Zereid about an hour after we drop you off." The words combined with a surge of comfort against my empathic nets as her dexterous, three-taloned hands clad in thick gloves tilted my head up so she could examine the hastily sealed laceration on my face. A warm trickle followed the removal of the plastiskin layer, which she discarded in a chute. "He's not in any immediate danger, but I don't have the equipment required to regrow his burnt skin. Melos will have to be treated in a medical facility."

I unsnapped the knife and its sheath from my thigh and tossed it in the drawer. My boots and pants followed. Last to go in were my wedding rings, and as I stowed the bands for safe keeping, they clinked against the drug vials concealed in the pocket of my coat. Had Tommi heard? I willed away the twitchy feeling and fastened the pocket shut. "Will these be deconned before I leave again? I hear there is a deadline."

"In a couple of hours, but you won't be able to wear the knife openly where you're going. Into the alcove. Arms up, legs spread." She aimed a thin nozzle attached to metallic tubing at my midsection.

I stepped into the stall and arranged my limbs Vitruvian style, bracing my bare feet on the cold metal grate. "Do you have any idea where I'm going? What can you tell me about this oh-so-important mission?"

"Above my pay grade. I know nothing."

My snort of exasperation turned into a whistling gasp as

the stinging spray assaulted my chest with ice-cold disinfectant. "Fucking hell! You can't heat this stuff up?"

"You warm-blooded species are real whiners, aren't you?"

Any formality between Tommi and me had long since disappeared. She'd become the sister I never had, and her sibling Ozzie, our pilot and second in command, was probably my closest friend on board *Thunder Child*.

"Turn around. This is going to sting a little more with those scratches."

No kidding. Out of sheer refusal to cater to her opinion of my whininess I stoically bore it even though the bite of the spray brought tears to my eyes. Tommi's directed water torture paid close attention to the skin between my fingers, toes, and ass crack.

"You get off on this, don't you?" I accused her.

"I want your body. For experiments, anyway. Shut up and close your eyes."

I complied. A scalp-scouring jet left my hair dripping before a gentle spray misted my face, though the open laceration burned like fire. I stepped out of the alcove and stood, shivering, with my eyes shut tight until a warm blanket enfolded me and a towel draped over my head. I wiped my face as Tommi shut the drawer filled with my clothes and gear bag and shoved it into the wall to be processed. The seal hissed. She entered the recess opposite the decon stall and robotic arms divested her of the suit. The upper and lower halves disappeared into their own processing receptacles as she directed me to the next airlock and sealed the hatch behind us, punching in the sequence that would irradiate the tube and kill any microscopic beasties.

"Let's go to medical and patch you up."

She drew blood, listened to my lungs, and checked all my orifices for parasitic stowaways before she finally let me dress in the gray fatigues we all wore on board the ship. Then she turned her attention to the cut on my face and gave a tongue-click of disappointment.

"This is going to need dermal accelerant, or it won't heal well. Lie down, and I'll clean it. While I work, we can start bringing you down for debriefing."

I reclined against the cushions. We were adept at our debriefing routine by now. There are few people of any species I trust as implicitly as I do Tommi. Unpacking the details of my first mission by virtue of its nature had been a traumatic event in itself.

Wire and the gel of the sensor pads lay cold against my forehead; the induction device hummed in soothing tones as she disinfected the wound and approximated the edges of the laceration. Dermal accelerant sealed the skin.

"Do you need something for pain first?"

"No. If you take me deep enough, I won't need any at all."

Her breathy hiss quietly urged me toward profound concentration as Tommi and I worked together on a light hypnotic state. It cleared the clutter in my mind and allowed me to relate important data I collected during my mission with a layer of clinical detachment.

We worked through individuals first: Kaisa and the cartel crest of the Pilean drug dealer. Then we discussed routines and small details I observed about the mine, the ore ship, and the operation itself as the tech on my head recorded our session. I talked about the drug pits of the camp but left out the part about becoming a regular customer. Even in my state of relaxation, the guilt of lying to my friend tasted like ashes. Tommi was gentle, discreet, and thorough and never judged me for the decisions I made.

Rion Sumner had no qualms about calling me out when I fucked up.

He strode in, blond hair freshly buzzed into a precise military style and PDD in hand, shortly after we ended our debriefing. "Tommi, do me a favor and send this to the *Nova Six* on an encrypted channel, please?"

"Yes, Commander." She took the PDD and favored me with a waggle of her talons. "See you at dinner, Dalí. Good to have you back."

Sumner fixed his attention on me with a piercing stare. "Turn off your implant. We need to talk."

Uh oh. Though I couldn't usually sense anything from Sumner, a prickle of distant heat brushed the edge of my empathic nets, and his body language betrayed the stiffness of anger. I tapped the bump behind my ear and stared back at him. He stayed silent until the med bay door slid into place behind Tommi.

"What happened today?" His voice held the crack of command.

"Some miners I had an altercation with yesterday followed us outside the camp. They started shooting and pinned Melos and me down behind an outcrop of rocks. Ziggy saved our asses, but Melos was shot as I hauled him into the ship."

"And before that?" He seemed to be expecting something.

Irritation flared as I shoved my feet into the boots waiting on the floor beside the bunk. "You know I can't read you, Commander. Is there something specific you'd like to discuss?"

"You're goddamn right there is." He shifted, his stance wide and his arms folded across his chest. "First, I'm not in the habit of having my orders questioned. When I pull you from the field, it isn't up for negotiation."

I stood, fury smoldering in the back of my skull. "I could have infiltrated the organization and found out where Skadi is hiding."

"Your mission was to gather intel about the mining operation and the identity of the Overseer, not to infiltrate the organization." A red flush crept up his neck. "Are you a member of this team or not?"

"Am I?" I didn't bother to try to conceal the sarcasm. "Everyone seems to know why we were pulled out, except me. As for my prior mission performance, I think I've proven I'm an asset."

"I won't deny it. But that isn't what I asked." Sumner cocked his head.

"I'm not one fucking step closer to bringing in the bastards who killed Gresh and Rasida. Not one."

"The Penumbra is not a tool for your private vendetta, Tamareia. Right now, I feel you're not really one of us. That we're just being used to fuel your own need for revenge, and you don't care who goes down with you."

"And I feel it's convenient when I get close to someone who might be able to tell me exactly where Skadi is, you pull me out of the mission."

His nostrils pulsed, the scarlet flush reaching all the way to his hairline. "What the hell are you insinuating?"

"I think you might not want to find your sister and bring her in."

The words slammed into him, a targeted strike that blasted a crater between us. He froze, stiff and silent. I immediately regretted what I'd said but couldn't take it back.

When he spoke, his quiet voice held the red-hot shimmer of molten metal. "I am a Penumbra agent. I will do whatever is required to fulfill my duty to protect the safety of the galaxy and its citizens and the lives of my team.

"Your blood tests show an illegal drug in your system. What I want to know is whether you were fucked up enough to let Melos get shot."

There it was. The statement hit me in the gut and took my breath away.

"The most important thing is knowing we can trust each other with our lives, Tamareia. If we don't have that, none of it works. This crew is a family. There's no room for someone with their own agenda."

I deserved every bit of this. "Am I being relieved of duty, sir?" My voice failed, suffocated beneath a heavy blanket of shame.

"Not yet. Consider this an official warning. There won't be another one. I haven't said anything to the rest of the team, but you know it's impossible to keep secrets on board *Thunder Child*." He regarded me through narrowed eyes. "You don't have a lot of time to decide if you can handle another assignment. Plenty of agents walk away like I told you. Pieces of each mission are embedded in our subconscious and change us whether we like it or not. But if you can't come all the way back from the next one, it might be a good thing."

"Sir?" Confused and dismayed, I watched him move to the door.

"A uniform is waiting in your quarters. We rendezvous with a Remoliad vessel in four hours. If you decide you are part of this team, meet me in my ready room an hour before we dock. Show me I didn't make a mistake when I offered you the job. Whatever drugs you brought into my ship I want flushed out the airlock. I catch one whiff of that shit during this mission and we head straight for Zereid, where I will personally kick your ass off the ramp."

He spun and left me. With an accusing hiss, the port slammed between us.

CHAPTER
SIX

THUNDER CHILD WASN'T a huge cruiser like the Remoliad ships. A Kadrelian-built blockade runner, she was slender, fast, and under the piloting skills of Ozzie and Sumner, slid through space like a deadly predator. The bridge level behind the cockpit housed the command center and medical. Crew quarters and mess occupied the central berth deck. On the bottom deck, the small bay sheltered *Three* between the hidden ventral gun array and the engines to stern.

Solitude could be hard to find in our haven between missions. I might have gone to my bunk, but that would be the first place someone looked for me, and I didn't want to face the rest of the team yet. The weight of humiliation bowed my back as I hurried out of medical. Instead of heading for the steep central stairwell, I turned aft to avoid my crewmates and skimmed down the ladder to the lowest deck.

I sat cross-legged with my back to the frigid bulkhead outside the still sealed decon chamber. A futile attempt to meditate left me frustrated, my mind too disordered and jumbled to make a clear decision about my future—but then again, it had been for two years.

Remorse lanced my festering guilt, and a foul deluge of self-disgust seeped out. I slammed the back of my head against the plating. "Fuck."

Melos and Ziggy could have died there on Bariish. If the ship's skin had been pierced by a lucky projectile or energy blast, *Owhra* would never have made orbit.

There was no one else to blame.

I could have given the Nos my ore bucket and walked away without picking a fight out of boredom. For taking up the goddamn vape again, I had no excuse. I hadn't been so high I couldn't function, like the dark days when grief stabbed a constant knife into my gut, and the vape's oblivion masked the pain. But the drug dulled my senses, my reflexes delayed under the influence. I couldn't deny that or the twitch in my hands every time I thought about the chems.

No apology or amends could absolve putting the lives of my friends in danger.

How could they trust me if I couldn't trust myself?

My solitude was short-lived. A brush of friendly concern against my empathic nets preceded a sound from the end of the airlock. I looked up, my vision dimmed through tears of self-reproach. Ozzie peered in and waved casually with one three-taloned hand as I hastily swiped wetness from my eyes.

"Hey. I thought I might find you here." Unlike his siblings, Ozzie spoke Sol Standard without the aid of his translator implant. His facility with languages made an impression since Cthash have no lips. His narrow tongue added a slight hiss to the *S's* of my native dialect, but otherwise, his command of the language was flawless. "Suppertime. You aren't drooling for Ra'sho's cooking after being planetside on that rock for the last eight weeks. Not hungry?"

I gave him a subdued smile. "Not really. Thanks."

"I made Sumner fly the ship so the rest of us can eat without getting indigestion." He squatted on the floor beside me. His bright-green eyes moved independently of each other on their stalks as they observed me, the tube, and my clenched fists. "He's been brooding in his ready room and biting off anybody's head who comes too close."

"He chewed off my ass. With good reason." Sighing, I tried to relax my knotted posture, hands flexed against my thighs. "I fucked up, Oz."

"I saw the blood test."

A short laugh of irony escaped. "So, the whole crew knows."

"That's kinda why I came looking for you." Both of Ozzie's eyes focused on my face. "How long have you been back on the vape? I thought you quit for good."

"I thought so too. About six weeks, and I'm already back to a daily habit."

"What made you pick it up again?"

"I didn't intend to. I had too much time on my hands. My usual trouble sleeping and the dreams ... " My voice broke. "I can't see them clearly, Oz. I'm forgetting what they looked like. How they smelled, how their skin felt under my fingertips. I'm not even sure it's them anymore. I don't want to forget."

Tears stung my eyes again, and I let them burn down my face. The sharp memory of Gresh, Rasida, and our too-brief life together kept the fire going inside me, the will to stay alive and bring the ones responsible for the bombing to justice. "When I went past the dealer's tent the first time, somebody was lighting up outside. Just the scent started my cravings again. I couldn't stop thinking about it. The next night, I went in."

"Did it help? Did the drug make them clearer in your mind?"

"No," I whispered. "Just ... made me not care as much."

Ozzie nodded once, solemnly. "And what would they have done if you had died? Do you think Gresh would self-destruct? What about Rasida?"

"No." The question seemed ludicrous. "They would have had our child to raise. Gresh's lobbying for human rights was too important. Sida had the new grant at the university. They were both passionate about their work and the things we accomplished on Luna."

"And you weren't? You were about to leave them for eighteen months, at least, and miss the birth of your child."

"No, I … " Frustrated, I couldn't find an answer. "Yes, I was that passionate about it. But it seemed pointless to worry about the future we wanted when it was destroyed in less than a heartbeat."

"Did they deserve that future?"

"Yes, they did." I impatiently palmed the tears away.

"What about everyone else in Sol Fed? In the galaxy?" He shrugged. "Most of them, at least. Those billions of young families holding the future in their arms and singing them to sleep every night. Don't they deserve the same vision of how things could be as much as Gresh and Rasida and your child did?"

His stern admonishment rocked me a little. "Of course, they do."

"That's why we do this, Dalí. When we dive into the ugly side of the galaxy, we're trying to make it better." Both of his bright-green eyes fixed on me. "You've got a gift for the work unlike few I've seen before, except when Sumner first came to us under our old commander."

He rubbed the scales underneath his jaw, a gesture I had come to learn accompanied an uncomfortable truth or confession from my friend. "In one of his first missions, Sumner infiltrated a ring as a drug runner for the Pilean cartel to find out how out-system drugs like the vape were getting into pre-Remoliad Sol Fed. We learned as much as we could about what he was running. Vaping is an extremely effective way of delivering the chemicals. Molecules are left in the nervous system for decades like a sleeping virus. Even years later, when the scent is encountered, the molecules reactivate and cause intense cravings. Humanoids like you guys and the Nos don't stand a chance when it comes to this drug. There is a synthesized pheromone component."

My head came up as comprehension flooded through me. Most humanoids are attracted by pheromones, a biological lure promising sex and propagation of the species. My changeling chemistry by nature is attuned more sensitively to these olfactory clues than other humans. No wonder this chemical and the spicy bait promising blissful, numb peace became my drug of choice.

In the attempt to exorcise the memories haunting me, I invited in another revenant, cloaked in sweet perfume.

His voice quieted. "Vape is one of the most highly addictive substances in the galaxy. The chemists who created this drug knew how to ensure repeat customers. We're still looking for the source so we can cut off the supply." He shifted, and his eyestalks waved back and forth before coming back to look me in the eye, his guilt crawling with prickly feet against the web of my empathic senses. "I probably shouldn't be telling you this, but you aren't the first to come back from a mission with a habit."

A current of disbelief zinged through my chest. For a moment I couldn't do anything but gape at him. "Sumner?"

Ozzie shrugged. "We do a lot of questionable things to fit in undercover. It comes with the job, and it's one of the risks we take. But we have to come all the way back afterward, and sometimes that's the hardest part. If he was hard on you today, he was just as harsh on himself. He felt he failed the team, and he almost quit. But we all knew, even back then, he would make a difference. So will you."

"Thank you, Ozzie." I meant it but shook my head. "I said something in there I don't think he can overlook."

"If it's the truth, maybe he shouldn't. Otherwise, he'll get over it. Sumner's not one to hold a useless grudge."

My breath hitched unevenly as the atomic countdown on the decon panel flipped and went still, an electronic buzz echoing in the tube.

Ozzie regarded me with a sideways cant. "Do you want me to get rid of them for you?"

"I appreciate that." He rose with me when I stood. "I should do it myself. But would you supervise? Just to be sure."

"Not a problem." He unlocked the hatch.

The decon box slid from its processing chamber. I unfastened my jacket pocket, fished for my wedding rings first and put them back on, one gold band on either hand. Then I withdrew the device and the chems. The vaporizer clattered into the chute to await consignment to the void.

But I hesitated and frowned at the unopened vials in my palm.

"Harder than you thought?" Ozzie's head tilted.

"No. This one. Something's different." I picked up the vial the dealer had given me—his 'gift' for my warning. The liquid inside had been as clear as water. After decontamination, a thin, cloudy sediment now rolled at the bottom, particulate that didn't appear in the other vial of amber fluid.

"That's odd." I explained to Ozzie the dealer's gift, which was suspect now I thought about it. He plucked the ampoule out of my hand and held it between two digits to examine the contents against the light, one eye telescoping in its flexible socket.

"We need to show this to Ka'pth and Ra'sho. Decon shouldn't change a chemical composition like that unless—" he hesitated.

"Unless what?"

Another shrug, and he hissed in puzzlement before answering, "Unless there was something alive in it."

———

I took a quick turn in the cleanser to rid my skin and hair of the tacky residue left by the decon spray. In the warmth and vibration, I shuddered as the last of the physical characteristics I'd adapted to pass as male shifted back into my neutral, sexless state. My crewmates didn't expect me to assume a gender, something for which I remained grateful. Without hormone stimulation to drive the change, the process was more painful, and my shoulders complained against the grind of bone and muscle.

I tamed my wavy brown mop as best I could, drawing it into a short, braided queue at the back of my neck before putting on the dress black uniform hanging in my quarters. The white starburst of diplomacy blazed in holographic relief on my left shoulder with the multiarmed spiral of the Remoliad's sigil on the opposite sleeve.

To be back in the uniform of an ambassador felt strange. Transient reflections in the narrow window showed a me I hadn't acknowledged in over two years. I barely recognized the echo of who I used to be, a transparent ghost against the stars outside.

The reason I had been pulled out of the field began to make sense, though I still didn't know what the assignment entailed. Time to find out. At the closed door of Sumner's ready room, I tugged at the tunic's high collar, squared my shoulders, and tapped on the panel.

"Commander. Permission to enter?"

"Granted." The door slid aside with his verbal acknowledgment. I stepped through.

Silhouetted by the flicker of busy data screens behind the desk, Sumner wore a black uniform with insignias of diplomatic service like mine, but without the starburst rank of ambassador. Instead, he wore the pips of an officer in the Remoliad Fleet on the high neck of his collar. He stared at the screen of a PDD, his expression dark and troubled.

Sumner glanced up and a crooked grin formed on his lips

as he rose. "Ambassador Tamareia. I haven't seen you in a while."

His vocal inflections sounded almost normal, but his eyes still held frost. We were never this formal with each other, a sign of the tension between us.

"I haven't seen me in a long time either. It feels very strange." I took a deep breath. "I would like to apologize for my insubordination, especially for what I said in med bay, Commander. I was out of line." Embarrassment burned in my cheeks, and I lowered my gaze. "I owe Melos and Ziggy more than an apology. I was under the influence on a mission, and I put the lives of my teammates in danger. I will accept the consequences of my actions as you deem appropriate."

"Grab a chair." He gestured opposite his desk, and I sat. "I think I owe you an apology as well. I've gotten used to autonomy. When some bureaucrat tells me to drop whatever I'm doing and pull my operatives in the middle of a potentially productive mission, it pisses me off. The order to recall you came from so far over my head I got vertigo. The rest is just the frost on the comet, and it pushed me over the line." He cleared his throat. "I'm sorry for the vendetta remark."

"No, you were right. I needed to be reminded why I'm here. You promised only that I will be involved when we take them down, not that I would be the instrument." No matter how badly I wanted the privilege, I had a bigger job to do. "Who told you to recall me?"

His mouth twisted in an ironic smile. "The Remoliad security council."

My eyebrows threatened to merge with my hairline. "The security council has authority over the Penumbra?"

"Technically. My superior answers to the secretary general, but it's almost unheard of to receive a direct order from any office."

"I don't understand." I frowned. "Did my mother have anything to do with this?"

"No, Ambassador Urquhart isn't involved as far as we can tell. We checked since the order was so specific. But I just received more details." He handed me the data device he'd been scowling at when I came in. "Against all previous declarations of disdain for galactic alliance, the Ursetu recently issued an emergency petition for their planet to become a member of the Remoliad."

I narrowed my eyes at him and took the PDD. "I saw something about that in my debriefing file. The crown princess is dead?"

"Yes. The queen and her grandson, Prince Razaxha, are still alive."

"What happened? Was the planet attacked?"

"Yes and no." He swept his hand and a heads-up display swirled into view between us. "I'll warn you up front, this is brutal."

The wreck of some immense ship blighted the forested grounds of a ziggurat-like palace, silhouetted against the backdrop of a sharp black mountain. Columns of smoke and flames traced the outline of warped and twisted debris. The recording lens zoomed in on a section of the disaster where tiny flashes of light sparked and died. As the picture enlarged, I sat forward in shock.

"Enhance this area." Sumner circled the spot on the heads-up and spread his fingers. The portion of the holovid expanded, grainy, blurred, and blocked by foliage, but I made it out plainly enough. Enormous, gray-skinned figures piled out of the wreckage.

Shontavians.

The four-armed beings appeared unstoppable as they swatted aside the Ursetu and their guns, snatched up the soldiers with their sharp-taloned hands and—

A psychic memory of the taste of blood and entrails hit me so hard I fought the urge to vomit.

"Stop the playback!" I drew heavy breaths through my

nose until the nausea passed and my heart stopped pounding. Sumner swept his hand over the enlarged holo, reducing details to a safe distance as my mind attempted to process what I'd seen.

A ship hadn't crashed in the middle of an Ursetu city. It was the orbiting laboratory where Shontavians were engineered and kept isolated until their sale to whomever bought their mercenary services. It crashed into the planet or was deliberately brought down.

By whom?

The Ursetu faced monsters of their own making—huge, intelligent creatures with the serrated teeth and claws of a predator, created solely for fighting wars. And they had a craving for sentient meat.

CHAPTER
SEVEN

SUMNER REACHED into to the locker beside his chair and came up with his precious bottle of whiskey and two glasses. He poured a generous shot into one of the small tumblers and pushed it toward me across the tabletop. "Can you handle this now?"

"Oh, hell yes." I slammed it back, not bothering to savor the novelty of real, old-fashioned, Earth-type alcohol.

"That is the royal city, the seat of government on Urset. Princess Arzalat led a group of warrior-caste troops against the Shontavians that survived the crash." Sumner refilled my glass and poured his own drink before he spoke again. "It was a slaughter. Once the soldiers were dead the Shontavians commandeered their weapons. The queen's evacuating ship was fired upon. The royal city is on an island, isolated from the mainland. Citizens were evacuated to prevent further loss of life. So far, the Shontavians are dug in near the wreckage of the orbiting facility and don't appear to be going anywhere."

"Not until they're hungry, anyway," I twirled the glass, thinking. "Somebody has got to be giving them commands. They're intelligent but conditioned to take orders. The targeted crash suggests the facility was brought down deliberately."

"It is a possibility." Sumner frowned. "Ka'pth and Ra'sho did some preliminary digging, but the Ursetu keep everything about their planet's culture and caste system close to the vest. Four and a half years ago, a civil war broke out. It has been smoldering ever since. If somebody did try to bring the facility down on top of the palace, maybe they intended the lab to burn up on reentry and kill all the Shontavians, but you see that didn't happen. The Ursetu estimate about ten survived the crash. Maybe fewer now since the battle on the holo, but those things are bulletproof to small arms."

"They engineered them that way. This certainly feels like a deliberate act. Whoever did it knew some of them would survive."

"The queen sent her grandson, Prince Razaxha, to present the petition for emergency membership to the Remoliad. He will be the new leader of Urset's warrior caste when he comes of age."

I hoped the grandson had a strong stomach and some serious firepower. "How old is Prince Razaxha?"

"Very, very young. Early teens by Sol Fed reckoning."

A groan escaped me. "Any military experience?"

"Unlikely."

A sense of foreboding etched lines into my forehead. "Exactly why was I recalled for this assignment, Commander?"

"Because the Council requested some rather specific help." Sumner's ocean-colored eyes glinted. "Only one person has ever successfully negotiated with a Shontavian and lived to tell the tale."

My jaw unhinged and dropped. "The Remoliad wants to negotiate with the Shontavians? And it wasn't me. Rhix made the deal. I just … " I stopped talking and studied him with suspicion as he regarded me. He was holding something back.

"News traveled pretty fast somebody had survived a death match against them," he said at last. "And when that person is something of a viral hero after fighting off a pirate boarding party, well … we live in a small galaxy. I think you should look at the file on your PDD."

I skimmed my finger against the screen and pulled up the data. A holo of the Ursetu queen and her family whirled into three-dimensional particles of light above the device. The regal female stood in the forefront, black-and-white-streaked curls caught up in a diadem mounted with blood-hued Ursetu rubies. Beside her loomed another female in decorative battle armor, geometric patterns inlaid in precious metals. Her crown bore a single ruby in the center. Between the royal adults stood a child on the cusp of adolescence. His bearing possessed the same hauteur as his mother and grandmother, but his eyes held laughter as if the image was captured in a rare moment of decorum. At least a score of other royals were pictured in the holographic image, but the figure standing just to the left of the queen, crownless, armored, and proud, made my mouth go dry. My pulse tripped unevenly.

Rhix.

"His real name is Nazhir." Sumner sat back in his chair. "He's the queen's son."

———

A moment passed before I found my voice again and made sure it stayed level. "Does the security council know what he's doing now?"

"Highly doubtful. Let's assume only we know for the moment. You and I are the only ones who saw him face-to-face."

Fumbling for the whiskey, I took a more thoughtful sip

and barely tasted it in my discomfiture. "When was this holo made?"

"Five years ago. He doesn't appear in any holos after that, which lines up with the time you estimated he became a mercenary and right up to the timeline for the civil war. Stories about why he left are impossible to come by since the Ursetu don't have much use for news media. Did he ever tell you why?"

"Not quite. He said, 'One can't abuse their subjects and expect them to follow.' He told me he didn't deserve his title."

"Was he banished?"

"I think he left of his own accord." My hand tightened around the glass. "Where is the royal family now?"

"The queen is on Urset trying to hold things together. Prince Razaxha is at the Remoliad. An emergency session is scheduled tomorrow to hear him out. The delegates from planets that faced Shontavian mercenaries in battle are threatening to block Urset's membership."

"The public nature of these negotiations could jeopardize any future undercover missions I take part in," I said with quiet dismay. "That's what you meant, isn't it? If I can't come all the way back from this."

"Keep away from broadcast proceedings, and it might be possible to stay anonymous."

"My mother is the Sol Fed Delegate to the Remoliad. I'm not unknown to some of the other delegates. I worked with them via subspace communications before the bombing." The memory of shattered glass and twisted steel got drowned in another slug of whiskey. "I'm not certain it will be possible to maintain a low profile."

But my mind had already begun to calculate what I needed to prepare for this short-notice assignment. My best assets were our Andari crewmates. A decisive tap on my implant opened communications. "Ka'pth and Ra'sho, can you compile as much data for me as possible on Ursetu culture, Shontavians, and previous rulings by the Remoliad on the bioengineered species of unaffiliated systems before we leave *Thunder Child*?"

"Of course, Dalí," Ra'sho's translated voice responded at once. "We anticipated it would be needed. The download is on your personal device." I found myself grinning. Ka'pth and Ra'sho's ability to "anticipate" was one of the things that made them invaluable to Sumner's team.

Did I bring anything to the team they didn't have without me? The grin faded.

"Thanks, Ra'sho."

Sumner didn't look at me now. "I had no idea what the council wanted until half an hour ago. Then I almost hoped you'd decide to walk away." His expression was still odd—a mixture of concern, anger, and something else I couldn't put a finger on.

"I don't feel I can turn down this assignment. The Shontavians are intelligent enough to negotiate. I'm glad the Remoliad recognizes this, rather than just destroying them. But I know what they are capable of."

"So do I." He rolled the whiskey in his glass. "Not just because of what we saw on the Market ship but what I experienced as a mercenary. I was part of the final troop surge on Lymo during the Scata Rebellion."

Aghast, I stared at him. He was in that bloodbath? The Scata Rebellion had been one of the deadliest conflicts the galaxy had seen in recent times, and the last known war to include Shontavian mercenaries. The ruthless dictator, General Moserok, amassed a list of atrocities rivaling anything recorded in Earth's bloody history. Lymo's freedom fighters and their allies eventually won but at the deadly price of a generation. I was still living on Zereid when the war happened. Sumner was only five years older than me. No wonder he didn't talk much about his mercenary tours.

"Seven hells. I had no idea." After a short hesitation, I

decided I wanted to ask: "Given your experience, what is your opinion of negotiating with the Shontavians?"

His jaw tightened. "I think you've been given a fool's mission. But I won't let you go into it alone." He gulped the last of his whiskey and finally looked up. "You will get to choose a diplomatic team before you leave for Urset. I called in all my favors and insisted on being assigned as your security advisor if you'll have me. I want to make sure you have someone at your back you can trust."

Relief sang a high song in my ears. "Yes. Thank you."

The stress of these revelations brought on a tension in my shoulders and the twitchy feeling in my hands. I was more appreciative of the last mouthful of whiskey. The warmth in my throat burned less fiercely than *agzi*, the naturally distilled liquor as mellow and smooth as I remembered. With a shaky sigh, I set the glass on the desk. It rattled against the surface with the tremors. Sumner noticed.

"You got rid of the drugs?"

"Yes, sir." I contemplated the shameful vibration in my hand before admitting: "I'm concerned about withdrawal during the early part of this mission. The first time, I was unconscious for the worst of it. I might have a rough week ahead of me."

"There's a procedure that speeds up the physical detox process. The doctor on board *Nova Six* is prepared for your arrival. I won't lie. It's going to suck." He appeared to want to say something else but instead ended with, "I'm sorry I didn't ask your permission. We don't have time to wait it out."

"Understood." I rose. "I'll go read the files until the rendezvous if you're finished with me, Commander."

He stood too. "You sure you're okay with this?" His head tilted as he scrutinized my expression. "All of it?"

"Of course," I lied. "Let me know when the *Nova Six* arrives, and I'll meet you at the airlock." I left his office and walked through the command center, my eyes on the PDD as if I were absorbed in the information, but the screen was blank. I descended the narrow stairwell to the second deck and turned into my quarters, my palm slapping the door release on the way in. It sighed shut as I dropped the PDD on the lower bunk and sank down on the mattress with my face buried in my hands.

A morass of whispering insecurities and doubt seethed in my mind. I would be stepping back into the deep end of the life I had abandoned when my family died—one in which I had been unable to function due to the still-raw loss of Gresh, Sida, and the child we created together.

I once told someone I didn't survive the explosion that killed them. I just took six months longer to die. The person I had been did not exist anymore, and the experience left me jaded, more reckless. Less concerned with the future.

Ozzie's gentle reproach had reminded me a future remained out there for countless other beings. Deep end or not, it was time to dive in and hope to hell I still remembered how to swim.

The Kadrelian doctor on board *Nova Six* was merciless. By nature, Kadrelians are no-nonsense beings of few words, driven by order and logic. My health history records left him shaking his head, but once he got over it, Dr. Muus became almost loquacious for one of his species.

After I changed into an examination tunic and climbed into the medical pod, he silently handed me a bucket. It seemed rather large.

"A precaution?" I asked as he exposed my abdomen.

"A necessity." Deft, sure tentacles wiggled a carpet of needles on the underside of the nanopatch into the skin near my liver, while a second pair of his appendages fitted one over my left side. "I cannot give you medications that distract the nanobots from the targeted molecules. This will be unpleasant."

Gritting my teeth, I endured the discomfort as the patches burrowed into my flesh. Penance isn't supposed to be pleasant. Pain is the just reward for being a dumbass.

He encircled my left forearm with a sheath fringed in tubing, jeweled in blinking readouts. It tightened against my skin with a serpentine hiss; unseen fangs inside the cuff pierced my veins and crimson flowed from one of the tubes into a device beside the bed. The filter blushed with my blood, spilled over into another set of tubing, and returned to the cuff with a strange, silvery sheen of nanoparticles surfing the scarlet crest into my body.

"When will I start feeling—" The last words came out as *blaaaarrrgh*, followed by an explosion of vomit.

"Now," he said mildly as one tentacle lifted the bucket closer to my face.

In the first hour I relived the deadliest hangovers I've ever had, all at once. My head pounded. My stomach repeatedly turned inside out until I was certain everything I drank in my life had come back to haunt me.

"If this is the worst, I can handle it," I managed to say between bouts of vomiting.

"That is yet to come," Dr. Muus gravely assured me.

I spent the second hour convinced something under my skin was trying to crawl out of me. Dr. Muus restrained my wrists to keep me from tearing flesh away with my fingernails.

By hour three, my muscles ripped themselves apart and tied the shredded ends back together in knots. Cold sweat rolled off my body, and I bit my lips bloody, breath coming in short, tortured gasps, eyelids clenched tightly against the pain.

Faces hovered in the red darkness behind my eyes. Delirium's surreal landscape was not unfamiliar to me. I'd visited that kingdom of nightmares and wishful visions before when I nearly died. I sensed Gresh and Rasida were among these hallucinatory presences. Better that they didn't see me like this. They would be disappointed. Turning my head away brought the inscrutable blue face of my Zereid crechemate, Gor, into focus. His lidless quicksilver eyes elongated into ovals, a loving but stern look.

"Peacemaker or peacekeeper," he whispered. "You will find your path again, beloved friend."

His visage dissolved into the fog of my mind. Another face took shape, this one gray, the wide maw full of pointed teeth. The sharp, black eyes of a Shontavian watched me as its mouth opened and sifted the air, filtering my scent.

It snarled, reaching for me with its four arms, the claw-tipped hands spread wide. A wordless cry of terror and anger rose in my throat.

Someone touched my hand where I grasped, white-knuckled, at a twist of sweat-drenched sheet. I opened blurry eyes to see Rion Sumner sitting beside the medical pod.

"It's the nanobots," Sumner said gently. "No shame in screaming. I sure as hell did."

His palm was warm against mine, fingers encircling my thumb. I squeezed, the hard pressure in return real and comforting. I rode out the pain, gripping his hand as if it were the last thing keeping my head above water. At last, hours later, my muscles unwound with a shudder when the nanos completed their task and returned to the dialysis filter.

Ocean-colored eyes swam in front of me as I blinked through sludgy exhaustion. He hadn't left. The shadow of a beard and the rumpled undertunic of his uniform proved he had been there for the duration.

"You still have beautiful eyes, even if you are a hallucination," I mumbled. He grinned.

"Hey," he said quietly. "You made it. The worst part is over."

"There will still be the psychological symptoms," Dr. Muus corrected as a tentacle-tip delicately entered a dose of sedative into his touchscreen.

"Joy killer," I slurred. The warm, sweet buzz of medication began to scramble my cracked thought processes.

A chuckle rumbled in my ears, and Sumner squeezed my hand. "Get some sleep. We hit the ground running tomorrow morning."

I couldn't keep my eyes open, but I knew when Sumner moved to disengage his hand from mine. I didn't let go and drew him back down.

"Don't let me fuck this up, Rion," I pleaded, my tongue thick and clumsy.

He smoothed the sweat-bedraggled hair out of my face. He said something else, but I didn't hear what it was, already floating away on the sedative.

The darkness behind my closed eyes faded from red to black. I slept.

CHAPTER EIGHT

MY BODY PROVED PAINFULLY sensitive under the vibration and heat of the cleanser the next morning. A dull headache pounded in the back of my skull. Despite those complaints, I felt unexpectedly normal, given eight hours earlier I tried to claw my way out of my own skin. After I ate a bland meal, and the doctor was satisfied I could keep it down, I tugged on uniform pants while he gave discharge instructions.

"You will still experience emotional lability, anxiety, and irritation for some time," Dr. Muus informed me. "The serotonin reuptake blockers left by the nanobots should be in full effect within two weeks, but the psychological needs which led you to the drug must be addressed. The human neurological system is uniquely susceptible to addiction, and danger of recurrence is constant. You cannot turn to chemicals to cope with your loss."

My empathic nets caught a wave of something from the stoic Kadrelian almost resembling sympathy. Of course, he knew everything about me. I'd personally handed him the holo record of my medical and psych history.

"I understand, Doctor."

His tentacles waved. "I have worked with Commander Sumner and the Penumbra before. My security clearance is high enough I know the nature of your work, if not the details." He paused. "Ambassador, may I speak frankly?"

I looked up, amusement quirking my lips as I pulled on the black tunic. "Do you speak any other way, Dr. Muus?"

Perfectly good sarcasm is wasted on a Kadrelian. He ignored the remark. "You must assume your own identity to thoroughly process these things. You cannot hide behind an alias and pretend to be someone else."

My fingers hesitated in their work, fumbling with the fasteners on the front of my uniform. "I don't know if that's a good idea." I wasn't sure I was ready to …

To be me again.

"There are sensitive galactic matters involved. I can't let my personal issues get in the way."

"They will get in the way again if you refuse to acknowledge them, Ambassador." Tentacles curled akimbo against his sides. Dr. Muus looked prepared to die on this hill, and I was not up to the fight.

"I will take your advice under consideration." I finished doing up the tunic and tugged on my boots. A series of tones sounded over the ship's com system; lights swelled and dimmed over the door. The Kadrelian glided over to a screen and nodded in satisfaction.

"We are on approach to the Remoliad. Farewell, Ambassador Tamareia. A safe journey to wherever you are bound."

I hefted my bag and winced at the residual soreness in my neck and shoulders. "Goodbye. Thank you, Dr. Muus."

The quiet of the medical facility shattered as the door opened into a busy passageway filled with gray-fatigued beings. Oxygen-breathing crew bustled about on their approach duties, most of them bipedal, but I encountered more Kadrelians flowing liquidly over the immaculate deck on whisper-quiet tentacles. I had to do a quick sidestep to avoid treading on sensitive appendages.

I realized I had no idea where to find Sumner and tapped the bump of the com behind my ear. "Commander? I've been released from medical. Where can I meet you?"

"Hang on. Coming your way now."

Clean-shaven and in a fresh uniform, Sumner's broad-shouldered frame was easy to spot among the rest of the crew. His own bag dangled from his hand. Sol Fed hadn't yet committed any human personnel to the Remoliad's fleet, and curious appraisals were cast at us as we met.

"We're going this way." He motioned down the passage, and I fell into step with him. "How do you feel?" he inquired.

"Surprisingly, not like I just had my nervous system stripped by nanobots."

"Glad to hear it. I was just informed there's an incoming shuttle for us. They aren't even waiting for the ship to dock at the hub."

I glanced up at him in alarm. "Are things really that dire?"

"I don't know yet. I'm not even sure who's on the shuttle, but I have a suspicion it isn't the minister of security."

Watching through the port overlooking the landing bay, I cringed as a short-hop vessel with a Ferian sigil on its flank lurched through the doors. Piloted like a novice sat at the helm, the craft's engines were barely cut before it landed clumsily on the deck.

"What the fuck?" I muttered.

Sumner gave me a side-eye. "Are ambassadors supposed to say fuck?"

I sighed. "This is going to be tougher than I thought."

We waited for the klaxons to indicate safe pressurization of the vast hangar in the underbelly of *Nova Six*. A Ferian standing awkwardly on his hind legs beckoned us from the end of the ramp as Sumner and I jogged across the bay.

"I am Lam Tiri, personal secretary to Delegate Mi Prinoya

of Feria." He began to extend his forepaw, swayed, and dropped to all fours, shaking his furry ruff in embarrassment. One lip curled over a sharp, white fang, and the slow burn of his embarrassment touched my empathic senses. "Forgive me. I am new to my post and still unpracticed at standing on only two limbs. She is waiting inside for you."

"A pleasure to meet you, Lam Tiri," I assured him with a grave bow of my head. "The Ferian tribes are represented with honor, whether on four limbs or two."

"Your kindness is appreciated." His tawny gaze avoided mine. "Please, we must not keep her waiting."

Given the Ferian insignia on the craft's side, I expected a utilitarian transport on the interior as we ascended the walkway. I was wrong.

Rich tapestry hung from the ceiling. Draped and fastened to the bulkheads, the material created a tent-like atmosphere. Four deep-cushioned seats were bolted around a table set with shallow cups in magnetic holders, and a tiny pot gave off wisps of steam.

Another Ferian uncurled with slow grace from one of the padded chairs as we entered. Female, she wore an artificial ruff, a glistening corona of fur and metallic fibers that collared her formal robe.

"Greetings, Ambassador Tamareia." She stood and extended her right forepaw with its long, clever digits. I shook it, the silk of fine fur between her pads trailing delicately against my fingers. A rub of her sleek jaw against mine and a trilling purr greeted me in Ferian fashion; then she pulled back and studied me. Her bright topaz gaze narrowed in curiosity beneath heavy, furred lids. "You are definitely Delegate Urquhart's cub. You have her strange, smoky eyes."

I smiled. "Delegate Prinoya, I presume?"

"Yes."

I presented my companion. "This is Commander Sumner, my security advisor."

She greeted him politely enough but omitted the Ferian cheek-rub. Leaving out the greeting was a slight and a clear indication Prinoya considered him the help. Ferian aristocrats were generally aloof and insufferably self-important. No exception here.

Prinoya motioned to the table. "Please sit. We must leave immediately to ensure we arrive in good time before the emergency session convenes." She waved at the steaming vessel. "I prepared *mirrba* for you."

Oh, seven hells. *Mirrba* was an interesting custom among the Ferian upper crust—few cultures serve shots of their own spiced, curdled breast milk to guests, but it is a mark of high regard, and to refuse the offer would be extremely rude.

"You honor us, Delegate Prinoya." I took the seat directly across from hers, and Sumner sat between us.

The young secretary sealed the hatch and brushed past me with an abject apology as he slipped through a slit in the tapestry to the pilot's compartment. Prinoya's upper lip curled back from both fangs as she watched him slink by on four limbs, her disdain sour against my mind. "Please strap in. We will depart in a moment."

The shuttle's engines began to whine, and outside the ports lining the cabin, flashing lights warned depressurization was under way. My ears popped. Prinoya's ruff whispered as she shook her head against the pressure changes and sank gracefully into her seat.

Our craft wobbled out of the bay, and I found myself clutching the edge of my seat as the shuttle lurched to port. The younger Ferian, a junior attaché by appearances, clearly had little experience as a pilot, which seemed strange. Surely Delegate Prinoya had access to the Remoliad's flight officers on official business.

Which implied this was not an official visit.

Once we cleared the ship's hull, my breath caught in my throat when I saw the view. To port, the enormous spherical hub of the Remoliad and its interconnected spiral rings hung like a jewel against a backdrop of stars, a physical representation of our galaxy in architectural form. It was impossible not to marvel at the construct, a feat of engineering created to house the interests of galactic peace. The structure passed from my sight as the shuttle executed an uneven turn and smoothed out into a direct approach.

Prinoya detached the magnetic pot and poured a lumpy, yellow-white liquid flecked with herbs into the waiting palm-sized cups. The rising steam carried a scent of exotic seasonings, but the undisguisable aroma of spoilage hit my nostrils. I suppressed a flinch. I had a feeling this was as much a test as an honor.

The trick was to swallow it as quickly as possible without gagging.

The dense, sour tang of fermentation on the back of my tongue mellowed with something that reminded me of ginger, but the experience still made my throat convulse. I hoped I wouldn't disgrace my species by heaving it back up. My still-sore abdominal muscles probably couldn't muster a decent upchuck, anyway.

Sumner was clearly no stranger to this custom and tossed it back, but I noted he swallowed hard more than once, his chiseled jaw tightening. Delegate Prinoya looked satisfied with our courtesy and curled back into her seat.

"May I ask why you've chosen to transport us in your personal shuttle, Delegate?" Sumner asked thickly. His cup clicked into the magnetic cradle as he replaced it.

"As a member of the security council, I wanted an opportunity to meet Ambassador Tamareia before the negotiations begin," Prinoya replied blithely. "There are so many delegates coming in for the emergency session, I did not think it right to request an official vessel." Her innocent explanation rang false underneath, a clear deflection and tickle of anxiety against my empathic nets. I noted the tuft of her prehensile tail flicking nervously beneath her robe.

Interesting. She had another motive for intercepting us prior to our arrival at the Remoliad.

Ah, intrigue. Most diplomatic communities have plenty of secrets. Clandestine meetings and private negotiations are conducted in the shadows before items ever reach the floor for public discussion. Policy and legislation passes or fails long before a single vote is ever registered in Sol Fed. But in the Remoliad, things were usually held to a higher standard, transparency valued more highly than in other arenas of diplomacy. With an agenda as sensitive as the Urset situation, and former victims of Shontavian mercenary troops like the Ferians already members of the Allied systems, the chambers had to be buzzing with very public discontent.

So why was she here?

A twitch of sudden impatience tightened my shoulders, and I decided to be blunt. "You could have met me with less trouble at the proceedings. I think it's clear there is something you wish to say in private, Delegate Prinoya. Shall we get to the point?"

She blinked. Her interest in me sharpened as her pupils dilated. "You are direct, aren't you?" She turned to Sumner, who had been giving me a surreptitious what the hell look. "Will you be so kind as to copilot Lam Tiri on approach to the Remoliad?"

One eyebrow rose as he registered his abrupt dismissal, but Sumner unbuckled his harness without argument. "Certainly, Delegate." He stood and ducked into the cockpit through the slit in the faux canopy, the murmur of his voice still audible in my head as he quietly spoke to the young pilot. He'd be able to hear most of the conversation over our implant coms.

"What do you want to discuss?" I sat back and steepled my hands in front of me, waiting.

"I would like to know how, exactly, you have experience negotiating with Shontavians, Ambassador." Her slit nostrils pulsed as if trying to catch the scent of my qualifications. "The data is vague, to say the least, and our new minister has been less than forthcoming with any information about your suitability for such a sensitive assignment."

"And I have not yet been briefed on the Remoliad's expectations of me. I can't tell you more."

"The minister's devotion to peace is admirable, but in this case, foolish." Her fangs glinted in a snarl. "It can only end in disaster. The Shontavians must be destroyed."

"I understand your concerns, but you do realize you are talking about the genocide of a sentient species?" I sat back, discomfited.

"Are there exceptions in Remoliad legislature for cases like this?"

My mouth twitched as I suppressed a horrified laugh. "No, the laws prohibit the purposeful extinction of any sentient species. Are you not familiar with those statutes?"

"It has never come up before," she sniffed. "There is a group of delegates on the security council from worlds like mine, which suffered under the Shontavian menace. We feel more decisive action must be taken. The vote was tied and broken by the minister in favor of his own plan." She growled deep in her throat. "What will you recommend if you cannot negotiate a peace with these creatures?"

"As I said, I can't even speak to that yet." Rising licks of heat flared behind my forehead as my irritation grew. "It would be inappropriate for me to speculate."

We stared each other down for a few breaths. Her righteous anger scraped against my senses in the same way her unsheathed claws whispered across the surface of the table. "It is the security council's responsibility to address threats to the safety of the galaxy. Ferian tribes were slaughtered by the thousands when our enemies introduced Shontavian mercenaries into their ranks, sold to them by the very caste of Ursetu who now beg for our help against their own abominations."

Abomination. The word was used against me often enough in Sol Fed to raise hackles on the back of my neck, my fingers tightening on the edge of my chair as she continued.

"The Ursetu will find approval of their petition difficult without our votes, Ambassador." The purr disguised a threat. "If we were to have assurances you will broker a deal with the Ursetu to eliminate the Shontavians should they refuse to submit—even in a painless and compassionate way, though those abominations—"

"Don't use that word again," I snapped, my palm slapping the table.

Her tawny eyes hardened.

"I apologize, Ambassador. I did not realize the word was offensive to humans."

"What is offensive is the ease with which intelligent beings invalidate another's right to exist." *Breathe, Dalí,* I reminded myself. *You're losing it.* I modulated my voice. "Pardon my harsh words. It is no more prominent in your species than in my own, Delegate. What is the Ferian saying? One should not roar … "

"One should not roar over the sound of another's pain." She regarded me coolly, less agitated now. "Forgive me as well, Ambassador Tamareia. You have an assignment none of us envy, and I shall not complicate it any further. You realize you may not survive?"

The taste of copper. *Oh, so much better than you know.* "Being an interspecies negotiator is not a safe haven. There will always be someone for whom violence is the only voice they feel they possess. My job is to help them find a new way to communicate."

Sumner's voice sounded in my head, echoed by the cabin's com system. "Please prepare for landing."

Prinoya hastily buckled her harness, the nervous flip of her tail tuft again evident. "Do you think Commander Sumner will take over the controls from Tiri? I would very much like us to reach the emergency session in one piece."

The edge of a dry smile lifted one corner of my mouth. "Don't worry, Delegate. He will make certain we arrive safely."

The titanic structure loomed above and below us, each curving arm that mimicked the spiral whirl of our galaxy vast enough to encompass the bulk of a cruiser. The throat of the landing hub swallowed us whole, a vista of stars outside replaced by striations of metal tubing and flashing lights, which guided Sumner and his copilot into the belly of the station. My nerves were jangling by the time the shuttle smoothly touched down in its private bay, but not from the flight.

I was two years late to my appointment with the Remoliad. My hands fumbled with the harness latch. Outside the port, the articulated teeth of pressure doors slowly closed behind us, and I hoped I wouldn't be chewed up and spit out by this mission.

CHAPTER
NINE

DELEGATE PRINOYA MADE a hasty excuse to part ways before we even exited the bay, eager to distance herself from us. "I must go to my office before the hearing begins. Lam Tiri will guide you to your destination. I will see you again soon, Ambassador."

She nodded regally, her ruff bobbing with a metallic rustle, and Tiri teetered carefully down the ramp on his hind legs as Prinoya walked purposefully toward a lift. The door whisked shut behind her.

Lam Tiri smiled hesitantly at Sumner, his fangs submissively concealed by his lower lip. "Thank you for your pointers, Commander. I think that is the smoothest landing I have ever made."

"You're going to be a good pilot, Tiri. You just need to log more hours," Sumner told him.

"I'm not really a pilot at all." He shook his ruff. "I'm an interspecies negotiator."

"Are you? Your qualifications are too high to be relegated to secretarial duties," I said in surprise.

"The Ferian council couldn't ignore my degrees when I requested an appointment to the Remoliad, but I'm the first

Ylaran to be assigned to a diplomatic post. They do not consider my tribe to be sophisticated enough to hold an ambassadorial position."

His difficulty standing upright made sense now. The Ylara were a minority among the Ferians, a genetic branch that still retained their ancestors' shorter bowed spines and long front limbs. While the major tribes were bipedal, the Ylara still ambulated upon three or four limbs.

"Those are impressive credentials, Tiri. I'm certain others will notice."

"Thank you, Ambassador." Tiri gave me a small smile. His eyes told me he knew he deserved more. Prejudice is no stranger to the majority of galactic society, even as sophisticated as most space-faring races are. Given my own experience in Sol Fed, I shouldn't be surprised anymore.

Not surprised. Disappointed, and pissed off.

He glanced between us. "Do you mind if I—" His front limbs dipped in a plea.

"No. Be comfortable," I reassured him.

"Thank you." His body relaxed into a lithe crouch, his weight balanced on all four limbs rather than two, discomfort visibly relieved. "I wondered, Ambassador Tamareia, and forgive me if I am out of line—what do you think of relocation to one of the uninhabited island chains on Therenato as an option for the Shontavians? They are too small for a large group to settle but fertile and removed from the mainland by an ocean."

"That is certainly a viable solution if we could ensure a suitable food source for them," I responded, a smile tugging at my mouth. "I like the way you think."

His pride and pleasure at my compliment radiated warmth against my empathic nets as I continued, "Assuming we can get the Shontavians to the table at all, we will have to discover what they want. The ones I negotiated with before simply wanted a place where they could see the stars outside the ship they served upon."

"That is remarkable and makes me sad," Tiri mused.

"They hadn't seen anything but bulkheads and corridors for a century."

"I didn't know they had such a long life span." Tiri's golden eyes widened.

"I don't think anyone knows how long they can live when they aren't on the front lines of battle."

Lam Tiri's quick mind worked on the problem, his expression intense. "Long-term food sources present another dilemma. I wonder if—" He stopped abruptly. My sensitivity illuminated a stab of chagrin as it flashed like lightning in the whirlwind of his thoughts. "Forgive me for delaying you. It is almost time for the session. Follow me, please."

The aide padded through the crowd in the busy corridor outside the bay. He moved in a quick, graceful lope, and Sumner and I trailed in his wake as he led us to a private lift. "This enters the secure hallway behind the Remoliad chambers, where the senior ministers' offices are located. Go to the sixth level screening area. I expect there will be someone from the minister's staff waiting for you there."

We thanked him, and he vanished back into the busy flow of diplomatic traffic.

"I can't imagine it's easy working for that particular delegate when he's probably more qualified than she is." I shot a glance in the direction Tiri had gone. "He understands the implications. This conversation was a lot more pleasant than the one I had with Prinoya."

"You'll have to fill me in on some of the details later," he murmured as we entered the lift. "I heard most of it. Some without the implant." He raised one eyebrow at me. "You doing okay?"

"I just need to stay busy." Anxiety tunneled its way

through my chest like an industrious worm. I hoped it wasn't going to burst out at an inopportune time.

The lift opened on a small security checkpoint. An energy curtain separated the lobby from the rest of the corridor. Beyond the intimidating crackle, I caught a glimpse of doors lining the curved passageway.

The Andari officer gave me a curious look as she scanned my bag. Apparently, most diplomats don't carry knives in their luggage, but my shiny new credentials bore a weapons permit. So did Sumner's. The commander must have had some unusual toys in his bag because the Andari's throat gills went flat and stiff before stuttering back into ruffled consternation. Dismay and alarm radiated against my empathic nets as she stared at the scanner in her webbed hands.

"Sir, I am afraid I cannot permit—"

"I will vouch for them, Officer Ni'ksh," a smooth voice interjected from the other side of the humming energy curtain. A tall being with skin shaded in hues of gray and lavender regarded us with interest. Carmine eyes gleamed in an ethereally handsome face as he encompassed us both with a regal nod.

I recognized him at once as my mother's seatmate in the holo vid. Even more attractive in the flesh, I found myself staring at him in a very un-ambassadorial way.

A burst of adoration tickled my mind, and I glanced in surprise at the security officer. Apparently, I was not the only one affected by that Tolkish beauty.

"They will be leaving directly after the session and have the appropriate security clearance for small arms." He favored the guard with a luminous smile. Her gills rippling so fast I thought she might take flight, the Andari nodded crisply.

"Of course, Minister Sim." She punched a code on her PDD, and the energy curtain shimmered from red to cool blue.

On my right, Sumner froze, his expression betraying shock. He stared at Sim, not in appreciation, but as if seeing a ghost.

"Everything all right?" I asked, concerned.

"Yeah. Fine. Go on. I'll be right there." He didn't meet my gaze though. I wondered what the hell was up.

I passed through the hair-raising prickle of energy. Sim extended his pale hand to me, palm forward, and I met it automatically with mine as he said, "Welcome to the Remoliad, Ambassador Tamareia. I am Alecto Sim, head of the security council. It is a pleasure to finally meet you."

His low, velvety voice, and Remoliad Standard brushed with a Tolkish trill to the R's ... It was sexy. I could listen to him speak all day—a very dangerous thing in a politician. A pretty voice can get away with a lot of ugliness.

"Minister Sim." The faint brush of his consciousness touched my senses, but a fuzzy blanket lay between his mind and mine. Against his smooth, hairless skull, a woven band of delicate silver wire encircled his temples. A psi shield?

In an environment such as the Remoliad, psi shields were not a bad idea, especially for someone privy to top-secret information. I had enough training with the Zereid to recognize an intrusion into my mind, but most beings do not, and not all telepaths shared the same respect for privacy.

Still, I found it surprising the head of the security council had come personally to escort us. I waited for Sumner to retrieve his own bag from the lovestruck Andari. He walked slowly, and I took measure of his approach, almost cautious, as if Sumner were uncertain how he might be received. Alecto Sim nodded at him, a gentle smile on his lips.

"Commander Sumner. I know it must have been highly irregular for me to order an immediate recall but necessary under the circumstances. I regret the inconvenience to you and your team. Thank you for your trouble."

Sumner blinked, his answer a beat late as he processed

Sim's contrite apology. "It was unusual, but the need is clear…Minister."

The body language, tension in his shoulders, the pregnant pause—these two had definitely met before. Seeing each other seemed like a surprise for Sumner, less so for Sim. My curiosity piqued, I tallied another point against my limited knowledge of Sumner's past.

"Are there any new developments in the situation?" I asked. Sim's head bent to the side in a delicate deflection.

"I think it is best if you are informed with the rest of the security council for the sake of brevity and confidentiality, Ambassador. There will be time for more private speech afterward."

He turned to the diminutive security officer. "Will you have their belongings conveyed safely to my office, please?"

"At once, Minister." The Andari had us place our bags into the belly of a waiting robotic porter, which zipped away to perform its task. Sim gestured down the corridor.

"Come with me, and I will show you to an area where you can listen to Prince Razaxha make his plea." Every motion of Sim's supple limbs was like a dance. I obeyed the gentle sweep of his hand and its invitation to follow the arc of the hallway. Sumner urged me ahead with the jerk of his chin, putting space between himself and Alecto Sim. I didn't hesitate. Sumner must have had his reasons for keeping a distance.

"The emergency session will begin as soon as all the members of the council are present." Sim smiled at me, the corners of his mouth hinting at some private mirth. "I must preside over the agenda, but I arranged for someone who, in my absence, can give insight during the proceedings."

The inner curve of the increasingly busy hallway was broken with smaller passageways. Through one of these entrances, I glimpsed a vast, circular chamber where delegates gathered for the session.

Minister Sim led us through a dim warren of passages opening into a private observation gallery. A familiar pattern of excitement and anticipation from someone waiting inside sparkled through my empathic nets before we turned the final corner. A huge smile stretched the skin around my mouth in ways I thought I had forgotten.

A tall human stood in the shadowed recesses of the empty gallery, the outline of their body broad-shouldered and soft, but I would recognize her anywhere.

My mother.

Marina Urquhart, Sol Fed Delegate to the Remoliad, stepped into the faint light emitted from the corridor. The surge of her joy against my mind overwhelmed me, and I fought for composure as Alecto Sim regarded us with a mischievous glint in his eye.

"I believe you are well acquainted with Delegate Urquhart. I must leave you and take my place on the floor, but you are in her capable hands. Wait here after the hearing is concluded. My ancillary will show you to my office."

"Thank you for this opportunity, Alecto," my mother said, and Sim bowed to her in grave formality.

"I could not possibly deny you this meeting, Marina." He beamed at her and then nodded at the still-stiff Sumner and me. "Excuse me." His attention lingered on the commander as he passed. I missed Sumner's reaction because as soon as Sim turned away, Mom vented all pretense of formality and threw herself at me.

I held her wordlessly, my heart full of too many things to say, to feel. It had been more than a year since we were in the same sector of space, two years since we'd been in the same room. The last time I was still so numb and bitter I had been unable to give her a proper farewell. I tried to pour all my regrets, my love, and my happiness to see her into our tight embrace.

She pulled back, her smile brilliant despite the tears

streaking her face. Lines etched delicate lace in the outside corners of her gray eyes, so much like mine, and there were more silvery strands in her short-cropped auburn hair than there had been when I last saw her.

"Oh, Dalí, I've missed you." Searching my face, the familiar, prominent V of Mom-worry etched between her eyes as she traced a thumb over the still-healing laceration on my cheek. "So many new scars. What in seven hells have you been doing?"

"Some very un-diplomatic things," I admitted, and changed the subject. Mom had only the vaguest idea of what my new career entailed. "How's Dad? Is he enjoying retirement?"

The swerve didn't fool her. She narrowed her eyes at me, but she didn't press the issue in Sumner's presence. "Oh, you know Paul. He's back to work, directing incoming traffic to the hub. He couldn't keep his nose out of the control center, so they gave him a job to do." She turned her smile toward Sumner, her arm still around my waist. "I'm sorry for the emotional display, but I haven't gotten to hug my child in ages."

I waved him over to join us. "This is my friend and colleague, Commander Rion Sumner. Rion, my mother, Marina Urquhart."

He offered her his hand, and Mom gripped it firmly. "An honor to meet you, Delegate Urquhart," he said. "I kept up with the negotiations and the final membership confirmation hearings. It was an exciting time for Sol Fed."

"Thank you, Commander. What colony are you from?" She tilted her head as she released his hand. "Do I detect a hint of Europan in your accent?"

"My mother was Europan, but like Ambassador Tamareia, I was raised off world. I'm serving as their security advisor for this mission."

As she glanced between us, I could almost feel the *click*,

click, click of her sharp mind as things fell into place, and a cold wave of apprehension came from her. All she said was, "I'm glad Dalí isn't alone."

"No, ma'am. There's a team behind us." A small smile relaxed the serious mien he'd gained after he saw Alecto Sim when he glanced at me. "We all look out for each other." Sumner's attention returned to Mom, and he nodded courteously. "Excuse me. I want to get a look at the room before things start."

He descended the ramp to the rail of the balcony. My attention followed him a moment as he walked away, and Mom nudged me with a grin.

"So, just a friend or a *friend*?" she whispered, giving the word suggestive emphasis.

"Mom, he's my commanding officer," I protested quietly, aware Sumner could hear both of us over the implant. He scanned the room below, his attention pointedly fixed away from us.

"I'm not so sure. That smile … "

"No, Mother."

"Okay, okay." She took a shaking breath. "I'm terrified. I can't hide that, but I'm enormously proud of you at the same time. Minister Sim said he can't tell me everything, but he has faith in your ability to reach an accord between the Ursetu and the Shontavians."

I'm glad someone does. "I'm not sure everyone on the council is invested in Ursetu membership or in negotiating with the Shontavians. We were offered a ride this morning I'm certain was not sanctioned by Minister Sim."

"Oh, really? Who?"

"Delegate Prinoya."

She rolled her eyes, and I allowed a smirk to twist my lips. My mother's opinion of the aristocratic Ferian was the same as mine. "I'll bet you were given an ultimatum," she said.

"Prinoya suggested the best way to ensure the entire

council votes to advance the petition for emergency membership is if I get the Ursetu to agree to slaughter the Shontavians."

Mom grimaced. "Half the delegates think Sim has lost his mind. I must admit, even I wonder if the plan is realistic. By all accounts, Shontavians don't respond when someone yells *parley*." She gave me the side-eye and squeezed my hand. "Well, not to everybody, anyway. Do I want to hear the whole story?"

"It might be best if you don't," I confessed and kissed her cheek. I leaned my forehead against hers. "Damn, I missed you, Mom."

She pulled away so she could look at me with a mother's concern. "I meant what I said. I'm glad you aren't alone. Tell me what I really want to know. How are you?"

My voice shook only a little. "Better. And if I don't completely screw it up, I have friends. I hope you can meet the rest of them, someday. I'm never going to be the same. But I'm trying."

"That's all I want, Dalí." She kissed the new scar on my cheek. "It's all Gresh and Rasida would want too."

The poignant sting of tears threatened to undo me. Mom recognized I was struggling and looped her arm through mine. "Come on, Ambassador Tamareia," she said lightly. "Let's see if Alecto can keep this galactic circus in order."

CHAPTER
TEN

WE JOINED Sumner at the front and took seats. The round amphitheater below our vantage point teemed with spectators who had no say in this hearing, drawn to witness the event out of concern or curiosity. Two media bots hovered above the proceedings, one of them the familiar globular chassis of Batterson Robotics. The sight of those goddamn things still made my stomach clench.

Only one empty chair remained at the center of the table where the twelve members of the security council gathered. A podium rose from the floor as Alecto Sim strode out of the shadows to take his seat.

A few moments later, a young Ursetu in scarlet body armor approached the platform. Metallic wire inlays traced angular designs over the breastplate, back, and shoulders, glistening in the harsh light. Tight black curls hid the spiral recesses of his aural tympanum. The prince's regal profile was a younger version of the being I knew as Lord Rhix, with the same dark, umber skin and sharp cheekbones.

The figure who trailed behind the prince gave me pause. His head shaven and his lips pursed in righteous disapproval, he had the arrogant bearing I expected of a nobleman despite his plain black armor. Priest, advisor, or both? Two black-armored guards, visored and faceless, arrayed themselves to either side of the podium in a vigilant stance as the prince hesitantly took his place.

"Members of the council: I am Razaxha—" he stumbled over the title, his lips tight, and corrected, "Crown Prince Razaxha of Urset. I speak for my grandmother, Queen Xahria, matriarch of Urset. This is Lord Khus, one of the queen's councilors."

His voice still carried the higher tones of youth, but would soon echo the basso richness of his uncle's speaking voice as his words were translated from Ursetu to Remoliad Standard via my implant. "We face a crisis on my planet. The space station where our Shontavian assets were created and housed was purposely de-orbited in a malicious act and crashed into the center of the royal city. Many lives were lost in the battle that … where my mother …"

He steeled himself and continued, "My mother, Princess Arzalat, led a group of warrior caste to investigate the crash. She and her soldiers were killed by the Shontavians. Queen Xahria and I narrowly escaped with our lives when our ship was fired upon. The royal city has been evacuated. We urge the Remoliad Alliance to accept our emergent petition for membership and provide us with diplomatic assistance to take back the royal city."

A mutter crawled through the assembled spectators. Alecto Sim raised his hand in a silent, eloquent plea for order before he spoke.

"First, Prince Razaxha, the council wishes to extend our condolences for the personal loss of your mother."

"She fought bravely and well to defend the queen and now walks beside the goddess." Razaxha lifted his head and squared his shoulders. "May I be so honored upon my death."

"There are aspects of your statement that must be clarified

before we can bring this matter to a vote." Sim leaned forward. "You stated the orbiting facility was deliberately brought down into the royal city. Is there evidence to support this claim?"

"The facility came down inside the walls of the palace grounds," Razaxha said. "The impact missed the building itself by less than a kilometer. It was too precise to be an accident."

Khus managed to relax his tight-lipped mouth long enough to grate out, "There is unrest among the casteless on the mainland. They have sympathizers in the ruling caste more than capable of this act."

I sat too far away to receive any emotional cues from the young prince or his advisor, but the Zereid consul seated on the panel was in perfect range.

"Forgive me. I am not intentionally listening to your emotions, Lord Khus," she said. "Your anger is too specific to be directed at an unknown entity. You believe you know who is behind this disaster."

"Who do you think brought down the laboratory?" Sim questioned.

"I suspect collusion by the exiled Prince Nazhir and the rebellious casteless on the mainland," Khus answered with a sneer.

A cold, leaden weight dropped into my stomach, and I shot a glance at Sumner, who already looked at me with a frown. I shook my head minutely. I didn't believe Rhix was behind it for a second. Did I?

The young prince glanced at his advisor and showed the first bit of spirit we'd seen. "The queen and I disagree."

"Of course. I spoke out of turn, my prince." Khus bowed to him, a sullen, resentful show of deference.

Huh. Mom and I traded glances, agreeing on Khus's lack of sincerity. I stole a look at Sumner and found him unimpressed, too.

"Are we discussing the civil war?" The Kadrelian emissary on the panel sat forward, tentacles curled close to his body in trepidation. "Prince Razaxha, the Remoliad cannot intervene in a domestic conflict."

"Our petition addresses only the emergent situation in the royal city," the prince explained. "We do not expect the Remoliad to intervene on the mainland in any way."

"We will continue to deal with the insurrection as we have always done." Khus dismissed the idea Urset needed help with a regal wave.

"Are the Shontavians not conditioned to follow orders?" the dry, papery voice of a Pilean interjected. "Can you not simply order them to stand down?"

"My mother tried." Razaxha's bleak response showed another crack in his composure. "So have others. Those that survived the crash do not respond to the commands to which they were acclimated during development." He cast a glance at Sim. "The minister suggested a specialized negotiator. We wish to ensure the Shontavians' voluntary surrender without further loss of life."

I doubted the Shontavians would let anyone put them back in a box now they had experienced freedom. I pitied the lucky bastard tapped to negotiate a compromise between these tasty aristocrats and their sentient meat-craving creations.

Oh, yeah. That would be me.

"In our preliminary hearing, we discussed the Remoliad statutes, which forbid the enslavement or sale of intelligent life forms," Sim reminded him over murmurs of disquiet from the spectators. "To be granted provisional status, you must agree to abide by these laws before and after your membership is approved."

Razaxha nodded. "We understand, Minister Sim. I discussed it with the queen, and she will agree to the terms."

"Minister Sim? May I speak?" a familiar voice purred over the continued whispers of the assemblage.

"Oh, here it comes," Mom sighed.

Sim's hesitation was so much more polite than mine would have been. No eye rolling or sighing, simply another of those fluid, dancelike gestures of his hand. "I see you, Delegate Prinoya of Feria."

Prinoya rose from her seat as a media bot zoomed in for a closeup, and she shook out her artificial ruff to full expansion. "I represent approximately half of this council, Minister Sim, and many others out there"—she gestured toward the amphitheater with a theatrical sweep— "when I say we harbor serious concerns regarding the Shontavian menace."

An ugly chorus of agreement rang out from some of the crowd, and even from my removed position in the gallery, the metal-biting sensation of their outrage tangled in my empathic nets. "As you know, the tribes of Feria suffered greatly in the past when those things were unleashed on our world by our enemies, as did your own planet, Minister. I am surprised you would even consider this path. After hearing Prince Razaxha's description of the battle and having just met the ambassador to whom this task is appointed, I am not at all convinced negotiation constitutes the proper solution."

My jaw dropped. "She went to all that trouble for a fifteen-minute shuttle ride just to be able to honestly diss me in council? You're fucking kidding me," I muttered to Sumner.

"Language, Dalí," Mom chided automatically, but Sumner snorted in agreement as Prinoya continued.

"Ambassador Tamareia, a human of Sol Fed, was chosen to lead this endeavor. I must formally register my concern a member of such an inexperienced species conducts these negotiations; indeed, that this is the proper course of action at all. The Ursetu created the Shontavians. Why should the Remoliad save them from their own folly? Before we can vote on emergency membership, we must be certain Urset will deal with the Shontavians in an appropriate manner when the negotiations fail." She paused dramatically and amended, "Forgive me. I meant to say *if* the negotiations fail."

I laughed quietly, the sound as dark as my opinion of Delegate Prinoya, who had just earned a top spot on my *fuck you* list. An uproar followed Prinoya's objection. The white underfur of her chin glistened in the harsh lights of the media bot as she lifted her head with a self-satisfied tilt and regarded Alecto Sim. The Ferian had gotten the reaction she wanted. Just as many voices from the audience of diplomatic staff and delegates shouted approval as were raised in dissent.

Lord Khus wore an expression of barely veiled contempt. Razaxha's young face showed bewilderment. His façade cracked to reveal an uncertain youth beneath the royal mask, a boy thrust into the role of leader far too soon. A pang of sympathy for the Ursetu prince went through me.

Sim raised his hand and commanded immediate attention. The crowd quieted at once. "If such disruption continues, I will have the chamber emptied of everyone but the security council. Am I clear?" His voice never rose, but the power in it was compelling.

"I won't be shocked if he is secretary general one day." Mom's tone hinted at reverence. "Alecto Sim is one hell of a friend to have, Dalí. Some pretty nasty antihuman sentiment exists among a few of the delegates, but Sim has faith in our ability to add to the greater good. I don't know how you got his attention, but with him behind you, there's no telling how far you can go."

"He is something else," I agreed in admiration.

"You have no idea." Sumner's voice, almost inaudible, sounded over my implant. I wasn't sure I was meant to hear.

My attempt to interpret exactly what Sumner's ambiguous statement meant ended as Sim continued to speak. "Delegate Prinoya, your objections are heard and registered. There is little danger the Shontavians will escape the planet without assistance. The ambassador must have time to assess the situation, and it would be inappropriate to extract such a promise. It is in direct conflict with Remoliad legislation against the genocide of any sentient species."

"The legislation is meant to prohibit the elimination of any *naturally evolving* sentient species, Minister Sim," Prinoya said triumphantly. "My allies and I believe the Shontavians do not fall under the current statutes. They are a bioengineered life form, and how Ambassador Tamareia expects to negotiate peace with mindless, silent killers is a mystery."

Damn Prinoya, anyway. I'd showed her where the ammunition was, and she'd just fired it over the bow. A flurry of nodding heads from Prinoya's supporters rippled through the assembly, and my face grew warm as anger blazed behind my breastbone.

Minister Sim peered up into the observation gallery. "Special Ambassador Tamareia? I know you have not yet had the opportunity to be fully briefed, but is there anything you would like to add?"

He'd just invited me to fire back. I raised my voice.

"Alpha Shontavians do speak when they wish, Delegate Prinoya." I stood and moved from the murky recesses to the edge of the rail, which overlooked the chamber. All heads turned toward me. For a moment I swayed under the bombardment of curious attention—and some undisguised, bitter outrage—against my empathic nets. The fucking Batterson media bot buzzed in and lit me with a blinding LED. I involuntarily flinched against the bot's sudden approach, my heart racing.

So much for anonymity. My face just got beamed all over the galaxy. "The Shontavians I have encountered are intelligent and possess a sense of self with wants and needs like any other species." I left out the part the two I met were telepaths and actually enjoyed their food alive and screaming. Whether this was true of all Shontavians or only those in the arena at the Market, I didn't hold enough information to determine. "Prince Razaxha"—I inclined my head with respect to the young nobleman— "stated these Shontavians no longer respond to the commands to which they were conditioned, and that says something in their nature has changed. Until we learn more, we must treat them with the same regard any other sentient species deserves."

"They are killers!" Delegate Prinoya seethed with resentment.

"They are purchased like weapons, Delegate, and denied free will. They are conditioned to do a job and do it well. They fight beside soldiers of other species without harm to their comrades in arms and even share the same living quarters in some circumstances. The Shontavians in the royal city are defending their position. It remains to be seen what happens when they are presented with an option not to kill." I couldn't keep my mouth shut. "But that appears to be a difficult choice for any sentient species. Wouldn't you agree, Delegate Prinoya?"

A titter of laughter rose from the assemblage, accompanied by a rustle of uncomfortable shuffling in the silence that followed. Prinoya blinked as she appeared to be working out whether I had insulted her or not.

"Thank you for your candor, Ambassador Tamareia," Minister Sim said. His lips twitched against a suppressed smile.

I returned to my seat, relieved when the media bot killed its spotlight and zipped away. One hand over her mouth, my mother shook her head at me, but I could read the scandalous glee in her eyes. Sumner's expression was more guarded. I wondered what went on behind his serious mask.

When I raised an eyebrow in question, he said, "You were half right."

Interesting. We needed to talk more about his mercenary service during the Scata Rebellion.

"We will deliberate in private before a vote is cast on provisional Remoliad membership," Sim announced. "Per our constitutional regulations, my vote will determine the outcome should the proceedings end in a stalemate, but I would plead the council consider the possible consequences of our inaction before they cast their votes. All who are not voting members will please vacate the floor as quickly as possible."

Minister Sim stepped down from the podium. The black-armored guards and Lord Khus swept the young prince back into the shadows. Delegate Prinoya, her dissenting faction of the council, and a handful of others from the now-departing audience clumped and muttered with mutinous glares cast like daggers at Alecto Sim's back.

CHAPTER
ELEVEN

"THE VOTE COULD TAKE away my cushy position as least senior delegate." Mom sighed as she stood and stretched. "Now I really need to get off my ass and to work."

"I doubt you've been slack," I scoffed as I rose. Mom had almost single-handedly negotiated the treaty making the reluctant Sol Fed a member of Remoliad society. Aid was already streaming into the overcrowded colonies in shipments of food, technology, and building supplies to ease the overcrowded tenements of Mars and dome-scraping towers of Luna. Approval of galactic citizenship had quickly multiplied once the general population recognized the benefits of alliance, silencing the protests of any remnant isolationism. Attitudes about contributions of third-gender citizens like Mom and me to the human gene pool were slower to change, but that was a problem no Remoliad intervention could improve.

"I should head back to my office. I have a meeting to discuss a joint operation in the Sol Fed and Pilean war on drug trafficking. Sim's Ancillary will be here to get you any moment." She cupped my face in her hands, the surge of her sadness bringing a sting to my own eyes. "I don't want to go.

I don't know when I'll see you again, and when I think of you negotiating with Shontavians ... "

"If there's any chance before I leave, I swear I'll find you." A nameless eruption of messy emotions flooded me. I hugged her hard and whispered, "Do you know how much I love you? How proud I am of what you've done here?"

"I love you so much." She kissed my cheek and stepped back to wipe her eyes. "Shit. I promised myself I wouldn't do this."

"And you wonder where I get my filthy language?" I gave her the side-eye, and she laughed.

"Guess I can't deny it. Stay in touch. You'll be given a private subspace communications link now that you represent the Remoliad. Send your foul-mouthed old mother a note now and then."

"I will."

Mom nodded at Sumner, who had discreetly removed himself to the aisle, his hands clasped in front of him. "Commander Sumner. I'm so glad to have met you. I hope to see you again."

"Thank you." He shook her extended hand. "I'm sure our paths will cross, Delegate Urquhart."

"Please, it's Marina. You're a friend of the family, after all." She winked at him. Sumner's telltale flush of embarrassment crept up his neck, but he grinned at her, laughter in his voice.

"Then it's Rion, Marina."

I'd never seen him so flustered before. I had to shake my head at them both, bewildered, but intervention came in the form of the minister's assistant.

"Ambassador Tamareia?" The voice was not as melodic as Sim's, his manner less soothing, but the slow, dancelike movements were the same. "I am Tikker, ancillary to Minister Sim." He bowed to my mother. "Delegate Urquhart."

Mom nodded at him. "Hello, Tikker." The band on her left

wrist began to peep insistently, and she sighed. "Delegate Lapahslo is waiting for me." Her whispery pronunciation of the Pilean's name rustled in the empty gallery like hollow bean pods swinging in the trees after harvest on Zereid. She touched my shoulder in farewell, her professional restraint laced with bittersweet worry. "If I don't see you again before you leave, Godspeed, Ambassador."

"Thank you," I whispered.

She edged past the Tolkish diplomat and disappeared into the corridor. My breath caught and wobbled unevenly. The sharpness of this parting ambushed me, and I turned away from the question in Sumner's eyes, dismayed at my jagged emotions.

"Go ahead. I'll meet you in a second." My voice betrayed the distress beneath.

"We'll be right outside."

Only when they left did I allow the hot overflow of tears to spill. My eyes squeezed tightly shut to wring the unwelcome burn of saline from my lashes.

Dr. Muus warned me the mood swings would intensify after the detox treatment, but they were an inconvenient symptom. It took a moment to collect myself before I wiped the telltale streaks from my face and joined Sumner and our guide in the busy corridor. They turned to me as I emerged.

"I'm going to check out the diplomatic vessel we were assigned," Sumner told me. "The ancillary is going to take me down to the bay. I'll meet you later."

My teammate was in no hurry to see the minister again. I quirked an eyebrow at him, and he flushed, avoiding my gaze.

"Let me show you something, Ambassador." Tikker turned to a small, concave depression in the wall and pressed his fingertips into it. A cool glow began to blink beneath his hand.

"Locate Minister Sim's office," he said.

A pearly line appeared beneath his feet, curving out of sight round the arc of the corridor.

"One follows that track. Your bio profile was scanned at security, and you may use the directional guide while you are here simply by touching the pad. I granted you permission to access his office. He will join you before the vote."

"Thank you."

Tikker turned in a swirl of robes, and Sumner followed him. The luminescent trail led me through the traffic of diplomats leaving the emergency session. Stares were directed my way, not all of them friendly. Uninterested in dealing with potential bullshit right now, I didn't make eye contact and kept my empathic nets furled.

My glowing guide terminated at a closed port. I pressed the panel beside it and the port slid aside, lights flickering on as I entered the room.

A plush Tolkish carpet in hues of blue and gray whispered beneath my feet as the port hissed shut behind me. I scanned the room, interested to see if anything clued me to a connection with Sumner. The wall opposite the port boasted a holographic projection of Tolkis, a green and white sphere rotating on its axis against a spatter of stars. It shifted to a forest view, the spiky, verdant branches of trees obscured by fog and then to a city sparkling in amber twilight, set like gems in a crown of mountains.

The minister's desk lay almost bare of personality, save for a cairn of stones arranged in a small tray. I touched the topmost pebble with one fingertip, careful not to disturb the arrangement. The cairn was a Tolkish tradition, a memorial. Each stone represented a regret, gleaned from the place where it happened. When the compunction was atoned for, the stone would be removed from the pile.

It seemed Sim had many regrets, some jagged-edged, some smooth, but all weighted by conscience.

The robotic porter had been and gone, our bags on the

floor beside a cluster of chairs in various configurations for Remoliad member body types. I retrieved my PDD from my belongings and sank into a deep, cushioned sling chair.

"Remoliad profile for Alecto Sim." The screen flicked up pieces of data, going back six years. The minister had moved up quickly from junior attaché to Tolkish delegate within two years. Remoliad commendations for his work toward security and armistice on member worlds were sprinkled liberally throughout his career. Four years later, he was voted head of the security council by a wide majority.

"Personal profile, same subject, birth to present."

The information struck me as sparse, but not unusually so. Sim had been born in the largest city on Tolkis, educated there, but a gap of twelve years spanned the completion of his education and his reappearance in the Tolkish diplomatic corps. He'd spent time off world, but in what capacity?

His voice startled me as Sim emerged from the alcove leading to the chambers. "Thank you for waiting, Ambassador."

A slight pressure against my empathic nets grew apparent as he came closer, but his psi shield was an effective one. I cleared my PDD screen and stood. "Is the council prepared to vote?"

"Nearly. I fear I have a condition to present you." Sim's lips curved in a rueful smile. "Delegate Prinoya and the dissenting members are agreeable to a compromise. You may not find it entirely palatable, but it ensures the Ursetu petition will pass."

"That doesn't sound promising." I waited for the bad news.

"They will vote in favor if half your diplomatic team includes members from worlds which suffered under the Shontavians."

"Delegate Prinoya wants a place on my staff." It took all

the decorum I had not to follow up the statement with choice obscenities.

Sim acknowledged the dilemma with a nod. "You must build a team which gives you the highest confidence of success. She cannot force you to choose her, but we have little time to lose. Lord Khus is adamant they return to Urset immediately."

"There is another candidate. Prinoya's secretary, Lam Tiri, is an interspecies negotiator. He is highly qualified and has some interesting ideas." I kept to myself the thought that as long as we didn't let him fly the ship, Tiri's presence was certain to be a more valuable asset. "There's no valid reason she can protest his appointment."

"I will not let her." Sim's smile revealed a little pettiness, which made me like him more. "Do you have others in mind?"

"I need a strong telepath. If my first choice is unavailable, we might ask the Zereid government to recruit a volunteer before we arrive at the hub." I didn't want to speak for my crechemate, Gor, and would not put him in a position of danger. Coming with me would be his decision.

"Then one other member must fit their criteria." Sim's brow creased in tentative hope, and he said, "I would like to offer myself as your fourth diplomat, Ambassador."

"Are you sure you should take leave of your duties at the Remoliad, sir?" I did not need an ambitious politician dogging my heels, no matter how charming he was. "The council appears to need a strong leader, and I certainly don't think Delegate Prinoya should be left unsupervised."

"Vice Minister Esh of Zereid is more than capable in my absence."

His answer seemed too quick, and I frowned. "We haven't had time to discuss any of this yet, so I will ask now. Why did you send for me, Minister?"

"Because of what happened aboard the Market ship. You

formed a connection with the Shontavians and were able to negotiate terms." Sim regarded me with open admiration. "It is incredible the story of your survival in the arena has not spread all over the galaxy by now."

"I'm certain anyone attending the Market prefers their transactions with Lord Rhix remain private, as do I." If he'd read the file, he already knew everything. "Exactly what do you hope to accomplish by negotiating with the Shontavians? Why is this so important to you?"

"Is the cause of peace not important enough?" Sim regarded me. "The facility has been destroyed, but this single platoon of Shontavians was enough to bring the ruling caste to its knees. Can you imagine the carnage, should they be used against the queen's own people?"

I didn't have to imagine. I had a vivid portrait painted in body fluids and shattered bones hanging in my memory. "It would be slaughter."

"And that is exactly what I wish to avoid." His eyes closed briefly against his own mental image. "I, too, have seen what they are capable of, not only on my planet but ... elsewhere." Focused on something in his mental landscape, the pain in his faraway gaze made me catch my breath. "The Shontavians must be removed from all potential battlefields in a way that does not encompass their destruction. And that, Ambassador, is where your experience is required. Their voluntary surrender is paramount to this endeavor."

"What you hope to accomplish will take more than a connection. It will require their trust. If we are going into hostile territory, I can't afford to worry about anyone's political agenda." I straightened and faced him with determination. "I want full authority over the negotiations, Minister. One misstep could mean we get eaten alive. If you join my team, it will not be as head of the security council but as an advisor. My authority, and Commander Sumner's as my security officer, will outweigh yours."

"You do not mince words." Sim's lips thinned as he considered. "I do not know you, only your reputation for remarkable, if reckless, deeds. I have no qualms regarding Commander Sumner's authority. I know he is a being of conscience and honor."

"How well do you know him?" The question slipped out before I could stop myself. He raised his head, eyes like bright garnets against his amethyst skin, and smiled faintly.

"I will let him tell you if he wishes. Our friend Rion values nothing more than his privacy, and I will not betray his trust." The fuzzy wall between his mind and mine left me guessing at the emotion behind the smile, but I wanted to say regret. One of the stones in his cairn had to belong to Sumner.

"Will you accept my terms?"

Behind the thoughtful gaze, I wondered what disadvantages were weighed and found an acceptable risk. Sim nodded at last. "I accept."

"Now that we have that out of the way, what the hell is happening on Urset?" I didn't bother to keep the exasperation out of my voice. "Their civil war must be heating up if someone tried to crash a facility directly into the palace. They aren't being honest with us."

"Prince Razaxha is eager to cooperate with the Remoliad, but Lord Khus is less than enthusiastic." Sim sighed and motioned for me to be seated again. "The prince told me Queen Xahria's decision to join the Alliance has strained her relationship with the other matriarchs." He sat too, his slender hands folded in front of him. "The sooner we can assess the situation for ourselves, the better."

I grimaced and admitted, "I actually agree with Prinoya on one thing. It's the Ursetu's mess. The Remoliad fleet should be on standby only if we have to evacuate."

"As it happens, the council also feels military presence is inadvisable given the internal strife on Urset. Permanent representation will hinge on how committed they are to work under Remoliad laws."

"Their other engineered species, the Simish, appear to be indentured servants, if not slaves. Their status will need to be addressed as well."

The chime of the port sounded a moment before the panel slid aside to reveal Tikker. "Minister? The council is waiting."

"Will you attend and announce your choice for the Ferian delegate?" Sim invited me.

"I wouldn't miss it."

His smile was almost luminous in those disarming, handsome features. "I am glad to see my instincts are affirmed. You were the right one for this task."

Despite Sim's ability to inspire devotion in the Remoliad —and especially because of my attraction to him—my own instincts said I shouldn't trust him until I knew why he wore a psi-shield.

I did trust Rion Sumner. If his avoidance of the minister said anything clearly, it shouted he wasn't sure about Alecto Sim either.

I wondered if he still trusted me enough to tell me why.

CHAPTER TWELVE

A DIPLOMATIC VESSEL with the spiral sigil of the Remoliad emblazoned on its side waited for us in the private shuttle bay below Sim's office. The minister clearly had more pull than the Penumbra. No rusting tin can of an *Owhra* here, but a luxurious Tolkish-made craft with twelve sleeping cubicles, padded jump seats, and a retractable worktable running the length of the aisle between the seats.

Sumner displaced the bewildered Remoliad pilot and stayed busy avoiding Sim with preflight checks as we waited for our passengers to arrive. Whatever the hell happened between them seemed pretty damned significant.

Khus's obsidian pupilless eyes fixed on me as he and Prince Razaxha entered the bay, flanked by the four guards. The drifting web of my empathic senses caught an oil-slick sheen of resentment as Khus regarded us. If he harbored such disagreement with the queen's petition for aid, why the hell did he bother coming?

Razaxha's emotional broadcast was also written on his face: the pride and excitement in his first official galactic duty as a royal fairly glowed. But there were cold spikes of fear embedded behind that outward layer, terrified by this new responsibility.

In deference to Razaxha's status, I gave him a reverent bow. "My Prince, I am Ambassador Tamareia. I offer my skills to your service." My tongue was still clumsy with the liquid syllables of his native language. The prince grinned at me and then, with a guilty glance at the disapproving Khus, stilled his features to a more regal mask.

"Thank you, Ambassador. You speak Ursetu?"

"Only enough to be understood," I admitted. "I look forward to gaining more experience with your language."

"I speak some Remoliad Standard," Razaxha offered haltingly.

"I suspect we will both earn a better grasp on communication by the end of this." I smiled at him reassuringly and gestured to my ear. His own translator device lay visible against the nautilus-spiral cartilage of his aural canal. "Until then, we can rely on technology."

Relief softened the lines of his body. "Thank you, Ambassador."

"We must leave. Every minute wasted talking delays our return to Urset," Khus snapped.

"Please, board the ship and prepare for departure. We are waiting for one more member of the diplomatic team to arrive." Alecto Sim turned to me before he followed the prince and his entourage into the sleek belly of the vessel. "Do we need to send security to rescue Lam Tiri?" he asked in a hushed voice. Wicked humor glinted in his eyes, and I grinned before I could stop myself.

"Here he comes." I caught sight of the young diplomat scurrying down the corridor leading to the bay, his personal bag strapped to his back.

"I am sorry." Tiri bowed his head in abject apology. "Delegate Prinoya insisted on briefing me before I left. Several times."

"I hope she wasn't too disappointed not to be invited to the party," I muttered.

Tiri cocked his head, his furry ruff swaying. A nervous bark of laughter escaped his throat. "She is not pleased. I have been reminded my failure to ensure an acceptable outcome will embarrass the whole of Feria." His tawny eyes shone as he peered up at me. "I want you to know how much I appreciate this opportunity, Ambassador Tamareia. I cannot tell you how important it is to me."

"Thank you for accepting the offer. I look forward to working with you." We walked up the ramp together. The ramp's hydraulics sighed as the port closed behind us.

Razaxha, Khus, and their guards occupied the six starboard seats, so Tiri and I buckled in quickly on the opposite side. I was surprised to see Sim up front in the copilot's seat. The familiar flush of discomfort reddened Sumner's features, but they appeared to be able to inhabit the same space without the commander undergoing spontaneous combustion. That seemed to be a positive sign.

After the vote at the Remoliad, I had sent an urgent message to Gor. There's nothing private about government communications, so I shared only a location and time to meet at the orbiting space hub with the invitation:

Will you join me on an emergency peacemaking mission that might end in blood and death?

Before we made our first transition to superluminal velocity, his reply arrived.

Of course. It will be fun.

. . .

From the sector of space where the Remoliad cruised in constant self-orbit, the flight to Zereid consists of one short Einstein-Rosen bridge jaunt, what the rest of the galaxy calls 'dark space', followed by a lot of slow-speed rock dodging. Sim turned out to be a skillful flyer and occupied the pilot's seat when Sumner didn't. Between the two of them, they navigated the asteroid field behind the ocean moon, an aquamarine brushing the mauve and white cheek of Zereid.

Prince Razaxha longingly watched our group. Early on, Lam Tiri extended an invitation for him to join us at our end of the table for dinner and share his insight on the situation. Though the prince brightened immediately at this idea, Lord Khus dryly informed us he did not make a habit of dining with peasants.

Well, not in so many words, but the sentiment was the same. Urset's rigid caste system was thousands of years old, and the sense of superiority radiating from Razaxha's advisor curdled my professional blood. Khus failed to endear himself to anyone on the forty-eight-hour trip, especially Razaxha, to whom he stayed glued in case the prince might be accidentally exposed to radical ideas like cooperation and equality.

My mood-swinging needle crept into the red zone around Khus, and I fervently hoped before we reached Urset— another ninety-six-hour flight from Zereid—the emotional seesaw Dr. Muus told me to expect would improve. Yes, I knew exactly what he had said. But I didn't have the leisure to plod through my neuroses right now, and mood swings around Shontavians could be fatal until I earned their trust. Maybe even afterward.

In contrast to Razaxha's reluctant segregation, Lam Tiri, free of the condescending restrictions imposed on him by Delegate Prinoya, proved to be a revelation. He spent most of the flight studying Ursetu culture and protocol with Sim and me and was the first to dive into what little we had available about Shontavian bioengineering and conditioning before anyone else. By the time we reached Zereid, a new confidence began to assert itself. This was his chosen field, and he reveled in it.

Sumner, on the other hand, withdrew.

Save for the brief moments he exchanged report with Sim in a cool, professional manner bordering on frosty, the shared job prevented them from occupying the same space for long. Sim's eyes lingered on Sumner a little too long when the commander came aft to get some sleep, and he caught me watching. The wistful smile Alecto gave me cemented the suspicion these two had once been very close. Perhaps even lovers. It hadn't ended well for Sumner.

With twelve hours remaining in the flight, I followed him when he retreated to his sleeping cubicle and tapped on the door.

Sumner slid the door open, shirtless and heavy-eyed. He didn't display his body freely, and I had never seen him without a shirt. Scars slashed in twisted red Lichtenberg figures from his right shoulder down to the flat, well-defined planes of his abdomen and disappeared beneath the waist of his pants. A blossom of mottled scar tissue to the left of his sternum displayed what must have been a near-fatal wound.

It was a struggle not to register my appreciation of the view. Our relationship remained a professional one, despite my tendency to involuntarily flirt with him under the influence. Mostly involuntary, anyway. I tried not to think about him that way. I didn't want to screw anything up.

"What's up?" he yawned.

"Can we talk privately?"

"Yeah." He waved me in. "Take a seat."

The narrow cubicle left little room for two; unless intimacy was the whole idea, two people would find it extremely close quarters. I sat next to him on the edge of the bunk and reached out to shut the door behind us.

"Did you hear from the team? How is Melos?" I spoke in

Sol Standard, our first language still not widely understood in Remoliad quarters.

"They're on Zereid. Melos is doing well. They expect his skin to be regrown in about thirty-six hours."

"That's great news." Relief sent a cool wash through me, releasing a tension I didn't realize I carried.

"It isn't the only reason you came, though." Sumner gave me the side-eye.

"Only part of it." I kept my voice low. "Commander, is there anything you want to tell me about Alecto Sim?"

He stiffened but met my gaze steadily. "We know each other. I'm sure you figured that out."

"When you saw him at the Remoliad for the first time, you were more than surprised."

"I thought he was dead." The short, quiet phrase painted layers of pain, anger, and bewilderment I could read despite the null. "I don't know him as Alecto Sim. That's a new identity. But he had to be aware it was me when he recalled the team." He rested his elbows on his knees, hands dangling toward the floor, and gave a sigh from the depths of his soul. "You're asking me if he can be trusted, and I can't answer. Fifteen years ago, the answer would have been yes. There are things I should tell you before we reach Urset. He's part of a past life I don't revisit. I'm not sure I'm ready to talk about it right now. I haven't even told Ozzie all of it, but I think some of the information might be useful when planning your negotiation strategy."

"Thank you," I said softly, acknowledging the unguarded moment as a rare glimpse of the genuine Rion Sumner beneath the efficient, professional armor he never lowered. "I'll let you get some sleep. When you're ready, we'll talk."

I rose to my feet in the narrow space between bed and door, an awkward angle necessary to avoid slamming my shoulder into the wall. I winced and uttered a short curse as a muscle painfully cramped in my midback.

"You haven't slept at all since we left *Nova Six*." He glanced up at me with tired eyes. "Get some rack time, too. That's an order. Your body's still processing the detox procedure, and you need all your brain cells."

"Yes, sir." I slipped out of the cubicle. He was right. Tired was stupid, and with my patience already sketchy, I might punch Khus in the face and cause a galactic incident.

I didn't give a fuck, but I really shouldn't embarrass my mother that way.

Easing open another sleep cubicle, I stripped off my jacket and boots before I stretched out on the bunk. My mind turned circles around who Sim might have been when Sumner knew him, whether his change of identity held commitment to a true, fresh start at a new life—or just concealing his past.

What part of himself had Sumner left behind, traced in those fractal scars?

I fell asleep with this puzzle in my head. It came as no surprise when my dreams were of Sumner and Alecto Sim.

We walked through the devastated Ursetu royal city, smoke, flames, and weapons fire all around us. Sim and I stopped to admire a garden through a shattered wall. Sumner kept walking down the street, alert for threats, a pulse rifle held across his body. Sim gave me a secretive nod and unzipped his civilized outer veneer to reveal a Shontavian inside, his second set of arms spread wide in a cruciform shape as lavender skin gave way to smooth, cartilaginous gray. Instead of threatening to devour me, the Shontavian only bared fearsome, serrated teeth in a gentle smile, put one talon-tipped finger in front of its mouth and hissed, *Shhhhhhh*.

CHAPTER
THIRTEEN

IN A SPACE STATION full of naked, fuzzy blue giants a little over seven feet tall, my crechemate does not stand out in any way that draws the eye. Gor wore the sash of priesthood over his broad, turquoise shoulders, but I could have found him simply by following the steady warmth of his love against my empathic nets or the answering spike of excitement when we saw each other. His presence is a beacon for me, promising all is well, and there are still beings in the galaxy who truly believe empathy leads to peace. The trouble is not everyone else does.

My confessor and conscience, Gor knows what I do with the Penumbra. How he still sees potential in a broken, ridiculous human is the mystery and grace of our bond. Then again, much to the chagrin of the temple school we attended, we've shared an appreciation for fart humor since we were three years old. That's a fine basis for any friendship.

Gor stooped and rested his forehead against mine, his massive hands gentle on my shoulders. I grinned so hard my jaws ached, his short blue fur tickling my nose. For a moment, we stood in silence and reveled in each other's physical and psychic presence as joy filtered between us in an isotonic exchange.

"Oh, my beloved friend," he murmured in the woodwind music of the Zereid language, soothing in my ears. "It is good to see you."

"I've missed you, my brother."

"And I, you." He drew back, the reflective silver-gilt of his eyes widening in the Zereid version of a grin. "Are we going on an adventure?"

"Maybe more than we can handle," I admitted.

"Nothing new then." Gor took in my diplomatic uniform with interest. "You are following the path of a peacemaker once more instead of peacekeeper."

"A detour, maybe." The confession stuck in my throat, and I swallowed. "Neither path is clear to me right now, brother, and I'm stumbling along as best I can. Will you help keep my feet steady while I walk this road?"

"Of course." His affection touched my mind. "You already know the path. You walked it many times, and it will unfold to you again."

I led him to the spacious lounge secured for the comfort of Prince Razaxha and Lord Khus. A transparent alloy window spanned from deck to overhead, overlooking the busy hub and the shorter arm of this private berth. Docked outside against the stars, the sharp-angled Ursetu cruiser dwarfed our little diplomatic ship. Khus sat close to the view with their four guards, and Prince Razaxha stood in front of the port, studying the royal yacht.

The sight of someone standing in the viewport of a space station still made my heart race with fear, my palms slicked with sweat. It was too easy to get swept away by the images of Gresh and Rasida, side by side in the window of Luna Terminal.

But I was getting stronger at turning those memories away before they became panic.

Sim and Lam Tiri were engaged in quiet conversation near the hatchway, and Sumner stood off to one side, his arms crossed over his chest. He relaxed when he saw us and grinned at Gor, whose lidless eyes became round O's of surprise.

"Dalí did not tell me you were coming," he said in Remoliad Standard. They exchanged an amicable greeting as each placed one hand on the shoulder of the other. "I see you, Commander Sumner."

"Friend Gor. Good to be with you again." Sumner withdrew his hand.

"Now I am even more curious to hear the details of this endeavor." Gor glanced around, taking in the rest of the group.

"We'll fill you in on the way—" I added a dramatic pause, "—to Urset."

"Urset?" A tremolo of wonder rose in Gor's throat. "That is new territory for peacemaking, is it not? I am honored to be part of your efforts, beloved friend."

"Meet our diplomatic team." I introduced both with a sweep of my arm as they approached. "Lam Tiri and Alecto Sim. This is Brother Gor, a *zezjna* priest and my crechemate. I invited him to join us."

"Brother Gor." Sim greeted my friend with a bow. The filigree of his psi shield glittered in the artificial light. With the customary courtesy of this telepathic society, the precaution made me wonder again what, and from whom, he was hiding. "It is a pleasure to meet you."

Lam Tiri stood on his hind legs and rested one forepaw on Gor's shoulder to exchange a brief cheek rub. "Brother Gor."

"How splendid to meet you, Lam Tiri." Gor beamed at him, the span between his eyes widening in the Zereid version of a smile. "What a wonderful collection of minds you gathered here, Dalí. I am honored to be among you."

The epitome of resentment, Lord Khus wore a sour

expression. "The ship is ready to return to Urset. Do not waste time with introductions. We have already been too long away."

"No, there will be time for that later," Razaxha agreed reluctantly, and started down the gangway. Khus stalked behind him like an impatient gargoyle as two guards flanked the prince. The other two waited for us to follow.

Sumner handed me my personal bag and hefted the large case containing my new subspace gear as he and Gor fell into step beside me. Alecto Sim and Lam Tiri trailed after us, the guards bringing up the rear. I couldn't suppress a shuddering breath, my nerves wound tight. My first diplomatic assignment since Luna Station, and what a cluster fuck it might turn out to be if I couldn't play the game anymore.

Though he didn't touch me, the brush of Gor's mind against mine was like a comforting hand on my shoulder. I smiled at him, glad for his presence, and led my motley band of peacemakers into the yacht.

———

Our first strategy meeting on board the Ursetu ship yielded intelligence useful to planning our approach, but Khus parted with every bit of data so grudgingly it was if the information were being surgically removed from his ass. Prince Razaxha, more confident in familiar surroundings, did his best to fill the gaps between what we already knew while his keeper ignored our briefing in favor of other duties.

"Why wasn't the palace evacuated with the first predicted crash trajectories?" Sumner asked.

"All initial data showed the facility would crash harmlessly into the sea." The prince pulled up a map on his data device and toggled a holographic image in the center of the table. "The sudden loss of communications suggested a catastrophic event just before the facility went into freefall.

The first projections showed it would pass south of the island and make impact here." He indicated a spot where a green line terminated in open water about twenty kilometers off the coast. "It began to change trajectory soon after entering the atmosphere. Subsequent projections showed the facility coming down closer to the island but still a safe distance away.

Two more lines joined the first, curving closer to the island. "The facility was never meant for atmospheric flight, but it did have engines, which allowed correction of its orbit when necessary. Those engines were observed to be in operation as it approached island airspace, and the crash zone was updated." He enlarged a portion of the image, a red line showing a termination point in the northwest corner of the mountainous island. "One of the crew had to have been at the helm. We were evacuated before the crash, and a warning went out to the rest of the island. Very few buildings outside the palace grounds were damaged. No one died, until ..." The tremor of Razaxha's grief sent gentle vibrations of sympathy through me.

"I am sorry you have not had time to properly mourn your mother's death." I ached for his loss. "If it is too painful to speak of it, we can move on to a different subject."

"No." He sat up straight. "I am fine, Ambassador. What do you need to know?"

"How soon after impact did the Shontavians attack?" I asked.

"The following morning. The hour of the goddess begins at sunset, and no military action may take place on the island until sunrise. My grandmother and I returned to the palace as my mother and her soldiers approached the wreckage after dawn. Her intent was to discover if any Shontavians were left alive after the crash and give command codes to ensure their cooperation. We do not know what happened to trigger the attack."

"Is it possible the soldiers attacked first?"

"We cannot be certain. The surveillance recordings are not clear enough to see what happened. I know they were involved in several skirmishes on the way to the palace."

Sumner's voice rose in puzzlement. "Skirmishes with the Shontavians?"

"With the other matriarchs' soldiers."

I exchanged concerned glances with Sumner and Alecto Sim before I questioned the prince. "Why were other matriarchs fighting Princess Arzalat's troops?"

"Some of them wanted to get to the wreckage first, to gain control of the Shontavians." Razaxha smiled ruefully. "But there is seldom a peaceful day in the capital city."

Gor's head cocked in curiosity. "The civil war has come to the ruling-caste island?"

"No, the unrest is confined to the mainland." The prince twitched his shoulders in a nonchalant shrug. "The matriarchs regularly battle for dominance against each other."

"Who fired on your ship as you escaped?" Lam Tiri's purr hinted at confusion. I was glad I wasn't the only one.

"We are not certain if the Shontavians fired on our ship with captured weapons, or one of the matriarchs did."

Sumner sat back in his chair, a grim furrow developing in his forehead. He cast an accusing glance at Sim. "Why weren't we told this before? I have no way to guarantee the diplomatic team's safety in an active combat situation."

"This is something you did not share in our initial conversation, Prince Razaxha." Alecto Sim's lavender countenance was grave and troubled, his slender fingers folded against his lips.

"I am sorry, Minister Sim. You only asked about the civil unrest on the mainland." Razaxha's bronze eyes were wide and innocent. "Does that change things? Will you not help us?"

"It makes our job a lot more difficult, to be sure." *If not impossible.* My tone carried the sharp edge of anger. It wasn't directed at Razaxha, whose genuine distress came through loud and clear to anyone with a shred of empathic talent, but my temper flared enough Gor's mental touch urged me toward calm. I released a slow breath and modulated my voice. "We cannot negotiate if they are under attack. All action near the Shontavians must cease before we arrive. Can that order be enforced?"

"I plan to speak with the queen before we enter dark space." Razaxha nodded earnestly. "I will tell her it must be so."

Great. No chance of reaching any sort of accord existed if the Shontavians were continually exposed to an active battle-field. It would have been helpful to know the entire island was a fucking war zone before I agreed to accept the assignment.

Would it have changed my mind? I had to admit, probably not. Looking at young Razaxha, I heard an echo of Ozzie's counsel. There were a lot of beings on Urset who deserved a peaceful future. I could help pave the way with this mission.

Whether or not I wanted to, I cared what happened. And I'd better not screw it up.

———

With my two favorite default settings to relieve tension being *fight it* or *fuck it*, there were very few appropriate options for a Remoliad ambassador to blow off steam. My sense of relief knew no bounds when I discovered the gymnasium on the lower deck and recruited Gor the next morning for *zezjna* sparring before breakfast.

The young prince and his watchful female guard wandered by while Gor and I sparred. Razaxha followed our movements with rapt attention.

"Ambassador, you fight *zezjna*? Brother Gor, did you teach

them this art?"

"We learned together as children," Gor informed him.

"If you are interested, we can teach you the basic forms." I scrubbed the sweat from my face and neck with a towel.

Razaxha accepted the proposal at once. "Yes, I would like that very much."

His guard sneered at the idea. "The prince does not need lessons in leaving one's enemies alive."

A familiar argument from another arrogant Ursetu. "On the contrary. Diplomacy and the art of *zezjna* present an effective tool for defense," I countered.

"What chance do they have against a blade?" The guard crossed her arms over her chest. A naked dagger gleamed at her waist, and a sidearm lay holstered against the thigh plate of her armor.

"Both gather more information without dealing death. May I demonstrate?" There were Ursetu training daggers in a rack, blunted instruments that would cause little harm. I took one and offered another to Razaxha. "I'm certain you know how to fight with one of these."

"Since I was five years old." Lithe and comfortable with the blade, he showed off his form for me in a rapid kata.

"One of the first things you must learn about your opponent are their strengths. Their weaknesses. Where they yield, and where they do not. The same is true of diplomacy." I took up the basic knife-fighting stance I had been taught in the Lunar Militia, deliberately holding the blade straight out rather than reversed in my hand the way the prince wielded his. "Show me what you've got."

Razaxha came at me with the serpentine Ursetu fighting style. This was the form I became familiar with on my first mission. I did not employ my sensitivity to feel for clues in his attack this time. Using Sol Fed technique did not provide ideal defense, but I managed to deflect his attack, not giving up any ground.

"What is my weakness?" I asked over our crossed forearms.

"The way you fight," he responded. "You are deflecting with both edges rather than one. You learned how to fight with a double edge, not with an Ursetu blade."

"Excellent observations, your highness. They are all true." I broke the hold and stepped back into a waiting crouch. "Again."

In my peripheral vision, I saw Khus arrive, but Razaxha was already on the offensive. This time, I employed the split-second advantages my empathic senses gave me. Flares of excitement limned the edges of his concentration when he thought he had the best of me and gave me clues to the timing of his strikes.

"What are my strengths?" I asked when I sensed his frustration.

"You anticipate better than anyone I have fought. But you are not following through. You never thrust or cut." He frowned. "You only defend."

"Again, true. Is that a strength or a weakness?"

"A weakness," he answered without hesitation.

"Shall I tell you what I've learned about you or show you?"

"Show me." He grinned, white teeth flashing in his dark face.

"All right then." I waited until he came at me again, deflected his arm with my left hand and smacked the flat side of my blade hard above his knee. He stumbled back with a grunt of pain and surprise.

"You lead with your right leg too far forward," I said and flipped the blade in my hand, Ursetu fashion, so the business edge now faced the prince. "I also learned how you fight. In diplomacy, observation and preparation are key to understanding."

I advanced this time, using the Ursetu knife style Rhix

taught me on board the Market ship, and gave no quarter. Razaxha was an excellent fighter, and his surprise only gave me an advantage for the first press. He came back at me hard. His attempt to reign in his right leg impressed me, but old habits don't break easily, and the more frustrated he became, the tendency to overstep resurfaced. I stepped in and forced his blade arm up, the edge of my dagger resting against his throat.

"Where did you learn *huya* fighting?" he panted, staring at me.

"What is my weakness?" I demanded, ignoring the question for now.

After a moment's hesitation, he said, "I am still alive."

"Is that really a weakness? Or is it a strength we share?" Shifting the practice blade away from his throat, I released him and stepped back, the weapon held loosely at my side. "What follows now is a universe of possibilities. One of us kills the other, and there are no other choices, no chances to learn about each other, or how we might benefit from working together. There is only an end to a fight that doesn't necessarily bring victory."

Razaxha nodded, sweaty and thoughtful. I was beginning to like this kid.

Gor threw another towel at my face. I grinned at him and mopped the dripping perspiration from my forehead and neck.

"You have learned new skills. I am not certain I approve, but well done," Gor said.

"Ambassador, where did you learn *haya* knife fighting?" Razaxha persisted, his bronze eyes earnest. He swiped a clean towel over his face. "You didn't master this just by watching me."

"No. I learned from a mercenary I met on a long jaunt through dark space."

Razaxha's head came up, and sparks of hopeful excitement fizzed against my mind. From Khus, however, a sullen explosion of suspicion and hostility almost drowned out the prince's response. He had not moved during the last bit of the lesson; just watched me with a dark expression and his arms knotted over his chest.

"What is this mercenary's name?" Khus demanded.

"Essek." I gave him the name of a mutineer, my first kill. "I was grateful for his insight about my form." A flashback on the first, rather sensual lesson with Rhix brought heat to my face, and I hid the flush behind the towel, scrubbing at my skin. Gor's interest in my reaction nudged at the edge of my mind.

"Essek." Khus grunted. "An alias if ever I heard one. What color were his eyes?"

"I don't remember," I lied. "Why do you ask?"

"Because that fighting style was developed by an exiled member of the royal family."

Shit and damn. Khus's resentful distrust pressed against my senses. Something malevolent beneath his regard clung to my senses like thick, greasy dust, but Razaxha's hopeful enthusiasm crowded out the nastier sentiments before I could identify them.

"Where did you meet this mercenary?" The young being's excitement lit his features. I hated to crush his enthusiasm but answered in the only way I could.

"It was a classified mission. I'm afraid I can't say."

"You consider yourself an expert in our ways simply because you know how to fight." A half sneer twisted the elder Ursetu's upper lip.

"On the contrary. I claim no expertise and will put as much effort into learning about your planet and culture as I did about how to fight." Maybe not quite so much, but ... everything suddenly seemed like a private double entendre. Gor's amused wonder burbling against my mind was not something I needed to deal with as Khus leaned in until we were almost nose to nose.

"You will find the ways of the Remoliad are not those of Urset."

The low boil of irritation began to gain pressure with his continued derision and loosened my tongue. "No, you are right about that. Most of us are far more polite."

Razaxha's eyes grew wide, his expression caught between laughter and trepidation. He swiveled away to hide his reaction. Even his stoic guard's mouth twitched. Khus said nothing for a long moment and glared at me. I was well on my way to becoming his least favorite human.

"It will be fascinating to learn where our cultures do intersect, nonetheless." Gor's lilting, musical voice offered a way out, and his mind touched mine with a private rebuke. "Shall we begin by showing Prince Razaxha the virtue of admitting when one is wrong?"

I sent Gor the empathic equivalent of a petulant raspberry. Aloud, I said, "Yes, of course. My apologies if I offended you, Lord Khus. My sense of humor does not always translate into other languages."

"Then perhaps you should keep it to yourself." The scorched edge of contempt in his voice rebuffed Gor's attempt to restore peace. "We will see how well the Shontavians respond to your sense of humor." He stalked away, a smoke-trail of resentment lingering in his wake.

"I truly am looking forward to learning something of *zezjna*," Razaxha said hurriedly. "Will you and Brother Gor be back in the morning?"

"We shall be," Gor assured him.

"Good." He flashed us a grin. Before they followed Khus down the corridor, Razaxha's guard favored me with a nod of respect. I had earned a few points there.

My crechemate cocked his head at me once they were out of hearing. "I think you and I have things to talk about. The person who taught you to fight is a source of many conflicting emotions."

"I'll fill you in later on what I can." Normally I would just let Gor mind-walk through my head, but I would need to prepare a few walls. Some things in the muck of my psyche were classified, and others, I was not ready for him to see.

Gor nodded. "The prince's mind is flexible. He will be a receptive student."

"I hope Khus hasn't influenced him too thoroughly. Flexible is not the adjective I would use to describe him." I had several in mind, not one of them flattering. "Do you get anything from Khus that worries you, other than he despises the fact the queen went to the Remoliad for help?"

"His resentment is poisonous," Gor agreed. "I do not sense he is hiding anything, if that is what you mean. His jealousy and outrage are surface features. What lies beneath is more of the same."

I decided to ask. "What about Alecto Sim? He never takes off his psi-shield." I dropped on the mat for a final stretch. "I don't get much of anything but static."

"It is a powerful device. I do not believe it is a psi-shield, but a suppression field that blankets his emotional state and thought patterns. The Tolkish use such devices for treating maladies of the psyche." Gor's unblinking eyes moved closer together as he pondered the question. "He appears to be harmless, and yet ... "

"What?"

"I cannot name my trepidation. There is something cloaked behind the suppression field. A need to prove something. To redeem himself." Gor's sad, fluting exhale added, "Your commander has the same need for redemption."

Dumbfounded, my jaw dropped. "You can sense things through that null?"

His oily, mercurial eyes drew apart in sorrow. "Only when he does not want me to."

CHAPTER
FOURTEEN

THE SHIP HELD the kinds of luxuries one would expect from a royal vessel: private quarters for each of us with efficient workspaces and comfortable beds. For once, I was sleepy and looking forward to inspecting that bed with the inside of my eyelids. My pants had just hit the deck when someone requested access at my door. I didn't unlock it but keyed the voice pad. "Yes?"

"Ambassador Tamareia." Surprised, I recognized Razax-ha's voice. "May I speak with you?"

"Just a minute." Cursing under my breath, I pulled up my pants and wrestled my undershirt back over my head before I answered the door, still shoeless.

Razaxha and his guard stood in the corridor. A cautious advance of my senses stubbed against her wary interest in me, but the prince's energy held a curious combination of excitement and fear.

"What can I do for you?"

"Forgive me for disturbing you." He cast nervous glances down the corridor in both directions. "I need you to come with me."

"Of course. Just a moment, let me finish dressing." I went

back inside. As soon as the door closed, I sat on the bed and tapped the bump of the implant as I shoved my feet into boots. "Commander, you still awake?"

"Yeah." His voice sounded in my head at once. "Anything wrong?"

"Clandestine meeting with the prince. Listen in?" I muttered, tucking my undershirt back into my pants.

"Will do."

I grabbed my fatigue blouse and exited the room. "I'm sorry for the delay." I hastily shrugged into the garment and matched their hurried pace.

"You could not have expected a summons at this hour." He held his hand in front of his mouth in a plea for silence and motioned for me to follow the guard.

We made a couple of sharp turns down other corridors and then rounded a corner, which signaled a change in venue. Where the corridor housing our rooms was far from spartan, this felt like walking through a portal into a palace courtyard. Thick carpets covered the deck. The overhead soared to two levels and a balcony with double doors in each wall, painted with bronze, sapphire, and crimson. Exotic foliage and over-stuffed lounges transformed the area into a little oasis, a holographic night sky projected above.

The guard opened the door and positioned herself outside. Razaxha beckoned me to join him. The quarters were opulent, full of cushioned chairs and colorful draperies. A sweet, smoky incense drifted in the confines of the royal apartment. Razaxha led me through the sitting area to a more private room behind one of the curtained alcoves where a vast desk lay scattered with data devices. The screens and circuitry of a large subspace array lay on a surface behind the desk.

"Thank you for coming, Ambassador. This may be our only opportunity for privacy. Please, sit."

My curiosity piqued, I complied. "What can I do for you, Prince Razaxha?"

"We are about to enter dark space, and the queen would speak with you." He touched his palm to an identification pad, and the screen lit up.

An older female with heavy-lidded bronze eyes, identical to Rhix's, regarded me with frank curiosity from the screen. Silver-gilded dark curls escaped from a band of metal set with small, blood-red cabochons and fell against her copper skin.

"Greetings, Ambassador Tamareia." Queen Xahria's voice was gilded with the arrogance I'd come to expect from my limited experience with Ursetu nobility. She dressed in battle armor, an outercoat draped over her shoulders and sparkled with embroidered geometric patterns in metallic bronze, blue, and scarlet. "I have given the command to prevent hostilities against the Shontavians as you requested. My warrior-caste troops have cordoned off the palace grounds to keep the others away. I cannot guarantee it will last until your arrival, but we will try."

"I understand, Queen Xahria. Thank you."

"Will you be prepared to make first contact upon arrival?"

"I believe so. Prince Razaxha has been extremely valuable in orienting us to the situation." I gave him a respectful nod, and his umber skin gained a pink tone, the tickle of his pleased embarrassment brushing my empathic nets.

"I have asked Razaxha to ensure Khus cooperates by providing any information you require. What else do you need?"

I sat forward. "We know almost nothing about Shontavian engineering and conditioning. Access to that information would allow us to craft a nonthreatening approach."

The queen gave a brisk nod. "Lady Darizh oversees the program. She is my closest ally and one of my councilors. She is still on the island. I shall arrange a briefing to take place upon your arrival."

"That would be helpful." We needed to pick the brains of someone involved in the process.

"Razaxha and I need your assistance not only with the Shontavian crisis but with more personal matters. We would ask this conversation to remain unknown to Lord Khus."

I tilted my head, intrigued. "How can I help?"

"First, I want you to teach my grandson the ways of conciliation as you work with the Shontavians. It is a lost art on Urset, and we need it now if our planet is to live in peace. He needs a guide familiar with those stars, and I am not."

"My team and I would be pleased." Tutoring a prince in statesmanship was not part of my curriculum vitae, but I had Alecto Sim to fill in where I lacked and Lam Tiri, young and eager to share his expertise.

Her voice mellowed, became less formal. "I am a relic of my mother's reign. Diplomacy has never been a word frequently used in the Razeha family vocabulary. Coming to the brink of collapse in our civilization has opened me to the idea."

"Is your safety at risk, even now?" I asked bluntly.

"There is no such thing as safety for an Ursetu queen." The corners of her mouth lifted in a mirthless smile. "Urset is not like the Remoliad. Balance within the ruling caste is never satisfied, and scales only tip with the volume of blood."

"There are seven families through which the monarchy rotates. Is that correct?" The dump compiled by my Andari crewmates on board *Thunder Child* held a best-guess cultural anthropology profile.

Xahria snorted in dark amusement. "It does not rotate, Ambassador, so much as it is wrested from one to the next by deceit and murder. Our family plays the game well and has held the monarchy for four generations—one of the longest successive reigns of any matriarchal line. I want Razaxha to make history by continuing our family's rule as the first male on the throne in four hundred years." The queen's flickering image smiled down at her grandson, who returned her regard, my empathic nets warming with his intense affection. "The Remoliad's vision of unity suits my desires for his future."

"Lord Khus does not share the same vision." I let my voice carry a hint of pessimism.

"Khus is my deceased mate's brother. His philosophies are not ours, but he is Razaxha's oldest male relative still on the planet and serves as regent head of the warrior caste until he comes of age."

Razaxha scowled. "His daughter is ten years older than me. Our houses formed many alliances over the years, but deals are easily ruptured. His mate's family would like nothing better than to place a queen of their line upon the throne now that my mother is dead."

"Some of the other matriarchs have tried to gain access to the Shontavians." The queen's voice grew bleak, all arrogance peeling away. "I fear there will be no return from chaos if we use our own creations against each other."

"What is your second request?" I glanced between the projected vision of the queen and the prince beside me.

Razaxha shifted in his chair, his eyes on his grandmother's projected visage. "I will be head of the warrior caste, but I have no experience. I am not yet old enough to be a soldier. Until I can take command, I need a general who will work for our goals and not his own."

"Command of the warrior caste must remain in my family." The queen leaned forward, her expression gaining intensity. "Razaxha told me you encountered someone who taught you *haya* fighting. I believe the mercenary was my son, Nazhir. I want to locate him and bring him home, so he can help me restore order. Do you know where he is?"

I blinked, speechless. Seven hells. Queen Xahria wanted me to find Rhix.

And I was probably the last person to whom he would listen.

"I do not know that it is your son," I stammered around my surprise. "Do you have any idea what he might be involved in?"

"He is above all else a leader," Queen Xahria said. "Wherever he is, he cannot stay in the background for long. It is not in his nature."

She was right about that. "With your permission, I would like to consult Commander Sumner to help me with the search. He is discreet, and I trust him with my life. I will need to know at what intervals the ship will emerge from dark space, so we can send and receive private messages."

"Razaxha will give you the information." The tension in Razaxha's body relaxed, and on the screen, his grandmother smiled.

"Thank you. Your willingness to aid us is encouraging."

"You are welcome, Queen Xahria."

"We will continue to speak on a regular schedule after you arrive." The queen raised her chin. "One last thing. Your name: Dalí." Her pronunciation gave it the Ursetu inflection of DAH-lee. "Tell me what it means."

"I understand the word translates to something different in your language. My name is pronounced da-LEE." I placed mild emphasis on the last syllable. I couldn't help but grin. "I was named after a twentieth-century Earth artist, not a vengeance demon."

"An artist." Xahria nodded. "I believe Nazhir would like you. My son has an appreciation for all things artistic."

My cheeks grew warm at that. "I look forward to meeting him," I said.

The screen flickered and went dark with static as I spoke. The vibration of the ship's electromagnetic drive wound up, setting my teeth on edge, and I gripped the arms of my chair against the disorienting flip-flop as we breached dark space.

Behind the desk, Razaxha screwed his eyes shut. The press of increased velocity remained noticeable until the ship's artificial gravity adjusted to a more comfortable level. The buzzing sensation in my teeth faded as the EM drive reached full speed.

Razaxha sighed in relief and stood. "Thank you for joining me on such short notice, Ambassador. I can show you back to your room if you like."

"No, I think I can find my own way back." I rose and bowed from the waist. "Thank you for trusting me with this."

"So, it is true you have negotiated with Shontavians before?" His eyes were bright and interested as he escorted me to the door.

"It is true." I grimaced. "But not on a battlefield."

"Still, you must have been very brave."

"Not at all. They terrify me, but I respect them as fellow sentient beings. One of them spared my life when it could very well have killed me." I bit back a shudder at the memory of the arena. "But I believe they will negotiate, given a chance."

"I hope so, for all our sakes." His face grew solemn, suddenly too world-weary for any adolescent child. The port slid aside, and his guard glanced at both of us. "If you need to talk to me in private before we arrive on Urset, you may contact Rhani. She is my grandmother's death angel. You can trust her."

The guard gave a crisp downward motion of her head in acknowledgment of the prince's words. "Follow the corridor." She motioned to the passage from which we had come. "Turn left at the first port, right at the second, and you will find your quarters."

"Good night." I bowed and took my leave. Turning left past the first portway, I muttered, "Still listening, Sumner?"

"I'm here."

"I know Ka'pth and Ra'sho keep tabs on the Market's

communications now, thanks to the bug you planted. Do you think they can get word to Rhix?"

"Probably, but it won't have as much weight coming from them."

"I'm not sure he'd even look at a message from me."

"I think he would." His voice held a strange note, and what he insinuated made me frown.

Rhix was not a draconian bastard like the last Lord of the Market. He abolished the slave trade and sex trafficking his predecessors had relied upon and proved himself open to considering new ideas, a character trait I had manipulated to my benefit whenever I could. Some of those benefits were fiercely erotic.

Bent on my mission to rescue the others, I betrayed him in a way that hurt him more deeply than I thought possible. No, Rhix wouldn't want to talk to me. I wouldn't either.

Simish might.

One of the droopy-visaged servants engineered by the Ursetu, Rhix's right hand being had the Lord of the Market's best interests in mind. If anyone could get his stubborn ego to bend enough to listen to me, it might be him. "The prince will tell me when it's possible to transmit communications. I'll work on a message we can send to *Thunder Child*, and then we can—"

I turned down the first sharp angle of corridor and came face to face with Khus.

"What are you doing in this part of the ship?" The aggressive thrust of annoyance thumped against my mind. "I thought you retired, Ambassador. To whom were you speaking?"

"Myself. I'm restless by nature." The truth rolled smoothly off my tongue. "I often walk when I can't sleep to sort problems. It helps organize my mind."

"This ship is crewed by warrior caste." A cold smile stretched his mouth. "If you are found stalking the royal apartments without an escort, they are likely to protect the prince first and seek answers later."

I nodded in bland apology. "Of course. I didn't realize this was a secured area. I will be more careful in the future."

"There are many who do not support the queen's decision to join the Remoliad. You will be wise to remember where you are welcome, and where you are not."

I returned his level stare without reaction until he gave a brusque nod, his shoulder bumping mine as he passed. My jaw clenched, and heat filled my veins with a sudden onslaught of murderous rage. *Damn, damn, damn. Get a grip.* These violent swings of emotion were going to get me killed.

Sumner's voice in my head reminded me he still listened. "Everything good?"

"Yeah. Fine. Let's talk about this tomorrow." I tapped off the implant.

Breathing in time with my slow-paced steps, the fire died down to ash and ember. My control reasserted itself by the time I reached my cabin, still thinking, *Hey, great. I am on my way to an entire planet full of arrogant, violent assholes.* If I couldn't harness my mood swings, the mission was completely fucked.

CHAPTER
FIFTEEN

ANY HOPE I'd had of a peaceful night dissolved in frustration. Thinking about Rhix brought on the damned sex dreams again. They were preferable to my shattered nightmares of Gresh and Rasida at Luna Station, but equally unsettling in their intensity.

The primal, violent couplings we shared slaked a need every bit as greedy for oblivion as the part of me that had turned back to illegal chemical highs. It hadn't been love, at least not for me. I wasn't capable then, still too raw and shattered by grief. It was a purely physical act of release, fueled by a reaction to his personal pheromones that hijacked my sex drive in a way no one else ever had.

Pieces of Rhix are permanently attached to the pleasure centers in my nervous system, just like the chemical signatures of the vape. There are no nanobots targeted to remove his traces.

Wide awake, I placated my body with a solo orgasm and gave up trying to sleep. I dressed and went to the conference room our team had claimed with plans to draft the message to Rhix, believing it would be hours before anyone else woke up.

To my surprise, I found Alecto Sim already there. He stood with his back to me in the darkened room, studying the projected holographic map of the crash site and its surroundings, his long, slender hands clasped behind his back.

"Good morning," I said quietly.

He whirled around, eyes wide and wild, body crouched and feral with alarm. The brief, icy burn of his fear surged against my empathic nets. For a moment, I thought he would attack me.

"I'm so sorry. I didn't mean to startle you." I slowly held up my hands where he could see them.

The filigreed metal of the suppression device glittered against his forehead, and he relaxed as the tech did its work, the fuzzy barrier thickening between my mind and his. Gor had told me it was used to treat maladies of the psyche. I suspected post-traumatic stress disorder, being intimately familiar with the taste of Sim's cold-sweat panic.

I stayed put until he smiled, the beautiful lines of his face still ragged at the edges as he sighed.

"Please accept my apologies. I did not think anyone else would be awake." He waved his hand at the map, a slight tremble evident in the gesture. "I could not sleep. My mind was preoccupied, and I decided I would try to be productive. You, as well, I suspect?"

"True enough." Slow, measured steps brought me to stand beside him in front of the map. A three-dimensional scan of the location showed the crash site on the palace grounds, thick with trees, spiderwebbed with avenues and what appeared to be government buildings inside protective walls of black stone. Towers of alloy and glass combined in architectural fusion with an immense stone ziggurat, thrusting up through the rain forest foliage. In a more manicured area of the grounds lay the wreckage of the orbiting facility.

My estimation of its size was perhaps a kilometer in diameter; an irregular mound of metal and composite alloy blackened and warped along the forward edge by the intense heat of reentry. The rear of the facility lay crumpled and streaked with char but almost intact. Burned-out vehicles lay on the leeward edge of the crash site, scattered in avenues pockmarked by artillery.

The front of the impact site came so close to the palace that ejecta from the plowed-up earth littered the immaculate lawns in front of the building. I rotated the image to see the area behind the crash site. The top of one of the government buildings had taken a direct hit, but the city outside the walls appeared unscathed. Whoever brought down this behemoth had deadly accuracy. They missed their target by a hair's breadth.

"This was definitely not an accident," I murmured.

"I fear not. Lord Khus may be the most suspicious of beings, but I do not see how this could be anything but deliberate."

One of the streets leading to the palace abruptly terminated at the crash site; heaves of rubble and twisted trees marred the once neat avenue. Close to the shadows of the ruined orbiting laboratory, I spotted the Shontavians. I enlarged the scan.

Smooth, gray faces with mouths full of sharp, serrated prongs lifted in observant interest of the drone that had made the reconnaissance holos. Standing gun arrays, presumed looted from Princess Arzalat's ill-fated assault, were manned by the engineered mercenaries but not pointed in the camera's direction. The bioengineered warriors did not appear to feel threatened. One of the armored figures, larger than the rest, seemed to be looking directly into the lens of the drone.

"That would be our alpha," I said.

"Yes, I think so."

"This avenue is an almost perfect approach to where they

are dug in." I swept my hand over the holo to expand the view.

"The buildings here can provide cover." Sim's fingers circled an intersecting avenue. "They are accessible from the east, out of the Shontavians' line of sight. A good place for a command post."

"I think Sumner will agree." I glanced at him. "You have combat experience."

"Yes." A shadow flitted across his face. "And you?" That transient darkness drowned in the light of his interested deflection.

"No. I was in the Lunar Militia, never in active combat. My military experience is limited."

"Yes, forgive me. I knew that information from your profile. And your mother, of course." He had recovered his charm, his eyes creased in mirth, and a quirk to his lips hinting at some intimate knowledge. It made me grin. He sat at the table, and I joined him as he continued, "The child of a diplomat, you were immersed in Zereid culture until you returned to Sol Fed." He chuckled. "I cannot imagine what a shock it must have been."

"It was that." I found myself laughing with him.

"Strange, is it not, that an upbringing in *zezjna* philosophy allows you to lead a life as dangerous and as violent as the Penumbra requires." He sat back, his expression mild and curious.

"*Zezjna* allows us to protect peace with whatever skills we have."

"It seems peace has an unusual definition on Urset." Even frowning, Sim was distractingly beautiful. "The prince is an innocent. He did not even consider the situation on the ruling caste island as something unusual."

"It's the only way of life he knows." I shook my head. "Razaxha may be young, but he has a sobering grasp of the situation on his planet. He requested we tutor him in diplomacy. I was thinking of having Lam Tiri take charge. He is passionate about the art of interspecies diplomacy, and his worldview is still positive."

"And yours is not?"

"Decidedly so."

"As is mine. The consequences of experience," he said.

"Tell me more about yourself, Alecto." I leaned back in my chair. "How did you become involved in politics?"

"I was assigned to the Remoliad as ancillary to Delegate Mara, six years past. A formidable politician, and a true advocate for peace. I learned so much at her side." His expression grew somber, the corners of his mouth drawn into a gentle curve. "Sadly, she was killed in a shuttle accident at the Kadrelian hub a year after I arrived. I took her place as the junior delegate. The Tolkish government formally elevated me to delegate four years ago when they determined I would be an adequate replacement."

"More than adequate, so I hear from my mother."

His visage brightened. "Marina is too kind. She and I became good friends during the ratification of Sol Fed's membership."

"You said you have combat experience." I knew the final conflict on Tolkis ended more than seventy years ago. Since Sim's species did not sprout hair until late in their life cycle, his smooth lavender pate meant he still had to be close to Sumner's age—too young to have fought in that war.

"Yes. My parents were barely out of infancy when the Weshka seized control and began a terrible period of violence on our planet. Peace came just after my birth, but my father and twice-father are warriors through and through. So was I expected to be, and I sought to fulfill our dreadful family tradition on other planets." His scarlet gaze turned to me, haunted with memory. "It is a legacy I chose to end in favor of a new cause. If you will indulge me, I prefer to focus on the present."

"Of course. Forgive me." I felt like an ass, probing what I already knew to be a tender wound to satisfy my burning curiosity. But I could probably confirm Sumner's connection with him to be a martial one.

"You did not have the benefit of learning about me before we met, as I did with your Penumbra profile." His skin tone deepened to lilac, and I realized he was blushing. "I admit I find you fascinating, Dalí Tamareia. I hope to come to know you better."

His warm eyes held something dangerously close to my more physical interests in Alecto Sim. His resonant voice frayed with a soft, intimate burr that curled around my already frustrated sex drive and set it purring.

Damn. It was going to be a very long mission.

———

More answers arrived unexpectedly in the bath.

The lavatories had both sonic cleansers and the rare luxury of a hot water filled tub, another benefit of traveling with royalty. A steaming bath was a meditation for the Ursetu. I wasn't about to pass up a chance to have a hot soak, capped off by a warm towel the thickness of the carpet under my bare feet.

Almost fully submerged beneath the water and relaxed by the heat, I jerked back to startled awareness when Sumner's voice sounded over the com. "What do you want, Naru?"

I sat straight up, sending water everywhere.

Implant coms are a blessing and a curse, Tommi warned me at the beginning. On board *Thunder Child*, a sign hung over the head in my lavatory, courtesy of Melos, proclaiming No One Wants to Hear This. I was terrible at remembering to turn the com off.

Sumner hoarded his privacy. Unless he needed the device for translation purposes or during an operation, his com stayed off. He wanted me to listen—he had purposely turned on his implant.

"We cannot continue this way if we are to work together. We must talk." Sim's voice, though Sumner had called him by another name. "May I come in? Please?"

The awkward pause in their conversation allowed me to scramble out of the tub with frantic haste and grab the towel. "I know you must have questions," Sim said.

"You're goddamn right." Sumner's voice crackled with electricity. "I thought you were dead."

"Naru Sabecc is dead. He died on Lymo, as he deserved." A pause. "As I thought you did. When I discovered you were with the Penumbra, I cannot name the feeling I experienced. I did not know you survived, or I would have sought you out."

"Somebody triggered the casualty chip in my armor. A drone picked me up. I still had a pulse when I got to the morgue, but just barely. They resuscitated me." Sumner fell silent a moment. "At times, I wished they hadn't."

"When they shot you, I had to think of the others under my command. I could not show my grief." Sim's words shimmered even over my implant, molten with the intensity of emotion. "Oh, my dearest Rion, forgive me. We all should have had the courage to stand or die with you. *I* should have stood with you. You paid blood price for your conscience."

"I didn't object soon enough. No matter how close they came to killing me, it will never change the fact we fought for the wrong fucking side."

Oh, god. I sat down hard on the bed, aghast, as what he said sunk in.

Sumner wasn't a freedom fighter on Lymo.

He and Sim were part of the genocidal wave the dictator unleashed on his own people. Sim's next words rocked me backward.

"What happened after that moment, in Amanosk... The

blood may be gone from my hands, but it will haunt my mind to my last breath."

Cold water dripped down my back, but the shudder that coursed through my body was a tremor of soul.

Amanosk. Of all the ghastly stories to come out of the Scata Rebellion, that one word is enough to elicit horror from any being with a shred of compassion.

The entire village had been slaughtered for aiding the enemy, ordered by General Moserok, and carried out by mercenary troops under his personal command. Infants. Children. Mothers. Aged ones. They were noncombatants clustered in a peaceful community where a small group of freedom fighters had received medical care.

Sumner's unit had taken part.

"You activated the morgue chip in my armor." Sumner's statement held certainty.

"Yes."

"It saved my life."

"I am glad it did." The smile in Sim's voice did not offset the pain beneath.

"What happened to the rest of the platoon?" Sumner asked.

"I alone survived the final push." The normal resonance of Sim's rich voice dwindled to a bleak, broken huskiness. "I did what I had to do to stay alive, but I could no longer fight. I fled the planet as soon as possible. The cause of galactic peace has been my work since then, but it is a lie I live instead of facing my crimes."

"Naru…" Sumner croaked.

"Show me no pity. I do not deserve it."

But the deep, wracking sounds of grief and remorse I heard over Sumner's implant did not belong only to Sim, nor did the wordless murmurs of comfort come only from Sumner. Tears burned in my own eyes.

"Thank you for trusting me, Rion," I whispered, and

turned off my com to give them privacy. But I sat on the edge of the bed for a long time afterward.

Alecto Sim had changed his identity to escape the acts of his past life. Whatever his reasons for capitulation, the cold reality of his war crimes would never be erased. Sim already knew it.

And so did Rion Sumner.

———

The evening before we arrived on Urset, Sumner told me about the battle gone wrong on Lymo.

"When you spoke to the security council, you said the Shontavians fight and bunk alongside other mercenaries without harming them." My commander squinted at me. "I disagreed."

"You said I was half right." I remembered the exchange in the gallery at the Remoliad.

"When our platoon rendezvoused with the general's troops, we discovered he purchased a weapons squad of Shontavians as well. They got dropped off by a drone transport the minute they hit planetside. The Lymon captain gave them their orders. None of us had ever fought beside them before, but we knew their reputation. In our first battle, the general gave us the objective of taking a mountainside where the freedom fighters were dug in."

He looked down, eyes fixed on the floor, fingers twined into a white-knuckled knot between his spread knees. "Late in the day we got caught in an intense firefight. The Shontavians provided cover for the rest of the troops, but as soon as it got dark … "

He paused and looked up at me, furrows lining his forehead. "The damn things suddenly stopped shooting and stared at the sky."

"The stars." Goose bumps prickled my arms.

"We were getting cut up. Rounds bounced off our armor like hail, and Naru … Sim … " he corrected himself, his voice dulled with memory. "He was my captain. He yelled at them to keep firing, but they just stood there and stared up at the sky like they expected something, for what felt like hours but probably only lasted a few minutes. The Lymon officer got to their position and gave them a coded command. They snapped out of it and started firing again. We took the ridge a few hours later but with heavy casualties." He ran his hands through his short hair, raking up spiky blond bristles. "We bivouacked on the mountainside overnight. The mercenaries on one side, the general's troops on the other, and the Shontavians on the outskirts, all sitting in a circle staring up at the stars. One of the Lymon officers lost his brother in the firefight when the Shontavians stopped laying down cover. He went over and started screaming at them. One of them pulled him in and broke his neck." The crisp sound of his snapping fingers echoed in my quarters. "You can guess what happened next."

"They didn't eat MREs," I said weakly.

"The general's troops practically slept in our shorts that night. From then on, it was two groups, not three, with as much distance as we could get between us and them. Only the Lymon captain had the code words, and he refused to share them with Sim or any of our officers. There weren't any other incidents. We held the mountainside for two weeks until they shipped the Shontavians out to defend the general's position. Then—" his ocean eyes darkened, shadowed like the depths where light no longer penetrated— "we became the monsters."

CHAPTER
SIXTEEN

THROUGH THE WINDOW of the landing shuttle, the first glimpse of Urset suggested paradise. A ziggurat came into view beneath patchwork breaks in the rain forest canopy. Solid and blocky, the lowest levels were fortified against assault. Glimpsed in the tree line, the architecturally ornate open columns and gardened terraces of the upper tiers gleamed like malachite set in black, volcanic rock walls. Beyond the palace, because it could be nothing else, a waterfall sparkled in filtered sunlight against the green and ebony face of the mountain. On the opposite side, the glint of a churning gray and white sea met the obsidian curve of a sandy beach.

The subtropical climate of the ruling caste's island hit me with a dense wave as soon as we stepped out of the royal shuttle. Midday sun streamed down, melting my shadow into a dark puddle beneath my feet. After a few breaths, I started to acclimate—Dad's Māori ancestors would have been appalled if I couldn't tolerate a little humidity, but even so, sweat already trickled under the high collar of my dress uniform.

We followed the prince and Khus down the ramp into the

wavering heat of the private landing pad where sleek armored transports hovered on the paved surface. On either side of the motorcade, warrior-caste troops manned tracked vehicles bristling with mounted guns, and more guards rode in gun turrets on the outside. Razaxha and his guard climbed into the first reinforced limousine with Lord Khus. My team and I were ushered to a second waiting vehicle, sealed into air-cooled, bulletproof luxury, and driven to the estate.

The beauty of the ziggurat was marred by gun arrays on the rise of its first level. The top of the wall crawled with armored soldiers. Our motorcade passed through a tunnel in the outer defenses and emerged into a paved courtyard where the prince's attentive guard hustled him inside as we exited our vehicle. Khus flashed a disinterested glance in my direction and vanished into the ziggurat's interior.

Abandoned by our hosts, save for the guards who had ridden the outside of the armored limousine, Sumner and I glanced at each other as Alecto, Tiri, and Gor joined us in awkward hesitation.

"Are we supposed to just walk in?" I muttered. "Or will that get us shot?"

"Ambassador Tamareia." One of the craggy-faced Simish exited the doorway at a hurried pace and bowed, addressing us in Remoliad Standard. "Commander Sumner. Brother Gor. Minister Sim, and Lam Tiri. Forgive my tardiness. The queen is busy on the mainland but welcomes you to Urset and into her home. I will be responsible for your comfort while you are here. We will convey your belongings to the suite. Please follow me. A midday meal has been prepared."

We entered a cavernous central hall, natural light streaming in from strategic skyward tunnels in the rock. Though the humidity was still high, the bowels of the pyramid were surprisingly cool. Staircases ascended against the walls in four directions, some open, others enclosed and artificially lit. The Simish led us up one of these flights to a spacious room bustling with more of the engineered servants.

Plump cushions with padded armrests surrounded a sunken table, which could have doubled as a landing platform for the royal yacht. At the head, an Ursetu waited. The rich jewel tones of her nanosilk robes proclaimed her as another member of the ruling caste. Of middle years with silver close-cropped hair bright against her dark skin, she frowned as she scanned the data device in her hand. Her golden eyes narrowed as she looked up.

"This is Lady Darizh, one of the queen's councilors and director of the Shontavian engineering program," the Simish said. "She will help prepare you for first contact, as requested."

"Thank you, Simish." I offered Lady Darizh a shallow bow. "I am Dalí Tamareia, Special Ambassador for the Remoliad." I introduced my team. "We are grateful you agreed to meet with us."

"Ambassador." Her head bobbed. A quick rake of her regard over my companions included them in the gesture. "Be seated."

I sank down to a seat as my teammates arranged themselves in varying degrees of comfort. Lam Tiri looked entirely at ease, half lounging upon one of the fat pillows. Gor sat cross-legged and folded the ends of his priestly sash neatly over his exposed bits. Sumner lowered himself to a cushion beside Alecto.

A number of Simish set out the courses of our meal: grilled shellfish on sturdy metal skewers, an unfamiliar red fruit something like an elongated strawberry, and globular clusters of crisp, leafy vegetables the size of my hand. The shellfish gave off an appetizing smoky aroma, making my mouth water. The meat was sweet and tender, flavored with spices for which I had no comparison but left mild heat on the back of my tongue.

The servants placed a crystal beaker filled with clear liquid and a shallow, stemmed vessel that reminded me of a champagne coupe before each of us. The glasses contained a pearly sphere. Darizh picked up her carafe and poured some of the liquid over the bubble, which disintegrated into vapor. Thick syrup held within the membrane fizzed and combined with the fluid. The rest of us followed her example.

"To the success of your mission." Darizh saluted us. I raised my glass in return and took a careful sip. The chemical reaction prickled my nose, the flavor an interesting mix of sweet syrup, a citrusy bite, and the unmistakable burn of high-octane alcohol. I set it aside and asked one of the Simish for some of the strong, aromatic tea I remembered from the Market ship. The last thing I needed was to go drunk into first contact.

"The queen says you need information about the Shontavians," Darizh said, draining her glass. She signaled the Simish for another pearl of syrup.

"How were they lodged on board the facility?" Lam Tiri asked, his eyes bright and interested.

"In group cells. It is not practical to house more than fifteen at a time. This last batch of twelve was decanted almost six years ago. The conditioning process works better if we pair newly decanted models with functional merchandise. But even functional items must be reconditioned if too much time passes between preparation and purchase." Her lips pursed as she waved the skewer of grilled chunks. "It is difficult to maintain a high level of preparedness for sale. To be lax is to devalue the product, though as more planets take up the banner of the Remoliad, the cause of peace has greatly diminished demand."

The way she spoke of the Shontavians as nothing more than inventory made my eyes narrow in distaste. "They are sentient beings," I quietly reminded her.

"Of course they are. They could not be conditioned otherwise. You cannot discipline something as stupid as—" Her teeth snagged one of the bits of seafood from the metal spike, and she harrumphed, her mouth full. "As one of these crustaceans, for instance. No, they must understand consequences and rewards if they are to be properly trained for mercenary service. This is achieved by a fairly simple process of neural stimulation, chemical reward, and induction in holographic environments."

"Chemical reward?" I didn't want to believe what that insinuated.

"Yes, a proprietary method using targeted nanoparticles. The Shontavians learn to associate battle with pleasure. Their endorphins are stimulated to secrete at a much higher level with the molecules we attached to their neurochemical organs. The drug reward is gradually withdrawn during conditioning. Their own endocrine system takes over and does the rest."

The Shontavians were quite literally addicted to violence by the same mechanism the Pilean drug cartel used to ensure human addiction to vape.

Unable to immediately process this, I listened in dull horror as Lady Darizh burbled on.

"I improved upon the method during my time. It is much more efficient if we restrict their choices to *either/or* rather than *if/then* scenarios. They come to understand consequences and reward eight times faster than under the old methods and inflict ten percent more casualties in simulation."

Her recitation fell on unappreciative ears, in poor taste given the members of our team whose species had suffered great numbers of casualties by Shontavian mercenaries. Across the table from me, Sumner's lips tightened. Gor's silvery eyes dulled with dismay at the relish with which Lady Darizh described the conditioning, his plate of greens forgotten. Lam Tiri's upper lip curled back from his fangs in a silent snarl of disgust.

Alecto Sim's gaze met mine, his expression mild and inscrutable. Having been a remote witness to the pain he shared with Sumner, I wondered how much of his calm demeanor could be attributed to the suppression field. "What do you believe happened here?" he asked Darizh. "The prince informed us the Shontavians no longer respond as expected."

"Undoubtedly a result of poor reconditioning habits. Someone became lax. I reassign the duty frequently so technicians will not become sympathetic to the merchandise. It is a brutal process but necessary." She pointed at me with her now-empty skewer. "I heard rumors someone recently survived a death match in the arena on board the old Shontavian Market. Clearly, that old pirate Lord Rhix let reconditioning lapse."

I risked a glance at Sumner. His mouth curled in a caustic smile.

"The Shontavians speak, do they not?" Gor tilted his head in question.

"In a limited capacity. The alpha line must speak in order to communicate with their masters, but many of the others never talk at all, save for sign language." She bit into a piece of the red fruit, sanguine juice running down her chin.

"Were they bred for psi talent?" I sat back with my fingertips pressed together in a steeple front of me. The tips turned white. It was all I could do to maintain a professional demeanor at this point.

Darizh laughed, spraying bits of fruit, and I lost my appetite. "There is no breeding, as such. They are without gender. They are not engineered for any useful psi talents. We know they possess a primitive group mind like some of the donor stock used in their engineering, which helps with the conditioning. What one learns about consequences, the others in the group sense as well."

"What genetic line is that?"

"A fallow species of primate here on Urset, called tavi. Big brutes, they are. There are smaller subspecies here on the island, but they are all forest scavengers, far too tame for the end product. It required some rather creative adjustments to achieve an aggressive nature in the beginning. I updated their existing genetic code, enhancing their physiology with most desirable traits from large predators and—" She stopped, and her eyes flickered over me as she hastily finished, "Other useful modifications."

Her abrupt self-edit sent up warnings of evasion, and I frowned. Across the table, Gor cocked his head in puzzlement. His adherence to telepathic courtesy meant my crechemate would never dream of listening in where he wasn't invited, but he too wondered exactly what Darizh avoided saying.

She changed the subject. "Perhaps I am a pessimist, Ambassador, but I do not expect efforts to negotiate with them will succeed. There is a chemical failsafe built into their enhanced physiology, created for situations such as this. An airborne agent, which enables a systemic poison triggered by the nanoparticles."

"A kill switch?" I muttered, passing a hand over my face to keep the shared horror of my teammates out of my expression. "Lady Darizh, we choose to believe there are other options."

Darizh's good humor vanished. "You do not strike me as a soldier, Ambassador Tamareia, and I do not believe you have ever been in battle. Shontavians do not understand the concept of peace. They embody remorseless killing."

"I have not faced them in war." My experience with them in the arena had been a much more intimate, close-up view of their capabilities. "I have the counsel of others who did, but you may not know them as well as you think." I leaned forward. "The pair with which I interacted not only negotiated a business contract but expressed a desire to be paid with profits like their humanoid counterparts. They spared a life during a feeding frenzy at the request of their employer in return for being granted the simple privilege to go outside and see the stars."

She blinked and snorted in derision. "I do not believe it."

"Before their employer and I negotiated with them, no one in a hundred years had ever asked the Shontavians what they wanted or needed. But they had thought about it. They did not hesitate to verbalize their terms when given the chance."

"One hundred years?" Lady Darizh's mouth dropped open. "But that is incredible. We had no idea they would live so long."

"They weren't purposely engineered for longevity, I take it?" Alecto Sim watched her disapprovingly.

"Of course not. They are front-line offensive troops, designed to be tough and resilient in battle. Thick, carbon-enhanced bones, skin like leather, and those famous teeth and claws." She grinned, bits of red fruit still caught between her own incisors. "When they are not armed, they are the weapon."

"I'm sure your genetic engineers thought of everything," I said. Sarcasm is something which doesn't always carry well across cultures. Lady Darizh's stiffening posture and prickly emotional output earned my scorn a near-silent sigh of disapproval from Gor.

There was another question I needed to ask and so delivered an apology. "I am sorry, Lady Darizh. I didn't intend to be rude."

Gor's mental nudge of *Yes, you did* indicated at least I hadn't fooled him.

I ignored him. "We appreciate your willingness to speak with us this afternoon. There is one more thing I wonder if you can answer. Again and again in our experiences with Shontavian mercenaries, we have seen them exhibit a fascination with the stars. Can you explain why that might be?"

She thought for a moment, frowning, and shook her head.

"I cannot offer a reason for this. There are no ports from which they could see space in the facility. The simulation programs contain no star charts. The only view of any stars is at the end of a simulation if they fail."

"What constitutes failure?"

"If they are killed in the simulation." She made a dismissive gesture. "It was a sentimental addition by one of the original technicians. We never bothered to change it. The warrior caste believes the stars where the gods reside is the final view of the fallen."

"Did this accompany another chemical reward?" Lam Tiri asked in a weak voice.

"No, just the consequence of deprivation from the battle simulations and their chemical rewards. Once they returned to conditioning, they would be eager to train again."

"Thank you." I favored her with a bland smile. "Would you be willing to provide more information should we need your guidance?"

"Of course." The glib affirmative response was negated by the resentment underneath. She didn't mean it. "If you survive first contact, Ambassador, I think I will have questions for you."

CHAPTER
SEVENTEEN

THE DIPLOMATIC TEAM was assigned a suite of rooms overlooking the central courtyard. Four bed chambers had stone steps descending into the cool, green verge, but Sumner insisted for security reasons I take the one with limited access. The dark, hewn-stone walls displayed pieces of bright geometric artwork, and a tapestry in the queen's bronze, crimson, and blue colors hung from floor to ceiling opposite the group-sized bed. I changed into gray fatigues, the subtle insignia of diplomacy and Remoliad Alliance at my collar rather than banded in holographic badges on my sleeves. The light material was cooler than the formal tunic, at any rate, and I doubted the Shontavians would be impressed by a dress uniform.

A digital chirp and a blinking indicator on the case of my private communications gear signaled an incoming message. My palm print on the security scanner toggled the display.

Transmission acknowledged by recipient. Now we wait. -O.

. . .

Rhix's Simish read the message then. It was a start. I tapped out a response of brief thanks and acknowledgment to Ozzie.

It would be bad form to forget the official reason I came to Urset. I dashed off a quick summary to the Zereid delegate overseeing the council in Sim's absence, updating her on the general instability of the current regime. But as I transmitted the message, something tickled my empathic nets. I had a strong sense of being watched.

A mind I couldn't immediately identify broadcasted a touch of curiosity and heightened anxiety as I turned to look over my shoulder. There was no one visible in the room, and no one requested entry.

I closed the case and secured the subspace equipment. Reaching into the bag on the foot of the bed, my fingers found the hilt of my knife and drew the blade from the sheath.

A firm knock on the door sent a jolt through me, forcing a pungent Zereid profanity between my teeth. The other mind gave an equally startled jump.

"Dalí?" Sumner came in. "Vehicles are waiting to take us to the crash site." His eyes narrowed beneath suspicious lids as he saw the blade in my hand. He cocked his head, a silent inquiry. I held up one finger and made a circular gesture, indicating we should search the room.

The tapestry on the far wall shifted slightly. Someone was behind it.

Sumner drew his sidearm without a sound, and we closed the distance.

He grabbed the banner's edge and peeled it back in one swift movement, his weapon sweeping the space behind. Shrill chitters sounded in the room, and he jumped back. "Shit!"

"What is it?" The unidentified presence I'd sensed now broadcast alarm and irritation.

He holstered his sidearm and raised the heavy material a little higher. "You have a visitor."

I sheathed my weapon and joined him. Behind the tapestry, a little four-armed creature covered in gray fur crouched and scolded, baring rows of sharp little teeth at Sumner. Its body was a strange shape, round in the middle with narrow shoulders and hips. The animal looked like the offspring of an old-Earth lemur if it mated with a pissed-off rugby ball.

A telepathic rugby ball, one that would have a fouler mouth than me if it spoke. This animal was the presence I sensed.

I laughed under my breath in wonder, and it turned its vocal assault on me. I knelt slowly, taking care not to frighten it. The creature's thought patterns were far from organized, but when I nudged its mind in greeting, the scolding stopped. Big green eyes studied me as its head tilted back and forth.

"What the hell is it?" Sumner muttered.

"A fallow sentient life form," I whispered. "What are you, little one?" The slit pupils in its bulging eyes dilated into saucers.

Then it leaped at me.

"Oh, seven hells!" I couldn't help but flinch as the creature landed on my shoulder and made itself at home. It didn't attack me though. One set of its hands gripped my collar, and the others searched through my hair.

The little beast nuzzled my ear with its mouth, a behavior I hoped was only scent-marking. "Please don't take a bite out of me," I warned and cautiously stroked its chest. The furry body leaned into me as a breathy cooing sound emitted from its throat. Its fingers curled around my hand and pulled me in for a harder scratch. I complied and the little creature's contentment spread in a warm glow across my empathic nets.

"You made a new friend." Sumner grinned and received a snarl and a snap of sharp teeth as he went to pet it. He jerked his hand back. "Or a bodyguard."

"Ambassador Tamareia?" the voice of our Simish

concierge called from the doorway. "They are ready for you." He caught sight of the little being perched on my shoulder. His eyes went wide in the drooping planes of his face, and he moved forward, flapping his hands. "Oh, my. Out. Out!"

The little gargoyle hissed and spat at him, bounded away from me and out the open window. The Simish hurried to the sill and pressed a button there. An energy field crackled and shimmered against the late sunlight. "I'm sorry, Ambassador. The little vermin are everywhere. Please do not feed them, or they will descend like a plague."

"What is the animal called?" I asked, curious.

"A satavi. Rainforest creatures. Thankfully, the ones native to the island are small. In the forests of the mainland, there are much bigger species."

"How big?" A suspicion grew in my mind.

"Just over two meters." He gestured to the door and inclined his head in respect. "If you will come to the courtyard, Lord Khus is anxious to reach the site."

The satavi peered in from the other side of the energy field as we hurried out. Vermin? Maybe, but I was certain we'd just met a swimmer in Darizh's Shontavian gene pool.

———

Urset's day star crept behind the jagged peaks in the early throes of a magnificent bloody sunset. The streets echoed with emptiness in the shadow cast by the mountains, an eerie, desolate atmosphere in which to traverse an otherwise abandoned city. The queen's troops maintained the secure perimeter two kilometers in each direction to ensure no skirmishes erupted while we reached out, despite the religious observation of the nighttime hours. We made base camp around the corner from the Shontavians' position, vehicles primed and ready for a quick retreat should things not turn out the way I hoped.

"Damn it, at least put on a vest." Sumner was exasperated with me.

"Do we have any that will fit Gor?" I countered. "No? Then I won't be wearing any either."

My Zereid brother was his usual state of naked. He had decided not to wear even his priestly sash for the mission. Only the two of us would make this first attempt at communication.

"You mean to go in without armor or weapons?" Khus eyed me in disbelief. "You are a fool."

"I agree with Lord Khus," Sumner admitted sourly, and the tone of his voice added a silent *for once*. "As your security advisor, will you let me advise you?"

"You already did. This time, I need to do it my way."

"Dalí and I will stop long before we are in reach," Gor reassured him. "I will be vigilant for any sign of agitation or threat emanating from the Shontavians' emotional and telepathic broadcasts."

"Emotions." Khus made an unattractive, guttural sound deep in his throat as if he were about to spit. "They possess none. I will watch you eat your words—perhaps as they eat you, Ambassador."

Lam Tiri and Alecto Sim, tucked safely out of harm's way in one of the luxurious armored transports, listened in via our group com. They would follow the feed from the body camera clipped to my shoulder. I'd ordered them to stay inside. Should Gor and I spectacularly fail, the rest of the mission would be up to them. Prince Razaxha remained behind at the estate, disappointed he was not allowed to accompany us tonight. Until Sumner had a chance to get a firsthand view of the terrain and the impact zone, neither he nor Khus wanted to risk the prince's safety.

Rhani returned from a solo reconnaissance mission and slipped into our grumpy huddle. "The Shontavians are outside the ruins of the facility, clustered in small groups."

She toggled a heads-up display from her wrist device. A three-dimensional scan of the crash site displayed over a map of the city with our position blinking in white. Rhani touched the diagram with her other hand, and red dots marked the location of the defensive sites at each major intersection. "The four standing gun arrays are unoccupied. They do not appear to be aware of our presence."

"What are the others doing?" I asked.

She shrugged. "Nothing. Just sitting."

"How many?" Sumner asked.

"I counted eight. The last report said there are at least nine."

"We'll lose the light soon." My breath shook as I blew it out. "Let's do this. Is the camera transmitting?"

"The feed has audio and video," Tiri reported over the group com.

"We have faith in you both." Even over the earpiece, Alecto's voice exuded warmth.

Gor reached for me. I moved closer to let him cup my head in his enormous, six-fingered hands as he assessed my mental state. "The psychic work we did earlier seems to be holding, beloved friend."

"Yes." It had been a long time since I tried to blanket the noise in my mind, too shattered and distracted after Luna Station. Gor helped me reach a focus point on the way to the site. I had gotten out of practice, having turned to chemical suppression instead. Too much of my subconscious was focused on keeping that state of internal calm. I'd gotten used to the chaos and in a strange way, missed it, but as temporary fixes went it felt relatively solid. I could do this tonight. "Thank you for coming with me."

Sumner's ocean eyes darkened beneath a furrowed brow as we rejoined the waiting group. "First sign of aggression, you get your asses out of there. Understood?"

"Do not worry, Commander. My ass can move very fast

when I wish." Gor's calm was not a façade, like mine. His serenity went all the way to the core.

"We'll be back soon." I gave Sumner a brief smile. "Greetings only, tonight, to make introductions and show them we mean no harm."

Here goes. I squared my shoulders and, with one last disdainful glance at Khus's hateful smirk, walked unhurriedly to the edge of the building with Gor at my side. We kept the same slow, steady pace as we turned the corner into view of the Shontavians. Still one hundred meters distant, we made way to the center of the street with our hands by our sides, palms presented forward. My crechemate extended his senses, reaching out to gather psychic intelligence on their state of mind.

Something moved in the shattered trees and foliage surrounding the crash site. I recognized family groups of the little, four-armed satavi as they clambered lithely through the branches, and some crept close to the currently equable Shontavians. The tiny creatures clearly found their enormous genetic cousins fascinating.

Weapons lay within the Shontavians' reach, but none of them had one in hand, save for the two sentries who monitored forward defense of their position. The rest of the engineered warriors calmly sat on the ground or atop piles of rubble. Most of them wore pieces of battle armor, but a few displayed only smooth gray skin exposed to the air.

"One would think they will be receptive in this state," Gor murmured. I remembered Ouros and its counterpart sitting placidly on benches in the mercenary barracks aboard the Market ship and hoped this was a good sign.

"Do they see us?"

"Not yet." Gor's mercurial stare fixed on the wreckage, towering over the other structures like a second mountain range of twisted metal. "There are others Rhani may not have seen, high above in the debris. They are armed."

"Copy that," Sumner replied over the group com as Gor relayed the observation. "Rhani says she counted the sniper positions. Be careful."

"And they are now aware of us." Gor didn't falter. My empathic nets were awash in his telepathic broadcast of calm. Ahead, some of the Shontavians came to their feet, alert and interested, spike-studded mouths sifting the air for our scent.

"They're reaching for weapons." Sumner's voice remained calm and controlled.

"I see them." None of them took aim, merely picked up guns and cradled them in two of their four arms. "Do you sense any aggression, brother?"

"Only curiosity and deep wariness. Understandable, given their previous experiences." A powerful nudge against Gor's mind was palpable even to me. He made a sound of understanding. "Ah. A response. They want us to stop here."

Fifty meters still lay between us and their encampment. Close enough for now. We waited.

Two separated themselves from the others and lumbered toward us. One held a pulse rifle, and the other, a makeshift club pieced together from scraps of debris. They were now within my range, and I caught drifts of their consciousness. Sharp barbs of assessment prodded against Gor's broadcast of welcome. Their steps quickened. I had an involuntary flashback: *the Shontavian barreling into the arena amidst screams of bloodlust from the crowd, ripping off the arm of my conquered opponent with its teeth, and—*

"Calm, my friend," Gor whispered. "They bear us no ill intent."

Breathe. In. Out. Don't blow this.

Instead of panicking, I concentrated on sorting what I sensed from the approaching pair. Interest. Caution, yes; suspicion glinted at the unyielding edges of their body language, but I got nothing that made me believe they would eat us. Darizh had grudgingly assured us the Shontavians had slow metabolisms and given the recent battles, were probably not hungry. Yet. Too late to run now.

I nudged their minds in greeting. The attention of both swiveled in my direction, sharp black eyes drowning in the first shade of evening.

"Do you speak?" I asked in Ursetu.

Heads tilted, but neither said anything. Instead, they circled us, weaving back and forth, their mouths open to taste the air. Rhix once told me they only did this with their own kind, after the Shontavians on board the Market ship greeted me with the same strange, dancelike movement. More probes bludgeoned my empathic nets, but not in a malicious way. Their interest in me increased as I returned the mental touches. I wondered if they considered any sentient creature able to touch minds as a kindred spirit.

"They do not know what to make of you," Gor informed me, barely audible above the shuffle of heavy steps. "I have been acknowledged as a telepath, like them. You, however, fascinate them. It is almost as if they recognize you."

"But in what way?" I murmured back.

He sighed in wonder. "How extraordinary. They are indeed a group mind, Dalí. I can feel them ... Oh." He went silent as one of the Shontavians ceased their weaving dance and turned, making intricate signals with all four hands.

"Don't stop there. Oh, what?"

"Another is coming to join us."

A psychic presence reached us before its physical form even left the ruins of the ship. This one wore complete battle armor. The approaching Shontavian loomed a full head over the rest, taller than Gor. I didn't dare flinch as it drew near. This one moved with purpose, intimidating in a creature of its size. Its black eyes assessed us with keen intelligence. The other two Shontavians got out of its way.

It bent close to me and inhaled, its mouth brushing my hair. I didn't react. It repeated the process with Gor and snuffled against the short turquoise fur and leathery skin of his neck. My crechemate shifted with a musical titter. Of all the times to be ticklish, I wasn't sure this was one of them.

"What are you?" it said in Ursetu. Its voice was deep and rough.

"My name is Dalí. I am Human," I said in the same language. "Gor is a Zereid. We mean you no harm. We would like to talk to you."

"Talk."

"May I return tomorrow with others, who wish only to speak to you? More like us, from other worlds. We would like to help you."

The Shontavian eyed us. "Why?"

"Because I am a peacemaker. I believe you can make your own decisions how to act. To choose not to fight, but to negotiate a different solution with the Ursetu."

"Choose not to die," it corrected, surprising me with its insight. The creature's sharp gaze pierced through me, the touch of its mind against mine keen with intelligence. "Ursetu." The Shontavian huffed a blast of breath, ruffling my hair with a sour breeze. If it had smelled like copper and blood, I might not have stood my ground. "They do not talk. They make war."

"Yes." I didn't deny it. "They do not know what else to do. I am here to help them find another way, as well."

"You are afraid. Inside." The timbre of its voice vibrated the air around me.

"I have seen what some Shontavians can do. But I also talked with them."

Before I could react, its mind rifled through my memories like a thief searching for one precious jewel among others made of glass. I reeled against the onslaught, my breath harsh in my own ears. Gor reached out to steady me as I stood fast. There was nothing I could do to keep the Shontavian out: its telepathic grip irresistibly strong, just as Ouros's had been. It plucked out my interactions with the Market's Shontavians—all of them, from the negotiation with Rhix, the gruesome encounter in the arena, and the last glimpse of Ouros and its counterpart as they peered out at the stars from the launch tube.

At last, it withdrew, and I shuddered as its presence slid from my thoughts like a blade out of flesh.

"That was extremely rude," I said tightly, careless and pissed in the moment after this unwelcome intrusion. "Next time, ask, and I will let you in."

"Ouros." The end of the name hissed experimentally against the Shontavian's countless needle-sharp teeth.

"Yes. I spoke with Ouros." I waited for it to say more, but it didn't. "Do you have a name?"

"No." It abruptly turned away and tossed back over its shoulder, "Give me a name tomorrow. Go. Come back before the star time. We claim it for our own."

As we turned, I noted dozens of smooth, gray faces lifted to the sky. I followed their motion and saw the first bright stars of evening had emerged from twilight.

No sense in overstaying our welcome just to see them stargaze. Gor and I walked away using the same slow gait, though the skin between my shoulder blades itched with the imaginary bullseye drawn on my back. I looked behind me once, surprised to note some of the wreckage still had power, lights visible here and there in the bulky shadow of the crashed station.

When we reached the armored transport, Sumner waited outside. We slid through the door, and I allowed myself to go boneless in cushioned seats. I leaned my head against Gor's shoulder after he folded himself in beside me and said, "Well done, my friend."

"Congratulations, Ambassador." Sim's beatific smile shone at me. Lam Tiri made a sound of pure relief, and I found myself with a mouthful of his ruff as I laughed against his energetic cheek rub.

"You were right," he said jubilantly. His carefully culti-vated Remoliad Standard relaxed into a purr in his excite-ment, and Tiri gently butted heads with Gor. As soon as Sumner crawled into the cabin, the door slammed, and the vehicle lurched into motion, speeding back toward the oppo-site side of the island.

"What do you think you accomplished here?" Khus dryly inquired. Though he continued to affect a bored detachment, beneath it all, he seemed impressed we were in one piece. The dull shine of his grudging respect was smudged with resent-ment. There would be no words of congratulations from him.

But I didn't need his approval. Damn, I was just happy our backsides didn't have bite-sized chunks missing.

"We laid the groundwork for trust." Gor answered Khus instead. "Tomorrow, we reinforce that foundation."

The release of tension left me limp and light-headed, but I knew it was not over by a long shot. "It's just the beginning. The alpha wants a name. Does anyone have a suggestion that won't get my head bitten off?"

CHAPTER
EIGHTEEN

THE INSISTENT BLEEP from my subspace gear dragged me out of bed the next morning. With a yawn, I padded to the table and opened the case. An encrypted message from Ozzie waited there.

Recipient states subject is no longer Lord Rhix. Gave no further details. Entering dark space enroute to Urset. Will contact you when we emerge. ETA 48 hours—O

Fuck. A flower of ice bloomed inside my chest, frozen vines snaking through my body.

The only way for someone else to earn the title of Lord Rhix was to kill the one who held it. Had he fallen to some ambitious challenger?

The idea left me unexpectedly hollow.

Outside, mist rose from the rain forest and swaddled the ziggurat in a heavy blanket of white. I stared at the blurred green foliage below and tried to decide what it was I felt.

A chitter above me interrupted my confused melancholy,

and I glanced up, startled, as a furry gray body landed on the sill. Enormous, pleading eyes peered up at me through the shimmer of the energy field, and I gave the little animal a half smile. I found the switch that turned off the barrier and a surge of moisture-laden air broke against me like the waves on the distant shore.

The satavi scrambled to my shoulder, snuggling into the curve of my neck, twenty tiny fingers sifting through my bed-snarled hair. It gave a croon of happiness as I reached up and scratched its chest. The creature shifted downward so I could cradle it in one arm, and it wrapped two of its appendages around my wrist to pull my hand in closer. Its eyes showed only a blissful sliver of jade beneath smooth lids, the cooing vocalization so loud it vibrated against my fingertips.

"Don't give me away," I cautioned. "You aren't supposed to be in here."

Simple joy radiated from the little beast and masked the tremors of confusing sentiment I wasn't equipped to handle this morning. Resting one hip against the window ledge, I closed my eyes and lost myself in the satavi's broadcast of contentment.

A quiet rap for entry ended the moment of peace and startled both of us. The furry creature in my arms gave a disgruntled *brrrt* as the queen's Simish called outside my door, "Ambassador Tamareia? Forgive me. I know it is early."

"Time to go," I whispered to the satavi. I set it on the windowsill. It leaped to the wall, nimble multiple limbs gripping tiny crevices in the rock as it clambered upward and vanished.

"I'm awake," I answered hastily as a second, louder knock echoed in the room. "Come in."

Terraced skin and droopy eyes appeared in the gap of the half-open door. "The queen requests you join her in council." His attention flashed over my bare torso and the formfitting shorts I'd slept in, then politely away. "There is no need for formal attire. I will give you time to dress."

While Simish waited outside my room, I attempted to push the unsettling news about Rhix into the back of my mind. The one lightweight set of dark-blue trousers and kurta I'd brought would be sufficient to cover skin. I captured my humidity-quickened mass of hair into a knot at the back of my head, a more femme appearance than what I'd affected so far. My boots were out of place with this clothing, so I fished a pair of squashy indoor slippers out of the corner of my bag and wore those instead. After some hesitation, I left my knife behind and joined the small being outside.

"This way." Simish led me down a long gallery of windows overlooking the rain forest. Down the coast of the island, I glimpsed the top of another ziggurat, a dark shadow above the thinning mist.

"Who lives there?"

"That is the Darizh family stronghold, the queen's strongest ally," he answered. "You met Lady Darizh yesterday. Each of the seven matriarchs has an estate on the sunset side of the mountain where night lingers. The goddess rises and slumbers later here."

We have claimed the star time. "Fighting stops at sundown and begins at dawn."

He caught my mutter. "Indeed, but that is only still true on the island. How long the ancient observations will continue to hold, I fear we cannot say. So much has changed in so little time."

"May I ask a personal question?"

"By all means." He stopped and turned, waiting expectantly.

"I understand Queen Xahria informed the Simish of their new status. How does the change affect you?"

"Our new autonomy, you mean. We are now able to choose for ourselves whether we wish to stay in service or go elsewhere." He pursed his lips, thoughtful. "I have attended Queen Xahria since she was a young girl, assigned when I was first decanted into service, and Prince Nazhir after her, until … " I received a sense of sorrow from him. He had been fond of Nazhir, I realized, before he continued, "I know no other life. We are caregivers, educated and encouraged to learn new ways to contribute to their well-being as we feel called to it: medicine, aesthetics, and culinary skills."

"But you could not leave their service."

"Nor did I wish to. Her family is very kind to us." He shook his head. "Here, the Simish have all we require and more in terms of housing, food, and clothing. We are not paid, but we receive all we need. I would call it a symbiotic relationship. Some may choose to leave, but no more of us will be created. We do not breed, nor live forever. The question of our freedom is a temporary matter."

His answer saddened me. We traversed the rest of the hallway in silence.

Outside the queen's suite, a silent guard waited. She swept me with a detector, her golden eyes narrowed in hostility. Satisfied I was not armed, she jerked her head toward the door. Before Simish could open it, a scream sounded inside the room. The lightning flash of someone else's pain scattered red sparks through my empathic web.

Startled, I took a step back. The guard and Simish did not flinch. "Unfortunate," the little servant muttered. To the guard, he said, "Please tell the infirmary to expect trauma."

"Is there trouble?" I asked.

"A policy dispute. Nothing serious." Simish gestured pleasantly for to me to enter as he opened the door.

Two guards hustled past us as we entered the high-ceilinged chamber. One supported a hard-eyed Ursetu whose fingers were bright with blood, clutched against the stump of his left arm. The other carried a dismembered limb. Red drips and puddles glistened in harsh contrast to polished black stone, an Ursetu short sword abandoned beside the mess. The scent of copper hung thick, trapped in my nostrils and throat. Swallowing against memories of the arena, I schooled my expression to neutrality.

Urset was not the Remoliad. In Khus's words, I would do well to remember that.

Xahria wiped blood from her sword with a nanosilk scarf, a victorious queen in black armor. On the wall behind her throne loomed a relief carving of the Ursetu goddess: barefoot, her gentle visage strangely at odds with unyielding stone. Yet in this rendering, one hand carried a knife, and the other, what appeared to be a heart. Fresh flowers obscured the statue's feet, and curls of sweet, pungent smoke rose from a tray of ebony sand before the altar.

"Thank you for joining us, Ambassador Tamareia." The queen's silver-gilded hair lay in disarray, and a light sheen of sweat honed the angles of her jaw and cheekbones. She sheathed her blade and indicated I should sit in the empty chair at the end of the table. "Shall we speak Ursetu, or Remoliad Standard?"

"At the risk of imposing upon your patience, I would like to try to carry on in Ursetu. Thank you." I lowered myself to a seat. In front of me, viscous blood spray gleamed against the black surface of the table. A servant appeared and wiped the sticky drops away as several other Simish worked quietly in the background to remove evidence of the policy dispute.

Eight chairs surrounded the hewn-stone table, only four occupied. The chair to the queen's right lay empty, draped by a pall in the vivid jewel tones of the royal house. I assumed the seat once belonged to Princess Arzalat. Khus sat in the second chair. His thin-lipped countenance carried none of the respect it held the previous night, my standing in his good graces a short-lived affair. Lady Darizh inhabited the seat to his right.

The servant who had escorted me returned and set cups of

steaming tea in front of us. I waited until the queen lifted hers before picking up mine, savoring the hot, bitter liquid.

"These are my councilors, Lady Aneszai and Lord Gerakh." A hawk-nosed Ursetu female and an elderly male occupied the chairs on Queen Xahria's left and acknowledged me with somber nods as she introduced them. "They have just returned with me from the mainland."

"Has the situation deteriorated further?" I inquired.

"News of Remoliad membership has sparked a riot among the casteless. They demand the election of representatives to the queen's council," Lord Gerakh said.

"That is none of the Remoliad's concern." Khus's razor-edged smile shaved a thin layer from my patience.

"I congratulate you on the success of first contact." Queen Xahria saluted me with her cup.

"It will take time to gain their trust, but the alpha did invite us to come back tonight. It was the best we could hope for," I allowed.

"We must conclude the matter of the Shontavians with haste." Xahria set down her tea. "Our attention is needed elsewhere. I received two communications this morning." The queen touched a data device on the table. "It seems word of the ambassador's achievement reached the other matriarchs. Onazheri offers an alliance of marriage with my grandson and full acceptance of Remoliad membership. Nexha also confirmed their approval of galactic citizenship."

"The idea you negotiate the Shontavians' loyalty is what frightens them." Khus's hand tightened around his cup until I thought it would shatter. "Razaxha's position is strengthened with a Shontavian presence behind him. As head of the warrior caste, I must urge you to reconsider."

"What are your plans for the Shontavians, my queen?" Lady Aneszai frowned. "If negotiations are in the wind, your council should know what they entail. I assume this is why we are here."

Xahria inclined her head. "Indeed. At this time, we will discuss their relocation."

"Relocation?" Lady Darizh sat back in her chair. The discord of her alarm jangled my empathic nets. "You would surrender them to the Remoliad?"

"No, we plan to negotiate their freedom, Lady Darizh." I kept my voice neutral, but secretly, I enjoyed her consternation after last night's sadistic recitation.

"My queen, these are the last Shontavian warriors ever to be created. They represent a significant investment." Lady Darizh's fist clenched on the table. "I can easily recreate the conditioning equipment and restore their obedience."

"The methods you described yesterday are prohibited under galactic law." It took effort for me to meet Darizh's glare without confrontation. "The queen agreed Urset will follow these statutes. Shontavians have the right to make an independent decision, as does any sentient species."

"You are a fool to believe them anything but weapons," she spat, a cruel twist to her lips. "I understand their nature better than you do, Ambassador. I engineered this brood. They will never be free of what they are."

"Nor will we," Khus muttered. "It is the sacred duty of the ruling caste to lead Urset. Inviting the Remoliad to interfere makes us appear weak to the matriarchs and our people. If we counterbalance that weakness with the force represented by the Shontavians, we can—"

"Enough." Xahria held up an imperious hand. "We must begin to embrace the thought of peace as strength. A Shontavian presence behind the throne will never allow unification to take root. My word stands unless anyone wishes to follow Lord Arzik's example and issue a formal challenge."

Behind us, dismayed silence fell as the cluster of servants paused in their cleaning.

"No, my queen." The elderly lord waved his hand and

chuckled. "It is only Arzik who can recover from such foolishness. My days of challenge are past."

The palpable relief of the Simish brushed my senses as the unobtrusive sounds of mop-up continued.

"We have yet to finalize the terms." Xahria grew somber. "We have done many things that ignore the teachings of the goddess, but none more so than the creation of life with no purpose but to take life. Through them, we spilled blood on countless worlds, and their transgressions will be held against us as our own. I hope it is enough to earn her favor before I die."

"Queen Xahria." Darizh squirmed in her seat. "Your devotion to the goddess is admirable, but you must think of Prince Razaxha's future."

"It is a future in which we have no place, my friend," the queen said gently. "We fought to keep our ways through isolation but no more. The galaxy is at our doorstep. Our people know what is possible and are not satisfied with the way things are. It is time for change. The ruling caste must ally with each other and adapt, or we will cease to exist."

"Instead, you would have the Remoliad insinuate its ways and assimilate our people into galactic society," Khus said bitterly. "Urset will bear no resemblance to what we have been for generations uncounted."

"That is not such a terrible thing, Lord Khus." Lady Aneszai's crisp rebuttal rang against the walls. "I am ready to lay down my weapons. Our daughters died together at the hands of the monsters Urset created, my queen. I will stand with you in all things as I have always done."

"Thank you, Aneszai." A stab of sorrow flitted across the queen's face. She turned her scrutiny on the dissenting councilors. "Half my remaining council registered their support. Only you, my closest allies, have not."

"As head of the warrior caste—" began Khus.

"Regent head of the warrior caste." The queen's brittle

interruption shattered on the tabletop. "Do not forget the title belongs to Razaxha."

"Perhaps the prince should take the responsibility from me, untrained and untried as he is, since you will not hear my objections." Khus's face twisted in frustration. "As your councilor, I disagree with you on this matter."

"And you, Darizh?"

"I cannot approve relocation for the Shontavians." Darizh straightened. "They are our responsibility. Ours for which to atone, as you said. Let them be sequestered here on Urset."

Oh, she was good. Lady Darizh unerringly went for an argument to which the queen would be receptive. Her discomfort over losing control of the Shontavians set off a warning in the back of my mind. I extended my senses a little more and got a dark taste of her apprehension. Why was she so worried about keeping them here?

Queen Xahria inhaled deeply, and I caught the bare hint of a wince. Her expression went blank and controlled. "Your thoughts, Ambassador?"

"My team and I have researched possibilities for relocation off world. But we have yet to hear from the Shontavians." I scanned the faces around the council table. "Their intentions may be very different from ours."

She nodded in terse agreement. "We will see what they want, but Lady Darizh is correct. They are our responsibility and should remain on Urset. Your team will be provided with all the data you need to find a suitable location here, Ambassador Tamareia. I would like to speak with you in private. The rest of you may go. We will reconvene tomorrow."

The councilors' emotional auras broadcast various attitudes as they departed. Lady Aneszai and Gerakh displayed a sober acquiescence to change. The press of deep resentment belonged to Khus, naturally. Darizh was relieved, but her eyes were on me, narrowed and calculating. I felt I represented a complication she did not welcome.

When the doors closed behind them, the queen stood, her right hand pressed to her side. The palm came away wet with blood, a slender puncture almost invisible in her black battle armor, and she swayed.

Alarmed, I realized she had not come through her challenge unscathed. I sprang from my chair to reach her side.

"How can I assist you?"

"I need to remove the armor, but I fear the bleeding will increase," she said tightly as her Simish servant appeared and opened a medical kit. "May I rely on your discretion? I wish to preserve my victory."

"Of course. Let me remove the armor. Be ready to apply pressure, Simish." My fingers found the hidden clips under the armpit and at the waist on her uninjured side, then the opposite, and I lifted the joined breast and back plate over her head in one quick movement. The queen stifled an exclamation of pain as the wound in her flank became visible beneath the clean slice in her under-armor. Simish pressed a pad of bandages against the rivulet of blood.

"I was almost too slow today," she rasped. "Razaxha's place must be secured, Ambassador."

"I understand." I set the armor aside.

Simish ripped a wider hole in the black material and applied antiseptic. Xahria winced as he probed the injury, her knuckles going white as she supported herself on the high back of her chair.

"A laceration to the ribcage, my Queen. The wound will not require surgical intervention."

"Thank you, Simish." To me, she said, "Do you think me foolish for believing in an omniscience?" I realized she attempted to distract herself from the pain.

"Not at all. Many find it a great comfort." Rhix's passionate devotion to the goddess had surprised me. It appeared to be a family trait.

"Do you believe in such things?"

"I try to practice the tenets of *zezjna* when I believe anything at all."

"The blue tube, please," Simish murmured, and I handed him the medication.

"Empathy is a curious basis for society." She grimaced, but tension began to melt as the servant applied numbing agent to the wound. "Brother Gor must consider us barbaric."

"He will be the last to judge anyone; believe me." I had the dermal accelerant ready for Simish. "Compassion is one of his more irritating traits."

She laughed; the sound went rough at the edges as Simish worked at sealing the wound. "Perhaps the Zereid can teach us to cultivate more compassion here. I fear it does not grow well in our soil."

A wave of anxiety preceded Razaxha's arrival as the young prince burst through the door of the council chamber. His bronze eyes widened in dismay when he saw Simish tending to the queen's injury, and realizing I was also there, tried to compose himself as he drew near. "I heard about the challenge. Are you all right, *Lumi*?"

His voice wavered on the endearment for *grandmother*, his concern for her littered with boulders of fear and anger in a near-avalanche against my empathic nets.

"I am well, Raza. It is nothing. Arzik wields a blade like a satavi swings a stick." The queen reached out and cupped his face tenderly with her unbloodied hand. "He will not challenge me again."

"If I were old enough to lead the warrior caste, I would have been the one to defend you." His eyes were bright with tears of anger. "Khus should have fought in your place."

"He disagrees with me as well, so the battle was mine alone. And this tradition will die with me." Her voice, smooth but unyielding, like warm steel, issued the gentle command. "Your reign will begin without bloodshed and with a united Urset, not with the ridiculous posturing of old women and men. How go your studies with—Tiri, is it not?"

"He says I have a gift for diplomatic thinking." Razaxha's face brightened, a tentative sunbeam through heavy clouds. "We are analyzing the unification of the Krish, from an imperial dictatorship to a parliamentary government. I think a similar approach will work for Urset. Tiri agrees." He turned a hopeful face to me. "After last night's success, may I accompany the team tonight and watch the feed from the command vehicle?"

I raised an eyebrow at the queen, who nodded firmly. "I will have Khus secure the area before your team arrives. The sooner we come to consensus with them, the better." She bit her lip as Simish finished sealing the edges of the laceration beneath a layer of dermal accelerant and foam.

"Are you certain housing them on Urset is wise, Queen Xahria?" Something about Darizh's eagerness to keep them here bothered me. "Once we make an agreement with them, it is imperative nothing changes. Can you guarantee they will not be exploited in any way?"

"I am well aware of the Remoliad's laws, Ambassador." Her clipped response gave me pause, and I realized I had come dangerously close to trying her patience. Oh, there was another family trait, the lightning-fast mood swings Rhix displayed. Added to the propensity for cutting off people's arms when they were angry, it appeared the genetic code did not drift far in this family.

As if she could read my thoughts, she changed the subject. "Have you learned anything of my son?"

The little Simish servant paused in gathering his medical supplies, surprise highlighting his craggy face as he glanced at me. Since the queen broached the subject in his presence, I answered. "Only that he is not where we last knew him to be." I kept my voice carefully modulated. I truly didn't know his fate and did not want to insinuate otherwise. "We are making further inquiries."

The queen lowered herself gingerly back into her chair, and Razaxha poured her another cup of tea. "I hope he understands I have come to realize he was right," she murmured and patted the hand he placed on her shoulder. "We cannot declare war on our own people. Nazhir must return not for my sake, but for yours, Razaxha."

CHAPTER
NINETEEN

RAZAXHA'S PRESENCE had Khus wound tight. All the roads leading into the palace grounds were blockaded. We passed through multiple checkpoints before we pulled into the avenue to set up command, and Khus continued to bark and growl orders over his com as we prepared for our approach.

Sumner thrust a lightweight armored vest into my chest. "You will wear that today, Dalí. No arguments."

"Why?" I kept my voice down. Tension skimmed the lines of his body like an outline of static electricity. "What is it?"

"Not sure." He scanned the vacant avenues and shook his head. "I guess Khus is making me paranoid."

I humored Sumner and put on the armor. He held another one out to Alecto. Sim's eyes glowed, his grin writing a lengthy tale of affection as his slender mauve fingers wrapped around the vest and took it from Sumner.

The commander had wanted to accompany me today, but I turned him down. Everything about Rion Sumner shouted *soldier*, and I didn't think we were ready yet to add him to the equation. Better to rotate the less intimidating members of our team in and out and allow the Shontavians time to get used to us before introducing another alpha.

I tapped Alecto to make second contact instead. I wasn't certain about the status of their renewed friendship or how far it went. With Sumner, it could be impossible to tell. The way Sim smiled said enough, and I was happy they had found each other again.

And a little envious of Alecto. Was envious the correct word? The emotion surprised me, nonetheless. Sumner and I flirted and fought, but we never crossed the line into physical intimacy. The thought had flitted through my mind on horny wings more than once, especially on long jaunts on *Thunder Child* with no target for my sexual energy. Rion was human— half human, at least, and I trusted him. I liked him. More than liked him, if I was being honest with myself, and that alone discouraged me from seeking Sumner out and trying to seduce him for casual sex. It would probably fuck up our friendship more than I'd already damaged it.

As soon as I realized the nature of their previous relationship, I kept my attraction to Alecto smothered. Though my liaisons were never exclusive, I respect not everyone else is willing to share. I didn't know enough about either of them to risk a misunderstanding.

So why the sudden attack of envy?

As I probed this unexplained bruise, I caught Gor's quiet amusement and flipped him off in an empathic equivalent. I wrestled my thoughts back in order while I fastened the camera to my shoulder. The mission was too important to be distracted.

Gor came with us to evaluate the Shontavians' mood before the point of no return. His reassurance came before we reached the halfway mark. The sentries cradled weapons in one set of arms and monitored our progress. Soon afterward, the alpha joined them.

"They are not agitated but highly aware you are here," he said. "Our friend seems almost eager to see you again."

"Go back to command, brother," I told him. We still didn't have armor big enough to fit Gor; not that he would have worn it in any case. "I don't want your ass to be the only one hanging out in the wind."

"Listen with your mind as well as your ears," Gor counseled me. His eyes contracted in focused attention on the alpha. "It may not be physically apparent if their mood changes."

"Believe me, I know," I reminded him.

Alecto Sim and I walked ahead. With nets unfurled to catch any mood changes in the Shontavian camp, I caught a fragment of clear emotion from my companion, an atypical occurrence that put me off guard. The sensation dissipated as quickly as it came: a hint of excitement, lined at the edges with bright fear.

"Are you ready for this, Alecto?"

He turned his head and favored me with one of his luminous, genuine smiles. It elicited a giddy twinge of delight in me, something new and confusing to add to the mess of my emotional garbage.

"Thank you for letting me accompany you on this mission, Dalí," he responded. "I have wanted to be part of something this meaningful for a very long time."

Movement in the trees and up in the wreckage caught my eye. Many more satavi occupied the site than I had originally thought. Instead of dozens, hundreds swung through the branches or groomed one another, nestled in the shade of their enormous Shontavian cousins. They regarded the furry animals with mild interest, but largely ignored them. The alpha carefully placed his feet to avoid stomping on the little creatures as he came toward us. The creature subjected Sim to the same snuffle of investigation from the razor-toothed mouth I experienced the day before.

The filigree of his suppression device glittered rhythmically in the heat of midday sunlight, shifted by the telltale pulse in his temple. It had to be unnerving for Alecto, but he stoically bore the inspection without a change in his beatific expression.

The weaving dance was reserved for me, cementing my suspicion mental touch meant something like kinship to the Shontavians. I nudged the alpha's mind in greeting and said aloud, "This is Alecto Sim. He is from a planet called Tolkis."

"Tolkis." The alpha cocked his head. "Battle simulation, objective seven."

"Not a battle simulation. A planet, where some of your forebears were sent to fight." Alecto's voice held cautious warmth as he said, "But I am not your enemy. We would like to know more about how you crashed here. What happened?"

The Shontavian regarded us with its shrewd eyes. "We happened."

I hadn't expected such a direct answer—and certainly not that one. Alecto and I exchanged a glance of surprise.

"You brought down the station," I repeated in wonder.

"Yes." It bared its teeth in a disconcerting imitation of a smile. "Targeted assault training program."

"Who instructed you to carry out this assault?"

The Shontavian raised all four of its arms and spread them wide. "We did."

Well, then.

"What was the final objective?" I asked.

"We looked for stars." It looked up at the still-light sky, though the shadow of the peak wept down the craggy face of the mountain as the sun lowered on the horizon. Sim and I exchanged a glance. Darizh had told us the only stars in the simulation appeared when they failed the mission. I couldn't parse exactly what meaning the Shontavian attached to it.

"What stars are you looking for?" I asked.

"Where the fighting ends." It gestured, and my gaze followed the sweep of its arm across the valley. Sudden, distant gunfire punctuated a dull explosion on the outskirts of the palace grounds. Black smoke mushroomed into the air.

The Shontavian grunted, almost like a sigh. "That place is not here."

"Oh, no," Alecto breathed.

The growl and grind of heavy engines rolled in the streets east of our position. The Shontavians swayed to their feet, instantly on alert, weapons raised in expectation. Their mood in my empathic nets changed from the stillness of waiting to the eager urgency of precombat. The surge of anticipation for battle grew heady in my senses, almost contagious. Even the satavi seemed to sense the change of mood, and their chittering grew louder, more aggressive.

This was not good.

"Sumner, we have approaching vehicles. What's happening?" I asked over the team's com.

"Stand by," his voice crackled.

One of the silent warriors came up and made urgent hand signs to its alpha. It signed back and turned to me, its dark resignation an ink stain spreading through the strands of my empathic web.

"Go, peacemaker. Retreat. These are not the right stars."

At the same time Sumner's voice sounded in my head. "Goddamn it! Get out of there, now!"

The flash and glint of the setting sun on metal reflected off the vehicle barreling across the palace grounds. I grabbed Sim's arm and took a single step before the rocket fired from the roof of the armored transport slammed into the wreckage above our heads. The blast knocked us to the ground, battered with a hailstorm of sharp, metallic debris.

———

Stunned, I realized I lay half buried in rubble with my legs wedged beneath something heavy, wet, and warm. A high whine pushed needles into my explosion-traumatized eardrums as panic assailed me and drowned my senses.

Thick, choking dust enveloped a silent panorama of battle unfolding. The Shontavians' weapons vomited fire through the hazy air, strange and bright in its soundlessness. At last, my dazed thoughts cleared enough for me to make sense of my surroundings. What lay across my legs was the dead body of the Shontavian messenger, a spear-like piece of metal debris through its chest, baptizing me in its dark blood.

Oh, we were so fucked.

With my recognition of just how sideways things had gone, I figured out the panic in my head wasn't mine. Alecto Sim lay just outside my reach, scarlet eyes wide and bulging in a rictus of terror, hands clapped over his ears. A trickle of violet blood ran down the left side of his face. His suppression device lay in the dust between us.

I struggled to free myself from beneath the deadweight bulk of the Shontavian, pulling myself toward Sim with my arms, but a sudden, tearing pain sent white lightning through my vision and stole my breath. The same piece of metal impaling the gray chest was also embedded in my left thigh.

I managed to free my right leg and dug my heel into the body to push the corpse up and away, lifting it enough to pull the other leg free. Pain drove red-hot bolts through my leg as the metal ripped loose, another stifled scream extruded between my gritted teeth. The Shontavian's pulse rifle lay on the ground beside it. I snagged the butt of the rifle and dragged it toward me. Cradling the weapon in the crook of my elbows, I high crawled to Sim, my injured leg dragging behind me. I scooped up the suppression device, the sharp edges of broken filigree stabbing into my hand.

"Alecto!" My own voice was still a faraway cry, my hearing full of hell's bells and whistles. "Minister Sim!"

He didn't respond to the name. "Naru!" I tried, then made my voice dark and steely. "Move your ass, Captain Sabecc. We're falling back."

Sim's gaze fixed on my face at last, some recognition returning to his agonized countenance. I nodded in confirmation and stuffed the broken headpiece into my fatigue blouse. "Let's go."

Together, we crawled toward a pile of rubble and sought cover on the lee side, opposite the firefight. The trunk of a slender tree bent under the weight of debris, the foliage hiding us from view for the moment. None of the Shontavians paid attention to us, focused on the approaching vehicles and returning fire. What came our way didn't feel like small arms either; it vibrated in my chest like thunder.

"Are you hurt?" I could hardly hear myself above the din of battle and the noise in my ears.

Alecto shook his head, a jerky movement. He raised his hand to his bleeding temple, eyes still wide and stricken. He hadn't spoken while waves of disorientation and fear cascaded through my empathic senses. Oh, I hoped none of these Shontavians got off on fear as an appetizer, the way Ouros and its counterpart did. The cold fingers of Sim's terror slid against my mind, a winter caress against hot skin.

"Your suppression device is damaged, Alecto." I ducked my head and made him look me in the eye. "You are not on Lymo. You are Minister Alecto Sim of the Remoliad Security Council. We are on Urset on a diplomatic mission of peace." *That has gone to shit,* I added mentally. "We're going to get out of here."

Another explosion rattled the ground, and his hand seized my forearm in a bruising vise. We curled up and covered our heads as dirt and rocks rained down around our shelter.

I cautiously raised my head in time to see the alpha with an enormous rocket launcher balanced on its shoulder. It took aim at the lead assaulting vehicle, a tongue of fire hissing from the exhaust tube. The missile found its target, and the vehicle disappeared in a blossoming column of fire and oily smoke.

I scanned the avenue from which we'd arrived. The street was clear, the command post around the corner and out of sight. Our escape route lay wide open but completely without cover. I didn't like the odds, not with my bleeding leg and Sim barely functioning. Just as I ducked back down, I caught a glimpse of vehicles racing by the point where Sumner and the others should have been, headed toward the attacking troops.

None of them were ours. Fucking hell. Where did they go?

We were stuck in the middle of a battle with creatures conditioned to kill for pleasure on one side, and an enemy trying to disrupt any hint of peaceful negotiation on the other. If we attempted to run, I didn't want to take bets on who would shoot us first.

We weren't safe here either, not with Alecto's innocent broadcast of fear on all channels. I slid back down beside him in the rubble, careful not to touch him.

"Alecto." I spoke gently and waited until his gaze met mine again. "Listen to my voice. Take slow, deep breaths. We're going to be all right." That was probably a lie, but I needed him more aware of his current surroundings.

"Where is Rion?" he gasped. "I have to find him."

"He's fine. Rion isn't in danger." I hoped it to be true. My gut twisted in knots of worry. Gor was too far away for me to reach his mind, but Sumner should have been yelling over my com, demanding to know if we were alive. I had no way to figure out what the hell was going on. "He's at the command post. Do you remember?"

Alecto nodded again. "W—with Brother Gor and Lam Tiri," he managed, gulping.

"That's right. Stay with me, Alecto. You're doing great."

We huddled together beneath the fallen tree until the shadow of the mountain overtook the palace grounds. The attack did not stop at nightfall. The sunset truce lay shattered, the hour of the goddess defiled.

CHAPTER
TWENTY

THE SHONTAVIANS RAN out of ammunition not long after dark. Return fire from our side of the battle line was sporadic, and at last, stopped all together. A bellow from the alpha ricocheted off the wreckage and the abandoned buildings. The ground shook with the impact of many heavy feet. I risked another glance over the rubble to glimpse the retreating mercenaries as they disappeared into the bulk of wreckage.

Seconds later, the heavy thudding steps of a Shontavian halted in front of our camouflage, and I heard the harsh and rumbling sound of its breathing. The nudge of its mind against mine did not feel friendly, blinded by battle lust. Reluctantly, I gathered the pulse rifle against my body in readiness. The last thing I wanted to do was shoot one of them. If I did, the mission was over, and we were both dead.

The tree shuddered and cracked, ripped away by the massive strength of one of the four armed mercenaries.

A coarse shout of furious defiance came from Alecto's throat. I threw myself on top of him to prevent him from rising. His agitation climbed to meet the Shontavian's. The shadowy bulk roared back. Starlight gleamed on a maw full of white teeth as its taloned hands reached for us.

A huge shape charged out of the night and snarled as it propelled the other Shontavian backward with a mighty shove. The alpha spoke in sharp, precise sign language. The now-submissive Shontavian vanished toward the wreckage, the brief altercation over. The alpha's eyes glittered in the darkness as a spatter of gunfire sent sparks ricocheting off the debris.

It crouched and dragged us out of our makeshift foxhole by our vests. "Come, peacemakers. Retreat."

I hissed against the white-hot pain flaring in my leg and staggered. "Go," I gasped out, and handed the Shontavian the pulse rifle. "I can't run."

The alpha sniffed the scent of my blood, lips curled back from the serrated spikes in its mouth. I waited for the flip of the switch into feeding frenzy. Which never came.

Instead, I got a surprising sense of its concern. The Shontavian shifted the gun to its superior right arm. Each lower arm grabbed Alecto and me around our waists and ran for the remains of the facility. Alecto cried out and struggled, his panic fresh and acrid against my mind as the alpha laid a screen of suppressing fire behind us.

"It's all right! Keep your head down!" I shouted, hoping to hell I was right to trust the alpha, and we weren't being taken inside for a post battle snack.

The gun ran out of ammunition as we reached a narrow crevice in the shattered hull, unfriendly fire pinging off the outside of the wreck. The Shontavian dropped the weapon and held us closer to its body in a claustrophobic embrace as it shimmied through the gap and dropped into dark, open space. My nose pressed against skin that smelled like leather and explosives. Far ahead, dim illumination shone on soot-streaked bulkheads and frosted the bare, twisted support struts in ghost light. The deck buckled in heaves of popped metal plates.

The Shontavian's pace slowed after a turn into a wide corridor. Other Shontavians milled about in after-combat chaos and from my place in the alpha's lower left armpit, I glimpsed many casualties. Some of the gray-skinned mercenaries moved among the living with medical kits, tending to wounds streaked with dark blood and torn flesh. Nearby lay the dead Shontavian beneath whose body I had been trapped. The sense of frustration and still-hot combat readiness plucked my empathic webs below the stream of Alecto's chaotic emotional broadcast.

The alpha carried us past its comrades, an act eliciting too much attention for my comfort. At last, we were set down in front of a half-open port that the Shontavian pushed wide with one enormous hand. A patina of emergency lighting dusted the room, recognizable as a medical bay. Everything loose lay in a drift of debris against one wall from the force of the crash, but the cots were anchored to the deck and stayed in place. From the size of the equipment, I judged the bay was meant for the Ursetu crew and not the Shontavians.

"Safe here for now," it said. "Do not evacuate unless my order."

A ripple of dismay went through me as I surveyed the dark room.

Not my favorite conditions. The Shontavian cocked its head at me. "Trust," it said quietly. "Do you trust?"

Wonder flooded through me. "Yes. Thank you." I put my arm around a still stunned Alecto to guide him into the bay, but he turned and stared at the alpha, his eyes wide. The alpha looked back at us. This time, the touch of its mind against my empathic nets encompassed Alecto as well. The deliberate gentleness in that skim of telepathic investigation made me believe the Shontavian somehow recognized Alecto suffered from battle fatigue.

"You have name for me," it said.

"Naru," Alecto quavered. Surprised, I stared at him. He gave the Shontavian his abandoned name.

"Naru." The Shontavian sampled the name in its mouth and nodded. "I will be Naru."

The newly christened alpha dragged the port back across the open doorway in a screech of metal. I limped over to one of the cots, and my breath emerged in a hiss as muscles shifted in a new way with the act of sitting, and fresh blood soaked into the leg of my fatigues.

"You are injured," Alecto said. Some of his dazed expression began to drain away.

"Yes. It hurts like hell, but I don't think it's too bad." I ripped the small tear in my pants wider to get a look at the laceration. Ugly, but not bleeding heavily. The room was too dark to see how far the metal had penetrated the muscle or if any debris remained. "There must be first aid supplies here, somewhere. The kits the Shontavian medics had were field packs."

"I think ... here." Alecto pulled down a case attached to the bulkhead and brought it over. I reached for the kit, but he swept my hand away. "No, let me see to your wound."

With silent efficiency, he tended to my leg. He was a skilled combat medic. His trembling grew less pronounced, graceful hands increasingly sure in their work as he dealt with the injury. Likewise, his mind's erratic broadcast began to ease its frenetic whine of panic as he focused on treating me. Antiseptic burned its way through my wound, followed by blissful numbness. Pads tamped against the bleeding, and he wrapped a pressure bandage around my thigh.

"That should do for now," he said. "I cannot tell if anything is left in the wound without more light. You are in danger of sepsis, but I do not know if any of these prepared antibiotics are compatible for humans."

"I'll worry about it later. Thank you, Alecto." I stood and

hobbled over to a communications panel to experimentally punch buttons and touch screens. "I was hoping we might have some residual power. More lights were visible from the outside."

"Deeper in the facility, perhaps, where there is less damage." Alecto wiped my blood from his hands with more antiseptic.

I tapped my implant com off and on again. "Commander? Can you hear me?"

Nothing. I sighed, running both hands through my disheveled mop to refasten it into a bushy knot at the back of my head.

"Something is wrong." Strain plucked at the words. Alecto's voice pitched again toward fear. "Why does Rion not answer?"

"He's probably out of range. Our coms only have a two-kilometer spread." I prayed that's all it was, unable to allow the black sense of dread for Gor, Sumner, and Lam Tiri to cloud my thoughts. The clips snapped crisply in the confines of the medical bay as I stripped off my vest to examine the tiny camera fastened at the shoulder. It still functioned, so I spoke directly into the lens.

"If anyone is receiving this transmission, we are alive. The alpha took us into the wreckage, and we are in—well, protective custody I guess, for the moment. I will turn off the camera to preserve the charge and update when I can. Tamareia out."

I stowed the little camera in the duty pocket of my fatigues.

"Is that another door?" Alecto pointed to the bulkhead opposite the port Naru had wrestled back into place. Both of us went to inspect it. The archway was narrower than the one leading into the corridor.

"Maybe. It might just be a closet." I strained against the metal to no avail. Alecto added his weight, and no matter which way we shifted, the port did not give. A crescendo of pain streaked through my leg, and I surrendered, panting. "No go. That one won't give without power."

"Not for us, in any case." Alecto let me lean on him on the way back to the cot. "Perhaps Naru would open it."

"We'll have to ask when he comes back. There are things I would like to inspect if they're still intact."

"The conditioning programs?" His interest sharpened.

"Among other things. Lady Darizh told us some of it, but I suspect it could be much worse than she let on." A fresh trickle of blood from Sim's temple glittered in the dim light as he regarded me. "Damn. Alecto, I forgot you were hurt too. Let me clean that up."

"It is nothing." He brought his fingertips to the small laceration.

"Still needs attention." I wet a sterile pad with antiseptic and cleaned the wound. Alecto winced. "Sorry. I know it stings like hell."

"You do not mean to hurt me." His breath was strangely sweet, brushing my cheek as I leaned closer to inspect the cut in the almost-not-there light.

This close to him, the warm vanilla-and-salt aroma of his skin beguiled me. His own gentle awareness of our proximity began to creep like sunlight against the strands of my empathic webs, and in the semidarkness, his eyes turned black and fathomless as they watched me. I sealed the cut with a dermal accelerant and stepped back.

"How are you feeling?" I asked, perhaps a bit too blunt in my speech.

"Strange. Very tired, suddenly." He touched his temple again, the absence of his suppression device still disconcerting. "Without the *riesh*, my mind is a tangle. I cannot concentrate. I am terrified my malady will kill us both in this environment."

"I don't know if it can be fixed." I drew the fragile tech out of my fatigue blouse and handed it to him. Alecto examined the device with a small noise of disappointment.

"Two of the connections are broken." He put it in his own pocket.

I hesitated a moment and plunged ahead. "If you read my psych profile when you chose me for this mission, you already know I have a similar illness."

"Your—what do the humans call it?"

"Post-traumatic stress disorder."

"My people call it *dreshmalahar*. The horror disease, I believe it translates." His mouth twitched. "Horror does not deserve a name that drips off the tongue like a sweet confection. Your term is more appropriate. More like stones dropped into a pit. The syllables break and echo."

"It's also called battle fatigue. I am almost certain Naru recognized you were suffering from this when he brought us inside."

"Perhaps the Shontavians are more like us than we realize. I hope Naru serves the name better than I did." His teeth flashed in a shadowed, rueful smile.

"Who was Naru?" I asked gently.

"The first Naru was a Tolkish general. The one who laid down his weapons in pursuit of peace between our planet and the Kadrelians. A philosopher, and a great leader. His act led to the eventual birth of the Remoliad Alliance. He was my sixth-father. The bearers of that name have always been great warriors, until the armistice." Alecto shook his head. "The most recent name bearer, a young male with dreams of becoming a person of importance, believed in the family tradition that the characteristics of a great leader can never be hardened in the forges of peace."

His voice pitched lower until I could barely discern his words above the noise in my still-ringing ears. "I was right, in a way. But I left the name behind, having proved myself unworthy of it, and took a new one. Our friend now has a name I bestow in hope they are more worthy of it than I."

I sighed, the harsh sound bouncing back from the bulkheads. "Somebody has all but dismantled the idea of a peaceful solution."

"I have to believe we can still salvage the effort." His emotional broadcast beat a rhythm of desperation, the slippery hint of mania against my empathic nets . Gor told me he sensed in Sim a profound desire for redemption. I wondered how high Alecto had pinned his hopes this mission would be the one to heal his wounded soul, and if failure would destroy him.

Assuming we survived it.

"Let's try to get some rest. I don't think Naru will allow any of the others near the medical bay." I moved to the next cot and groaned as I swung my legs up into the bed. "Oh, fuck, that hurts."

"Do you need something for pain? I believe there was a compatible drug in the kit."

"No, I'd rather not be impaired now." I controlled my breathing, urging muscles to relax. I heard Alecto settle into the cot next door, his respirations slowing toward an exhausted sleep. My mind still spun in circles, hoping my trust in Naru was not misplaced. It took a long time before I stood on the cliff of drowsiness, ready to fall.

A stray thought jolted me out of near slumber. The attack had come without warning, either from within the warrior caste troops guarding the perimeter or from someone the queen's soldiers trusted enough to get close to the checkpoints. I thought I might know who attacked us.

Lady Darizh. The sadistic bitch who came up with the training program, and the queen's closest ally.

CHAPTER
TWENTY-ONE

I DIDN'T GET much rest. The oppressive, motionless air in the closed room carried an odor of Shontavian waste and a whiff of what I hoped might only be decayed food storage. Alecto thrashed and moaned in a shallow doze, never truly sleeping. Bleary-eyed, we gave up and called it morning though my wrist chronometer said the world was still dark outside. At least the head wasn't blocked by the wall of debris, but the evacuation system did not work. Conditions would deteriorate to a health hazard in short order. I hoped we would not be there long. While Alecto relieved himself, I tried to reach Sumner again on the implant com.

"Commander? You copy?"

Nothing. If they were alive, Sumner, Gor, and Lam Tiri must be at the queen's stronghold with a mountain and several decks' worth of metal between us. If they were dead ...

White explosions burned beneath my eyelids as I pressed my palms against them. A panicking herd of thoughts stampeded through my head, and I slammed the door against the destructive flood of emotion. I refused to entertain it as a possibility. I had work to do.

Assuming power still functioned in less damaged areas of the facility, I anticipated I could find a working communications panel and send a message to Ozzie and my teammates once they reached orbit. How to get there presented a problem I hadn't solved yet. I had no idea of the facility's schematics, nor any guarantee Naru would allow me out to wander. More pressing issues concerned food and water. Alecto and I had last eaten yesterday afternoon. My mouth was as dry as Bariish's parched surface had been, with a strange metallic taste on the back of my tongue.

Our Shontavian host returned a couple of hours later, the friction of the port loud and shrill in the enclosed space as Naru shoved it back into its housing. A wave of cooler air, as pungent and humid as ours but fresher, swept in.

"Good morning, Naru." Alecto greeted him with grave respect.

Naru and I exchanged mental nudges. In one set of hands, it carried a sealed, hard-sided container almost half the size of one of the cots. The Shontavian slid the box through the door.

"Emergency supplies," it said in its rumbling voice. "Food."

"Thank you." I sent a pulse of gratitude toward Naru as Alecto snapped the seals on the box and dug out water rations for both of us. We drank in deep, greedy gulps, and Naru stood protectively in the open doorway as we each consumed a dense nutrition bar.

I limped to stand before the Shontavian. My leg smoldered with dull fire, but I ignored the pain for now. Looking up, I met the alpha's regard. "Are we safe to leave?"

"No. Surrounded by Ursetu, but they do not fire yet. Safe here."

"How are your wounded?"

"One dead." A sense of emptiness came from Naru. To lose a member of their group consciousness had to be like losing part of oneself, and I could not imagine it.

"I'm sorry," I said.

Naru grunted. "Not made for peace." It eyed me with a wary shift. "You work for Ursetu."

"No. Not for them but with you both," I carefully corrected Naru. "It is my responsibility to negotiate acceptable terms to which you and the Ursetu agree. I do not think you were attacked by the ones who brought us here. Their objective was peaceful."

"What terms for peaceful Ursetu?"

"That you do not fight. You surrender and will be taken somewhere else to live."

"But those outside?"

"I don't know what they want." My voice cracked. I let the Shontavian feel my outrage. "We did not expect this."

"Peaceful ones betrayed, or changed terms?" It weighed these options. The intelligence of this Shontavian exceeded my expectations—so different than Ouros or how Sumner described the bioengineered warriors in his mercenary days.

"I would like to try something," I said. "Is there a part of the ship with power where I can send and receive messages outside?"

Naru said nothing. It wanted to know if I could be trusted, the careful probe of its mind setting off vibrations in my empathic webs. Wordlessly, I lowered my mental defenses and invited contact.

More gently than before, it rifled through my thoughts. I let Naru see the meeting with the queen and her councilors. Once again, the alpha encountered Lady Darizh in my memory, and the consuming heat of hatred rose in Naru. It absorbed my abhorrence for her methods of conditioning, the horror of my team at her descriptions, and my concern that she seemed unwilling to relinquish control of the Shontavians.

It paused in its review of my memory and pulled back to fight against the blind rage building in its mind. This made

Naru special, I realized: its ability to check its own reactions, to exert self-control and choose to do something besides allow the conditioning to take over. The knowledge didn't prevent my pulse from quickening as its agitation flared.

Naru recognized my discomfiture and released an avalanche of memories, a shared vision of Lady Darizh seen through its own eyes. She smiled in triumph while the alpha was decanted; its first memory, and it gazed on her with wonder and adoration.

It imprinted on her like a parent and its hatchling. But that trust was betrayed with pain, again and again. Darizh's beaming visage appeared, her smile of cruel benevolence behind a protective observation screen in a control booth as the alpha emerged from neurochemical conditioning, shattered and remolded into a vessel for rage and bloodshed, desperate for another hit of the narcotic reward.

I watched as a new batch of Shontavian warriors were decanted and imprinted upon Naru as the alpha, who knew they would be subjected to the same pain. And pain did happen, offset by the pleasure of chemical bliss for violence. But the faces hovering above them were not always Ursetu. The triangular, insectoid skulls of Pileans peered down at them with glittering, multifaceted eyes.

Naru destroyed the machines which tortured its brethren. The bodies of Ursetu technicians lay broken and bloody on the floor, the memory of its revenge violent and satisfying.

A brutal score of days when Naru and the others suffered through the abrupt withdrawal from the chemicals, only the strongest wills among them surviving as the rest fought and killed each other in search of release. The strength of Naru's mind ushered it unscathed through the group's agonizing detoxification, but its witness of the others' suffering, a bloody civil war of desperation, lay raw and bleeding in its mind, an unhealed wound.

Its first meeting with me and Gor: the soothing touch of

my friend's mind elicited an immediate trust, but with me ... something else. Naru recognized me as more. Familiar.

Kin?

Naru released its telepathic hold on me, and I swayed. The implication of its revelations devastated me, the stark cruelty with which Darizh rendered these sensitive creations into killing machines.

Someone had to have known about the takeover. The facility was overrun by the Shontavians almost a month before it de-orbited and crashed into the palace grounds. No possible scenario existed that Lady Darizh, head of the bioengineering program, did not have prior knowledge of the mutiny.

What the fuck did the Pileans have to do with this?

I said aloud in Ursetu, "Naru, it is imperative I find computers and outside communications still working anywhere on board the ship. I think if we have any chance to make it out of here without a fight, we must discover exactly what Darizh was up to."

Black eyes glittered in the dim light.

"Trust." The magnitude of Naru's reply sent a shiver through me.

———

Naru escorted us out of the medical bay. Before we left, I checked the battery and memory level on the body camera. Even if no one received the feed, we could still use it to record images of what we discovered. If we found what I thought we might, I needed to back up our evidence.

We walked past the other Shontavians gathered in the hallway, placid and calm, no longer agitated. The body of the fallen messenger was missing, only a large finger painting of dark ichor on the deck giving testament to its former location. Nausea crawled through me at the thought of where the body went, and evidently Alecto's thoughts were the same. His purplish skin took on a distinctly gray hue as he went pale. Naru's massive head swiveled in my direction, catching our unspoken trepidation.

"They are dead. We live." Its eyes gleamed at me. "We will not eat you. Yet."

Humor? I hoped Naru made a joke, but it was difficult to tell.

"My own species once consumed the dead, thousands of years ago," I said. "It was an act of respect for loved ones. They believed it would keep them close by making them part of you."

"Part of us. Yes." Naru agreed solemnly. "No choice. Food chambers were destroyed in crash."

The Shontavian guided us back to the first narrow corridor. Alecto and I could stand comfortably, but our shepherd had to crouch to continue, its bulk filling the passage. The tilted decks and uneven slant of the wreck had my injured thigh begging for mercy before long, and I stumbled. Alecto moved in quickly to catch me. He wrapped his arm around my waist and supported some of my weight. A glimmer of light grew brighter as we entered a portion of the derelict station where curved bulkheads still blinked with the red-circuited eyes of half-awake control panels.

Flickering white illumination glared from an open port. A crumpled door lay on the deck outside what seemed to be a central hub for this level, ripped from its housing by the unimaginable strength of one or more Shontavians.

"Command center." Naru motioned us inside. The room lay in shambles—the Shontavians' objective to disable the command center had been successful. Some equipment lay torn apart in a mangled mess, but the facility no longer needed orbital control or propulsion anyway. A head-sized hole spattered with blood and chunkier, dried organic material made a shattered bullseye in the screen of what I recognized with dismay as the now-defunct communications panel. Damn. I was relatively certain that one would not work.

Alecto helped me to an intact bank of screens, and I lowered myself into the anchored chair, tilted sideways on the uneven deck.

Two of the holo screens flared to life under my fingertips, splashed with a dark-red substance. The rest reflected my visage in sullen, blank surfaces. I swallowed my revulsion and scrubbed at the dried fluids with the sleeve of my fatigue blouse to clear the screen. Nothing looked like a comm system here, only some sort of database. A flatlined sound-wave cursor pulsed in anticipation of verbal instructions. I groaned inwardly. This was not Kua technology: those were the best computer systems in the galaxy, with machines so intuitive they were practically an extension of one's brain. This was Micso tech. I despised the voice interface on these things. They always sounded inconvenienced.

"Display most recent Shontavian neurological upgrade," I said in Ursetu. The waveform danced across the tab.

"The data is not available at this station." The artificial voice dripped with annoyance.

"Up yours," I muttered in frustration, slamming my fist on the arm of the chair.

"I do not understand this action," the tech replied.

"Where is the data available?" I said, enunciating each word with sharp consonants.

"Level six, bioengineering control." I swear the thing sounded as if it rolled its eyes behind the screen. "Minimal power. Damage to the mainframe. Some files may not be available."

"Of course," I grumbled. "Is there a communications panel there, and does it have power?"

"Communications are online. Limited auxiliary power at twenty percent."

Just enough to research and send a message out if we got lucky. "Naru, do you know how to get to bioengineering control?"

"Climb." The Shontavian pointed upward with one sharp-taloned digit. "Tubes designed for small bodies, not ours. Lifts do not work now." Naru showed us where to access the ladders.

The tube stretched impossibly far as I peered up the dark shaft, angled by the wreckage in such a way that climbing would be a pain in the ass—especially if I slipped off the rungs. "What level are we on now?"

"One," Naru said.

Of course.

"Are you up to a climb like this?" Alecto's brow creased with concern.

"I think so." Maybe. I had to get up to that computer station, find the answers, and send a message before the power completely drained. We had one shot.

"I am coming with you," Alecto said.

CHAPTER
TWENTY-TWO

BY THE THIRD LEVEL, one of the little satavi would have had no problem hanging off the proverbial monkey bars at their slanted angle, but Alecto and I were forced to hook our arms through the rungs to stay attached. Muscles cramped, palms slick with sweat against the metal. My injured leg played a discordant symphony of pain each time I used it to anchor myself.

The sun beat down on the outside of the hull and made the area ridiculously, uncomfortably hot, my fatigues already drenched in sweat under my arms.

The temperature increased to sweltering levels the closer we got to the top. By the time we pulled ourselves through the access hatch on the sixth level, exhausted by the climb, I retched from the heat and the distinct odor of rotten flesh coming from somewhere on that deck.

Alecto was not in much better shape than I, but he kept me from sliding down the steep angle of the corridor and forced another fluid ration on me, his cool fingers cupping my neck beneath the ear as I swallowed. His concern flowed against me as he drew his hand away.

"Dalí, I think you are feverish. I fear your leg may be infected."

"I think so too," I confessed around another heave, but the water stayed down. I handed him the container. "Let's find the lab before I vomit again."

"Tell me what you hope to discover there," he said. "If you become incapacitated, I will not know what to look for."

"Anatomy scans. DNA profiles. I suspect our friend Naru and the rest of Darizh's new, improved Shontavian mercenaries have a secret ingredient she doesn't want the Remoliad to find."

"If that is so, the information may not be in the open," Alecto panted. He took another swallow of water and handed it back to me. "Drink."

I took another sip. Water squelched around my insides with unpleasant certainty it wouldn't remain there for long. I capped the ration and gave it back to him to stow in the bag. "I promise I'll drink more later. Right now, we need to find that console."

I stripped down to my sleeveless undershirt and knotted the arms of the fatigue blouse at my waist, unable to bear the heat any longer. Alecto helped me stand and we slipped and slid up the curving corridor. This port, too, gaped open, though the door was not ripped from its track like the other. Most of the screens stayed intact, the overhead lights dim but steady.

"There is the communications panel," he said with relief. "It appears to be undamaged."

I lurched my way to the bank of windows overlooking a central bay, the floor three meters below. Jagged piles marked the remains of the conditioning devices Naru smashed in the memories it shared with me. Twelve platforms with immobilizing straps and cages, the equipment overturned and scattered awry. More technology lay in fragments, unrecognizable as anything but flattened scraps of alloy, glass, and circuitry. That had not occurred on impact: this was sheer fury, savagery inflicted against the mechanism of injury.

Alecto joined me at the gallery window and stared. "What happened here?"

"So much pain." My eyes burned with tears born from stinging sweat and outrage. "They were essentially infants. Naru showed me how Darizh conditioned them. She tortured them, addicted them to drugs to make battle-ready mercenaries who get off on killing." I turned to him. "But they kicked the habit and came home for a reckoning."

"They must know they will not survive." Alecto's eyes went wide with horror.

"I don't think they expected to. But they had nobody to intervene for them either. Now they do." I leaned forward in question. "Are you willing to go against our directive and do the right thing? Even if it means the end of your political career?"

His mouth tightened. "I will fight on the side of freedom this time."

"Then let's start looking for ammunition." I motioned to the bank of screens behind us, and we struggled into tilted seats.

A tap on my screen brought it to life, the waveform cursor ready and waiting. "Display a readout of auxiliary power level with audible warning at ten percent. Review the most recent Shontavian neurological upgrade."

"Acknowledged," the interface sighed.

Beside me, Alecto relayed instructions to his interface to display DNA lines used in current bioengineering. It may have been the heat, maybe the fever, but I swore it was more polite to him.

Scientific Ursetu vocabulary stretched my fluency to its limits, the crabbed alphabet swimming in my vision. I resorted to instructing the computer to read portions out loud for me to translate through my implant. Slow, too slow. The power readout crept steadily down with our use of the tech.

This got me nowhere fast, until, "Dalí ... " Alecto's voice was grim. "I believe I found something."

"What is it?"

"A string of genetic code. More than a string. An entire genome sequence for the Shontavians' neuroendocrine system." He stared at me in trepidation. "I think it may be important."

I hobbled over to examine the screen. There are certain evolutionary patterns repeated all over the galaxy, one of them being the double helix arrangement of DNA. For most humanoids, the pattern of amino acids is strikingly similar, but there are telltale combinations which denote the species origin.

I'd read enough of my wife's published work on her research to recognize genomes when I saw them.

This was not just a sequence of physically similar genetics. This was human DNA.

―――――

So, the Shontavians were cousins to humanity. That was going to make any future family reunions interesting and a little terrifying.

"Contact with unincorporated planets for the collection and sale of genetic material is forbidden by galactic law," Alecto said in dismay.

"It never stopped the Elusians." I referred to the slender, gray alien race which once harried precontact-Earth's citizens and had soon moved on to greener star systems. "Are there image files?"

"Display images of Shontavian neuroendocrine system," Alecto instructed.

A map of organs and nerves popped up on the screen. I

recognized those organic roads, and a flare of shock went through me.

"Put a human neuroendocrine system side by side with the Shontavian's." A cold, hard lump formed in the pit of my stomach as he complied.

"They are identical," Alecto breathed.

"I knew Darizh was hiding something," I said through gritted teeth.

One idiosyncrasy of the human species concerned our neuroendocrine system. It developed differently from most other humanoids with the ability to create new biochemical roads. This fairly unique trait predisposed humanity to different kinds of addiction—a quirk with which, unfortunately, I was all too familiar. These pathways rewarded certain behaviors, like emotional states. Overindulgence in food and alcohol. Sexual activity. Drug use.

Darizh created the perfect addict for her conditioning program.

With a shaky hand, I fumbled the camera out of my fatigues and gave it to Alecto. "Will you make a record of it, please?" I returned to my own interface while he captured the information.

"What research was in process at the time of the last entry?"

"The growth of organ systems for ongoing product development," the system replied.

I frowned. "Define product development?"

"Chemical reward drug manufacturing."

Holy shit. I had a strange feeling of dread. "Display that."

It was horrifying to read. They created chemicals tailored directly to the Shontavians' brain and nervous system. Human systems. I had a very strong suspicion about the identity of the Pileans in Naru's memory.

Drug cartel.

"They manufactured drugs out of this facility, using the

Shontavians as test subjects." My voice almost failed me, outrage thick in my throat.

"Barbaric. This is a crime against a sentient species." Alecto pointed at a clip of hologram; tiny, writhing cells dividing and subdividing under microscopic observation. "Why are they putting living organisms in the drugs?"

"That is some kind of bacteria," I said, shaken. "I think we just stumbled into something very ugly. We need to record this too."

"No matter the acts Shontavians perpetrated in the name of war, no sentient being should be subjected to torture and experimentation." Alecto's fury reached out in a haze of red, condensing on my empathic web like drops of blood. "As representatives of the Remoliad, we must offer them protection and legal recourse."

"Where is the laboratory where the chemicals are produced?" I asked the interface.

"Level six. Room two."

Just a bit farther in the corridor, but it would be a downhill climb. When Alecto finished recording the images and chemical sequences, I held out my hand for the camera. "I'm going to look for evidence in the lab." I lurched out of my seat, and the inflamed muscle in my thigh protested immediately. I sat back down with a hiss and massaged the cramp.

"You can hardly walk," Alecto chided. "Let me go instead."

He wasn't wrong. I didn't like the way I was starting to feel. My leg burned hot to the touch above the bandage, and the noxious, humid environment made me dizzy. The metallic taste in my mouth hadn't been relieved by the water ration.

With my forearm, I wiped away the sweat rolling off my forehead and admitted defeat. "All right. I'm hoping they might have a Frankenstein-type lab with brains in jars."

"I am sorry, but I do not know what a Frankenstein is."

Alecto's brow creased delicately. I waved my hand, fighting off the urge to giggle.

"Never mind." Getting delirious would not be helpful. "Document whatever you find. If possible, grab evidence and come back as soon as you can. We need to get out of this heat. Be careful."

"Yes. You drink this while I am gone." He handed me another water ration.

"Power at ten percent," the artificial voice interrupted.

"Damn it," I muttered.

"Try to reach Rion, or anyone. I will be back." Alecto made his way back to the corridor, steadying himself on the consoles and fixed apparatus as he went. The sound of his cautious footsteps on the deck faded, and I wrestled myself over to the communications console. Full range on this thing would quickly drain what we had left of auxiliary power. I could not be sure how far the signal would travel in the shadow of eight thousand feet of volcanic rock.

I set my frequency to the private band used by my team's coms and toggled the mic. "*Thunder Child*, are you in orbit?" I said. "Is anyone receiving this message?"

Only static answered. I guessed it was still too early for Ozzie and the team to be here, but it had been worth a couple of tries. I set the transmitter to a standard Remoliad frequency.

"This is Ambassador Dalí Tamareia, attempting to reach any Remoliad vessel in the system. Please acknowledge."

Silence. I repeated my message for five minutes and the power display ticked downward another notch into the red zone. I moved the frequency to a broad band that would be more widely received but would suck down the last of the power in minutes.

"This is Ambassador Dalí Tamareia of the Remoliad Alliance requesting urgent assistance. I must get a message to Queen Xahria. Does anyone receive me?"

Silence reigned. Where the fuck was everybody? I repeated my distress call. Then, suddenly, a deep, cultured voice emerged from the void, spoke in Sol Standard, and sent shivers of recognition through me.

"Ambassador Tamareia. How may I be of service?"

"Rhix?" I whispered.

"That is not my name." Warning tinged his voice. "We have not met."

I collected myself. This was not a secured channel. "I'm sorry, I was mistaken."

"I learned from a reliable source the queen requested my presence."

Thank you, Simish, I breathed silently. I continued in Sol Standard—with our relatively new status as members, the language had not yet been added to most galactic translation programs. With any luck, none of the matriarchs would understand it, but this particular Ursetu was fluent. "I don't know what is happening out there right now. We were attacked while attempting a peaceful negotiation on behalf of the queen. I am currently on board the wreck with a number of Shontavians and the head of the Remoliad Security Council, who is part of the negotiations. We lost communication with the queen's troops and the rest of my diplomatic team. The alpha and I reached an accord, but we are pinned down by someone who seems more interested in killing us than making treaties."

"What do you require, Ambassador?" Clipped words, icy tone.

"Please tell the queen, based on discoveries made here I must insist her original plan of action be reinstated. She will understand, but she may not agree. I need her to trust me and come to our defense if it's possible." I couldn't help but wince, considering what once passed between Rhix—Nazhir —and me in terms of trust. "Do you think you can convince her?"

"The queen is a strong-willed matriarch." His voice remained crisp and formal. "But I will make my own determination if it is the right course."

It was all I could hope for. He owed me nothing.

"I can't communicate again," I said in a low voice. "The auxiliary power is nearly depleted. I don't know how long the soldiers outside will wait before they try to drive us out. Can you get a message to this vessel?" I rattled off *Thunder Child*'s com frequency. "They will be entering the system soon and might be able to help."

"Anything else?"

"Guns. Ammunition," I found myself saying. "I won't let them be slaughtered. We should at least have the means to fight back."

"We, Ambassador?" Gentle mockery gilded the rich basso tones. "This does not sound like *zezjna*."

"A friend recently told me it's impossible to kick people in the head while they're shooting at me."

"That friend is wise." A pause. "I will see what I can do ... *dali*." I wasn't sure if he said my name or called me a demon.

"Thank you." The last of the power drained away as I spoke. The communications console and the touchscreens went dark and silent, the faint glow of emergency lighting all that remained.

He was alive. No matter how or why he'd left the Market, it seemed to be on his own terms.

CHAPTER
TWENTY-THREE

I STOOD and steadied myself against the consoles, giving my leg time to adjust to weight bearing before I made my way to the open port. The corridor was dark now, illuminated with patchy emergency lighting. In the silence, Alecto's sliding footsteps and ragged breath chronicled his struggle back up the slanted deck.

"I'll meet you at the access shaft," I called. Rather than attempt to walk down the tilt, I sat and slid on my butt, controlling the descent with my uninjured leg.

"I went down the same way," Alecto said around a breathless smile as he arrived. "Did you reach Rion?"

"No, but I did contact a friend. At least, I hope they are. They are getting a message to the queen."

"I must ask you something." He gave me the camera. "How did you know there would be brains in jars?"

"I didn't," I said in surprise. "It's a stereotype. Old-Earth science fiction. They were really there?"

"Yes. Entire organ systems preserved in upright cylinders. Only one remained intact, but I filmed them all. That room is the source of this terrible odor. And something quite unexpected. Three dead Pileans are in the room or at least, the remains of their exoskeletons. I documented them as well."

"What did their forehead crests look like?" I would have taken bets on what clan they belonged to.

"Wavelike."

"Pilean drug cartel." I almost hated confirming my own suspicions.

"That explains these." He reached into the pocket of his fatigues and gave me a handful of small ampules. "I found cases full of them. Hundreds, if not more than a thousand vials."

The little tubes held clear fluids. Even in the dim light, one shone a familiar, glistening amber. It set my pulse tripping a little faster despite the detox procedure.

This was vape.

The others were as colorless as water like the one the Pilean drug dealer had given me on Bariish. I divided them up between us.

"There's a better chance of getting it out if each of us carry evidence. We need to get these to Rion and the Penumbra team." I stowed the vials in the duty pocket of my fatigues with the camera and sealed the flap. "They've been looking for the missing piece of the puzzle for a long time." Alecto did the same and swallowed the last of his water ration. His skin was violet flushed from effort and glistened with sweat in the half-light. I gave him what remained of mine.

"Finish this before we go back down," I said.

"You need to drink this." He held up the water accusingly. "The fever will dehydrate you if you don't keep up."

"I've just been sitting on my ass. You've been climbing in this heat. My stomach won't handle it just now. It won't help either of us if I throw it up."

"Can you climb down safely?" His brow creased. "I do not want anything to happen to you. Rion would never forgive me."

His earnest proclamation made me laugh quietly. "Likewise. I'll be all right."

"I will go first. If you become unsteady, you must tell me."

The temperature decreased as we descended, almost cool compared to the searing heat up top. It seemed easier going down, but my grip was less sure, my injured leg shaking and lanced with pain each time it bore my full weight. Alecto never moved out of arm's reach, steadying me every step of the way. When we finally reached the first level, the fresher air in the corridor was almost sweet in my painful lungs as I leaned against the wall, so grateful to be off the tilted ladder I could have kissed the deck.

"Where is Naru?" Alecto began, but I held up a hand. "Wait. Listen."

A disembodied voice floated in echoes through the silent facility like a ghostly presence. I could not make out what they were saying. Alecto supported me as we made our way back to the broad passageway from which we'd come. We found the survivors of last night's attack clustered near the fissure in the cracked hull, Naru rising like a mountain in their midst. The group mind shifted and flowed between my empathic webs like a rush of water, splashed in surges of tension. Their quick hands made signs to each other. As we emerged from the shadows, eight pairs of eyes turned in unison to us.

"They call for you, peacemaker," Naru said.

It had taken us the better part of thirty minutes to climb down. I doubted my message garnered so rapid a response from the queen. The complicated miasma of hatred rising from Naru and the other Shontavians told me they knew who was outside.

"Is it her?" I asked Naru.

"Yesssss." Its teeth bared in a snarl, echoed by the rest.

The amplified voice from outside rang clear to me now. "Ambassador Tamareia. Come outside if you are able. We received your transmissions." Darizh's tone attempted to sound reassuring.

"I am a terrible spy," I muttered to myself. I dug the camera out of my fatigues and gave it to Alecto. "Well, let's make certain everyone knows what happened here. Broadcast this little summit, and we'll see how it goes."

"You do not mean to go outside," he said in alarm. "She must be aware she is compromised."

"If I can barter for more time, we might be able to fend her off for a while." I turned to the Shontavians. "Please stay here where you are safe. I plan on coming back, but if anything happens to me, take cover and hold your ground. Help is on the way."

I hoped.

Alecto supported me as we picked our way along the twisted, broken struts and metal plates. "Keep out of sight," I told him. "Don't stop recording. If they shoot me, get your ass back to Naru and the others. Go as far into the wreck as you can and guard that evidence."

"Do not die," Alecto said.

The pile of soil and rock mounded up by the crash landing presented another unstable climb, but I made headway on hands and knees. Blinking against the bright sunlight, I struggled to my feet and raised a hand in front of my eyes to shade the glare.

"Well, fuck."

Half a dozen armored vehicles fanned out before the wreckage. I counted more than thirty armed soldiers in battle gear. A standing missile battery rose behind them in deadly, bristling menace, manned and ready. The projectiles would easily penetrate far enough into the facility to eliminate us— or the banks of sleeping computers which held key evidence. Darizh had not been idle in the nighttime hours, defying the after-dark peace in every way.

In full battle armor, Lady Darizh stepped cautiously out of

a nearby vehicle and approached. Her soldiers clustered around her; their weapons pointed at me.

"Ambassador. Thank the goddess you are still alive." Her voice dripped with false relief. "Queen Xahria will be glad to know you are unharmed. Where is your comrade?"

"Inside. We reached an agreement with the Shontavians."

"Indeed. What terms?"

"I'll let you know after they speak to a solicitor," I responded. "They are currently under Remoliad protection, in accordance with the galactic statute which prohibits unethical research on a vulnerable sentient species."

Her body language changed immediately, stiffening her back. Her head came up, and she watched me through narrowed eyes. "The Alliance is not here."

"Yes, it is." I spread my arms in a shrug. "I am their appointed representative. I will not permit the Shontavians to be harmed. Their case will be examined through the appropriate channels."

"You are but one person, Ambassador Tamareia."

"Perhaps. But I stand for them. I asked Queen Xahria to reconsider her intentions."

"Whoever you spoke with earlier was not the queen. She will not be coming." Lady Darizh sneered. "Xahria is weak, so desperate to retain her family's power she sought Remoliad interference. It is time for a stronger hand to take control of Urset and show the casteless who their masters are."

"I don't see how collaborating with the Pilean drug cartel makes you the better ruler."

Her face twisted. "You understand nothing."

"How long did you condition the Shontavians for this exact mission? In all the years you allowed the Pileans to test new drugs on them and torture them with withdrawal, you never expected they would be strong enough to break the cycle on their own, did you? Certainly not before you were prepared to overthrow the queen."

I hoped someone was listening to the broadcast. The look on her face told me I hit pretty fucking close to the mark.

Her voice chilled. "Since you are such a skilled negotiator, I present my terms. The Shontavians will submit to me as their sole commander, defending my claim against all other matriarchal clans who fail to recognize me as queen. They will undergo reconditioning to ensure their obedience to me."

I shook my head. "I am certain they will tell you that is a deal breaker."

Her eyes glittered, cold and hard in the remorseless sunlight. "I offer them an incentive to accept my terms." She held up a canister. "Do you remember at dinner we spoke of a failsafe? This is designed to be launched inside an artillery shell. If you do not return in thirty minutes, or my terms are refused, I will fire this into the wreckage and activate the catalyst in their bodies. I cannot guarantee it will not kill you and your associate as well."

I wasn't close enough to get a sense of her threat as a bluff, but her body language suggested a deadly conviction to her plan. "What happens to your claim to the throne if you kill the only potential advantage you have left?"

"I have faith in your skills. Oh, and Ambassador … if that is not enough cause to be persuasive, perhaps this will inspire you." She made a sharp motion with her hand.

Two faceless soldiers dragged a third figure out of Darizh's vehicle. I didn't recognize the bruised and bloody face at first until one startling, blue-green eye met my horrified gaze.

Sumner.

CHAPTER
TWENTY-FOUR

THEY FORCED him to his knees in the sandy earth. I could only stare at his misshapen jaw, the blood crusting his bright hair. Cold rage boiled in my veins like liquid hydrogen.

"The others are safe," Rion slurred, a lopsided grin of defiance on his lacerated mouth. "Don't give up anything on my account."

Behind me, Alecto's emotional broadcast went from quietly watchful to red alert in the space of a breath when he heard Sumner's voice.

I stumbled forward half a step. One of the battle-armored soldiers pressed the barrel of his weapon against my commander's skull.

"You have work to do, Ambassador." Darizh smiled. I wanted to erase her smug expression with my fists until nothing remained but a bloody pulp. My nails cut half-moons into my palms, the ring of rage a war song in my ears.

A stir of violence emerged from the group consciousness in response to Alecto's fear and my blind, burning fury. In the wreckage above me, the little satavi screeched and bared their canines as they added their warning to an already turbulent atmosphere. Naru's inquisitive probe against my mind was too aggressive. I forced myself to breathe, to push the conflagration in my head behind a wall of stone and think of something.

Think.

I couldn't think of anything except Rion Sumner.

"I will present your terms." The words escaped between my clenched teeth.

Darizh stopped smiling. "Thirty minutes, or his life ends."

Sumner nodded at me. I stared helplessly, my memory flung back to the moment in my first mission where he faced me, rescue impossible, believing I would die in the arena. Our positions were reversed now.

I feared this monster was far less reasonable than Ouros.

I managed to return the nod, hoping my expression conveyed what burned in my chest. Skidding down the loose soil back to the facility, I ran into the blunt force trauma of Alecto's panic against my empathic nets.

"What can we do?" Fear glazed his features.

"I don't know. I'm stalling for time." I pushed past him to thread back through the twisted supports.

"I cannot let him die again, Dalí." His composure teetered at the edge of reason. "Not for us. Not for them."

I stopped short, took a deep breath, held it, and blew it out before I turned back to Alecto. "We both need to calm down. We won't be doing Rion or the Shontavians any favors if we incite a battle rage. Can you do that?"

His head jerked in assent. "Without the *riesh*, it is difficult to keep these emotions at bay. I am sorry."

"I understand. I have to talk to them. Neither of us can afford to distract them this way. We don't have time."

Naru waited for us when we arrived. The tension of the other Shontavians generated a crawl of electricity that threatened to erupt in thrumming, pulsing arcs.

The alpha listened to me recount Darizh's demands and her deadly incentives before I said earnestly, "Naru, am I correct some of your conditioning was for this exact scenario? You were trained to disable the command center and bring down the facility, but it missed the palace and did not kill the queen."

"Failure to execute. We expected stars here."

"You intentionally failed." A sudden understanding flooded me. "You thought you would die. That's what the stars represent to you, isn't it? A permanent end to fighting. Peace."

Naru exhaled a grunt of confirmation. It signed to its brethren, all four hands moving in rapid speech, and as one, they made a sign back: fingers of the right upper hand spread out, then clenched tightly into a fist.

"Tell her: peacemakers go free. Accept terms." Naru cocked its head at me, black eyes fathomless in the gloom, jagged teeth glinting in the diffused light. "Let her be queen."

The sharp flux of the Shontavian's satisfaction behind those words piqued my dismayed interest.

"What are you thinking?"

"Other ways to find right stars."

The weight of despair constricted my breath. "No."

"Trust."

"You can make a different choice. There is still time. We can think of something."

"No." One of Naru's massive hands enveloped my shoulder, razor-tipped talons whispering against my skin with surprising gentleness. The Shontavian moved past me into the fissure. The others went with the alpha, their anticipation of violence a rising tide in my head.

My eyes burned with despair as they filed out.

"What are they doing?" Stricken, Alecto turned to me for answers.

"Fulfilling their own objective." I followed the gray-skinned warriors through the gap in the broken hull to the mounded soil. For a moment, Naru stood silhouetted against the white-hot sky, all four arms displayed open-palmed and empty before moving forward. The rest of the squad slowly joined the alpha, displaying their limbs in a similar fashion. I limped behind, Alecto at my side.

The hundreds of little satavi in the trees and the crumpled shell of the facility screamed defiantly as the phalanx of eight Shontavians moved with Naru at their head. They stopped halfway between the wreckage and where Darizh waited, an expression of triumph on her face.

Every one of her soldiers had weapons trained on us, quivering with attention. Sumner still kneeled on the ground. His unsupported form sagged between his captors, but he raised his head to let his good eye appraise the Shontavians. Alecto's attention fell immediately upon Sumner's brutalized face. His anger scorched my empathic nets.

"Calm," I reminded him in a whisper as I walked forward to join Naru.

"With time to spare, Ambassador. I am impressed," Darizh called.

Loathing for this transaction churned my insides. Words piled up behind the knot in my throat until I choked out, "Naru has additional terms before they accept and recognize you as their queen and commander."

"Who?" Her expression contracted in puzzlement.

"I." The single syllable rolled in a thunderous, defiant assertion of self as Naru shifted to stand in front of me.

She studied the alpha in consternation. "Very well. You may speak."

"Peacemakers go free."

A short, humorless laugh from Darizh left me no doubt we would end up dead, no matter what she promised. "They will be released immediately after you swear your allegiance. Does that satisfy your terms?"

"No harm," Naru snarled. "Let go now."

The other Shontavians bared their teeth, the hiss of their breath making the hair stand up on the back of my neck. The satavi shrieked in crescendo behind us, shrill cries echoing through the battle-scarred streets. The incandescence of Naru's hatred for Darizh crisped my empathic webs, but the alpha did not move.

"So be it." She nodded at the soldiers holding Sumner. "Release him."

They hauled Sumner to his feet and pushed him toward us. He staggered, and I lurched to catch him. Alecto was there, too, supporting Rion at his other side. Sumner's one eye glared at me.

"I told you not to make a deal," he growled thickly.

"I didn't. They did," I muttered back. "Take him into the facility, Alecto. Find cover."

I turned back to Naru. "Goodbye, peacemaker," the alpha said. The Shontavian's mind touched my senses, a brief, warm nudge of reassurance we had done all we could.

"You don't have to do this," I said in desperation.

The hand that had been so gentle minutes earlier now swatted me away as Naru roared. "Go!" I staggered back with the force of the blow, my injured leg almost buckling beneath me.

"It seems the Shontavians, too, are finished with Remoliad arrogance." Darizh's cold laugh was echoed by shrieking satavi. "Leave while you are still in one piece. You are no longer needed here."

Fuck.

I turned my back and limped away. My eyes burned with fever and with impotent rage, but no tears came. Come to think of it, I wasn't sweating anymore either. Not a healthy sign. I couldn't tell if the hollow ring in my ears was born in the forge of my anger or the infection creeping through my system.

Too quiet now. The satavi had stopped shrieking and observed the spectacle, motionless, waiting. My empathic webs shuddered violently with the approach of a vast earthquake convulsing to the surface. I picked up my pace and hurried toward the shelter of the facility, grimacing as pain burned through my thigh at each step.

"Swear your allegiance to me," Darizh's voice commanded.

Naru's inflectionless response followed. "You are queen."

The hair on my scalp tingled and crawled on my neck as Alecto gathered me in. We slid partway down the mound of soil with the half-conscious Sumner cradled between us. I kept my head above the peak, compelled to see and hear what was happening, to be witness to the storm about to break.

Darizh smiled in triumph as she stepped forward. The deafening silence carried her words to me. "Yes, I am the queen. You will follow my commands and no other's."

"We swear." Naru's voice reverberated in the unsettling silence. "Urset objective will now be completed."

My confusion surrounding the Shontavian's plan coalesced and dropped into sudden, sharp clarity.

"What objective?" Darizh began. Her face went blank as she, too, realized she had just been outplayed.

The building tempest against my empathic nets broke open in a savage crescendo of bloodthirst and consummation.

The satavi wailed in hair-raising chorus. Alarmed warrior-caste soldiers stumbled back as a mass of furry bodies leaped from the trees and wreckage and poured across the ground in a fluid, leaping gray tide filled with needle sharp teeth and claws. The soldiers didn't know where to aim as the creatures fell upon them, scratching and biting wherever they found purchase. The satavi couldn't do damage through the battle armor, but the soldiers' attention was distracted from Naru.

The alpha seized Darizh by the throat. A savage twist, and

the self-proclaimed queen of Urset lay in two bloody pieces at its feet.

The rest of the Shontavians charged into the wall of soldiers. Pure carnage. A handful of warrior caste disappeared in an eruption of gray rage and blood spray, torn limb from limb before the others could react. Eight Shontavians against a platoon of Ursetu warrior caste was more than enough to make a hole in their defenses.

But they were still unarmed.

Only seconds passed before Darizh's troops overcame their surprise and realized the satavi couldn't hurt them. They began to fire on the Shontavians with the large caliber weapons mounted on the vehicles. One gray body jerked and fell as shells punched gaping holes through its chest and head, but the Ursetu could not hit their targets without collateral damage. Some of their soldiers were ripped apart by the same powerful artillery that took down a second Shontavian.

In the center of the maelstrom, Naru rose like some ancient god of chaos, four upper limbs streaked to the elbow in scarlet gore. I refused to look away. I would witness this end they had chosen of their own free will.

Three tones sounded in my skull.

"Dalí, Sumner? You copy?" Ozzie's sibilant voice rang in my head. "You guys need some help down there?"

"Fuck, yes! Do not fire on the Shontavians!" I screamed, delirious with relief. "It's close quarters. Repeat. *Do not fire on the Shontavians.* Take out the mounted guns."

The raptor-shriek of engines echoed against the mountains. *Thunder Child* swept in, ventral guns blazing. The missile battery came up, but Ziggy's aim was true, melting the weapon to slag with a well-placed blast from the directed energy cannon. A second vehicle followed it to hell. Projectiles whined off the hull as some of the troops turned fire on the hovering ship. We were forced to slide farther down into the shelter of furrowed earth. Alecto and I covered Sumner with our own bodies as chunks of debris fell around us. The sound of guns ricocheted in staccato reverberations through the fissure.

"Two vehicles leaving in a hurry, and we have a dozen retreating on foot," Ozzie said tersely over the com. "The Shontavians are pursuing and … whoa, I did *not* need to see that. I don't think you're safe down there."

We needed to get Sumner immediate attention. I wasn't doing so great either, my heart hammering in my chest and the edge of my vision full of white sparks.

"Sumner needs medical, stat. Can you land?"

"There's a lot of trees. I'll have to get closer to the Shontavians than I'd like. You have to move fast."

Grit clouded the air as *Thunder Child*'s engine wash gusted through our shelter. As soon as the tempest died down, Alecto and I helped Sumner stand, and we made our way to the outside. Not far away, the smoldering remains of vehicles sent heat plumes into the sky. I caught a glimpse of the remaining Shontavians.

Naru's head turned as the ship landed. I staggered toward the lowering ramp, and our gazes locked for a moment. A powerful telepathic nudge of farewell hit me right between the eyes.

Damn it. I couldn't abandon them now.

Tommi and Ziggy met us on the ramp with a stretcher. I stepped back to let Zig take my place at Sumner's side and ease him on the cot.

"Leave me a medical kit with broad spectrum antibiotics, Tommi," I shouted over the engines. I fumbled the vials out of my pocket and handed them to Ziggy. "I think we found the missing link in the Pilean cartel. Have Ka'pth and Ra'sho analyze these along with the footage on the camera. Alecto has it."

"What are you doing?" Tommi's surprise was evident, one

eye assessing Sumner, the other scanning me and the torn, bloody leg of my fatigues.

"Dalí, you cannot stay!" Alecto protested. "You need fluids and medical attention."

"No. If I leave, there's no one to speak for them. They'll kill them."

"Then I stay as well." Alecto placed the vials and camera he'd been guarding on the commander's chest, and placed Sumner's hand on top of them. He swept one slender hand over Rion's head in a tender gesture.

"You two get your asses on my ship," Sumner growled.

"I must see this through," Alecto insisted. "I am sorry, Rion."

"Uh, Dalí? They're picking up weapons over there," Ozzie said. "I am not comfortable."

I craned my neck to see. Though Naru still monitored us with mild interest, the others gleaned through bodies and vehicles, collecting pulse rifles and armaments.

"Go!" I waved them on, and Tommi and Ziggy carried a feebly protesting Sumner into the ship. Alecto and I moved away as quickly as we could, his arm around my waist to steady me as the wash spattered our backs with gritty earth. "I'll take my chances, Ozzie. We've been with them two days. The alpha trusts us. I don't think they'll harm us, but they don't know you. Keep in touch on my com, please. I don't have any other way to communicate right now."

"We'll be ready for evac," Ozzie promised. "You sure about this?"

"No, but it's the right thing, Oz."

As the ship hovered, I spied Tommi at the top of the still-open ramp. She tossed down a field pack and another hard-sided container. "Be careful, you idiot," her voice said over my comm, the whispery Cthash words full of concern beneath the mild translated voice. "Call if you need medical consult."

"Thanks, Tommi."

Thunder Child pulled away from the earth. As the ship grew smaller against a clouding sky, I couldn't help but wonder if the right thing and the smart thing to do were as at odds as they seemed right now.

CHAPTER
TWENTY-FIVE

THE SHONTAVIANS WATCHED the ship soar away. Naru regarded me a moment before rejoining the others in their search for ammunition.

Alecto eyed the returning satavi, no longer slavering beasts full of teeth and screams but chittering excitedly as they swung through the trees with four-armed athleticism. "Our surprising allies. Why did they attack?"

"I'm guessing their group mind meshed with the Shontavians' since they share a genetic link." I groaned as Alecto lowered me to a seat on the mound of earth in front of the wreck. He hurried back into the open, keeping an eye on the surviving Shontavians as he shouldered the medical bag and grabbed the hard-sided case. He put it on the ground beside me and scrabbled through the kit, pulling out a pump pack and fluids.

"Give me your arm." He swabbed the inside crook of my elbow, peeled a nanopatch and slapped it against my skin. The sting of needles faded into coolness as the fluids traveled through the connected tube. I stared at Alecto's dust-streaked, lavender countenance as he worked, mesmerized by its perfect proportion and serious mien in concentration. Yeah, definitely on the edge of delirium because for a minute I thought I was in love with him, thankful he stayed with me. He chose a vial of antibiotics and a transdermal patch to reduce the fever, holding them out for my approval. "Do you agree?"

I nodded. The potent antibiotic would be rough, but I felt like shit and no doubt needed the meds. "You treated humans in the field before?"

"Only one other." He quirked a smile at me as he snapped the vial into the pump's receptor. "Nos, primarily, but you are so similar in physiology."

"Did you do all right during the battle?" I'd never stopped to think how Alecto fared while the fighting went on.

"I focused on Rion. I am fine." His quick, sharp movements told me a different story of tension barely held in check. He applied the patch to my neck and glanced worriedly at the Shontavians, still rooting through the bodies and vehicles. "Do you think you will be safe if I go to the medical bay to get water and nutrients?"

"I think so. Be careful, Alecto."

To my surprise, he gave me the same gentle sweep of his hand against my head he'd given Sumner, and my empathic nets sang with his affection and regret. "You are a brave being, Dalí Tamareia. So much like Rion. It is no wonder he cares for you."

He vanished into the dark recesses of the derelict facility. Too damned confused from the fever and the chaos of the last hour, I couldn't process his words now. Shaking the thought out of my head, I turned to the second case and unclipped the braces. Nestled in the padded interior lay two small, deadly, energy sidearms capable of drilling holes through rock. Tommi did not fool around when she chose this case, or maybe Ziggy had. Either way, we were newly defensible.

So were the Shontavians. They made their way back to the wreck, twenty-four huge, gore-streaked arms lugging pulse rifles and ammunition cases. Naru had another missile tube slung over its shoulder like a club. Their mouths and razor-prong teeth were stained red with fluids and tissue. I swallowed, dark, queasy memories flitting through my feverish mind like night insects.

I didn't close the case. My hand rested against the butt of a weapon, and I cast out my senses to catch a hint of the warriors' current setting: murder, mayhem, or neutral?

What I sensed as they got closer was surprising calm. Contentment in the afterglow of their violent outburst, the climactic rush of conditioned biochemical release. That part of addiction I understood too well. As Darizh told me when she still had a head, the Shontavians' own neuroendocrine systems would provide the reward for the desired behavior—perhaps not as potent as the drugs had been but no less satisfying.

The chemical habit had been broken. The killing habit remained, reinforced by the mutilation of Darizh and her soldiers.

"Peacemaker." Naru's greeting touched my mind in puzzled reassurance. "Why stay?"

Clouds veiled the sun, the promise of rain so heavy in the air I could taste it. "I won't leave until you are safe. It's what I came to do."

The cycle would never end here on Urset. We had to get them out.

———

Darkness came early with the rain. Rather than face the stifling conditions inside, we camped beneath the wreckage for the night.

The six surviving Shontavians, weather ignored, sat in a

closely arrayed group, their number so much smaller than at sunset the day before. They gazed at the sky, their throats issuing a low, atonal moan echoing the thunder out to sea. I was certain we witnessed a memorial of sorts for their fallen. The day ended without stars, the mountain shrouded in mist and low clouds. Night rolled in with more rain, and sullen flashes of lightning traced upturned, gray faces.

I dozed off and on, lulled by the droning of the Shontavians and the counterpoint murmur of the satavi. But with intravenous hydration and strong antibiotics, my guts became restless. I was forced to find a private place to relieve myself. The Shontavians didn't care, but I had developed a sudden fastidiousness around Alecto, careful not to wake him as I pulled off the nanopatch connecting the now-spent IV fluids to my arm.

In the darkness, I limped a dozen meters downwind around the side of the facility and dug a suitable spot in the dirt with a piece of debris before the cramping hit without compromise. I had to yank my pants down in a hasty fumble, supporting myself against the wreckage.

It was an ugly thing. I thought I managed to stifle my vocalizations, but as I cleaned myself up with supplies out of the medical kit, the dry voice over my implant com let me know otherwise.

"For the sake of all intelligent life, Dalí, turn off your com when you shit. Why is it always on my watch?"

"God, Melos, I'm sorry. That was brutal." I pulled up my pants and fastened my belt. "How is Sumner?"

"He is resting. Tommi is seeing to him. A concussion, dislocated jaw, fractured orbital, broken ribs."

I closed my eyes, thanking whatever gods were listening that Darizh lay sprawled in two bloody pieces somewhere to my right; otherwise, I would have hunted her down. "Did he say how they captured him?"

"Apparently, Lord Khus left you behind in retreat. Sumner

demanded to be let out of the vehicle. He was trying to reach you and Minister Sim when he was captured."

That sounded like Sumner. I paused a moment. "And how are you feeling?"

"Better, now your expulsions have ceased."

Oh, yeah, Melos was still pissed at me. I couldn't blame him. "I meant your injury." I scraped dirt back over the hole and drenched my hands in antibacterial gel.

"I will have a scar." His cold voice dropped a few more degrees than usual. "It is healing."

"I owe you an apology words cannot express." I leaned against the hull of the ship. "If you still want to kick my ass, I will stand there and take it. I deserve it."

"Have you given the drugs up for good?"

"Yes." I meant it.

"That is all I need to know." He dismissed it.

On the subject of knowing, I wanted confirmation. "How did you guys learn we needed help?"

"We were contacted by an anonymous party. Is that who I thought it was?"

"Probably."

"He was quite forceful and specifically mentioned you asked for weapons. It appears the Shontavians were able to solve that for themselves. I am sorry we did not have anything larger to give you."

"No, those are more than enough if anything goes down. Thanks, Melos." So Rhix—damn it; I would never remember to use his real name—had done exactly as I asked. The life-debt balance between us tipped again in his favor, and I owed him.

"There was a reason I opened the channel to be met with your defecation," Melos said. "Ka'pth and Ra'sho have analyzed the chemicals you and Minister Sim liberated. The dark one is vape, as I am certain you suspected, but the clear formula is identical to that which you were given on Bariish.

It is similar in composition to the original vape, save it contains a live bacterial component. The first sample was destroyed by the decontamination process, but this one is intact. The Andari need more data on the engineering of the bacteria. They want to know if you can still access the system."

I groaned. "No, the power is completely drained. The Micso tech memory core for the bio lab is on the sixth level, and there is a lot of information in it I need to defend the Shontavians. I'm not sure I could climb back up with this leg. There may be a way in through the hull, but I don't know that. *Three* should be able to land up there without settling the wreckage."

"I can make a hole if one does not exist. Perhaps this should be done before morning."

"I agree. The more information we can extract from their core, the better proof, and if another attack comes, it will be after dawn. There's a sort of religious truce on the island until then." It hadn't stopped Darizh, but I didn't think Queen Xahria or any of the other matriarchs would break the taboo.

"I will consult Ozzie. Tell your Shontavian friends not to shoot me down."

"Copy that."

A shriek sent ice through my veins. Muffled Tolkish shouts assaulted my ears, and the shockwave of Alecto's panic and disorientation zinged through me like an electric shock.

"Trouble?" Melos asked sharply.

"Not that kind. I'll keep in touch if needed."

I tapped off my com and made my way back to Alecto in a double-time limp. He sat straight up on his bedroll, his breathing quick and shallow in the throes of what appeared to be an ugly flashback. He heard my clumsy approach and spun into a crouch with a snarl, red eyes glinting like a cornered animal's.

And then, his body became a missile in the darkness. His shoulder hit me mid-abdomen and took me down, unable to brace on my injured leg. Slender fingers wrapped around my throat and squeezed. I gripped his wrists and tried to pull them apart.

"Alecto!" I croaked. "It's me, Dalí."

His fingers tightened, cutting off my air. I wasn't convinced he was even awake, his eyes blank and unfocused. The last thing I wanted to do was punch him, but it was going to happen in five … four … three … My hand curled into a fist.

"Peacemaker." A gentle gray hand enveloped Alecto's arm. Naru's voice echoed the quiet storm out to sea, compelling and powerful. "War is inside. Not here."

Comprehension slowly returned to Alecto's eyes. With a cry, he looked down at me and cast himself to the side. I sat up with a convulsive inhalation, caught between relief and wonder as the Shontavian released his arm.

Alecto's ragged gasps slowed and melted into soft, heartbroken keening. His long fingers covered his eyes, and he shrank against the earth in a knotted crouch. Though his source of pain was much different, the empty despair flayed my empathic nets and left me raw. I moved closer, unable to speak for a moment against the onslaught of his pain.

"You aren't alone, my friend." My voice finally emerged, hoarse and breathless.

A shocked moment of silence as he raised his tortured face to me. He collapsed into my side, raw moans of grief and shame torn from his throat. I managed to guide him back to his bedroll and wrapped my arms around him. I held Alecto with the knowledge words meant nothing. When I looked up, my face streaked with tears, the rest of the Shontavians had shuffled closer to us, drawn by the outpouring of Alecto's distress.

Naru squatted on its haunches and began to croon. The

others followed suit. It seemed they mourned not only for their own dead, but those victims of the Scata Rebellion who died over and over in the war for Alecto's soul. The basso vibration of the Shontavians' lament quieted his anguished moans, and the strange lullaby pulled both of us into sleep at last.

CHAPTER
TWENTY-SIX

IN THE MURK of reluctant consciousness, I woke with someone in the curve of my arms, my lips pressed against the top of a smooth head, a source of warmth in the chill of yet-dark morning. It felt right; safe and somehow familiar. I raised my head to find Alecto curled against my shoulder, dark plum-colored circles beneath his eyes, but peacefully asleep.

A pang of loneliness went through me. I missed my husband and wife, a visceral ache that brought tears to my eyes. But more, I realized I longed for the intimacy of a relationship, waking to find myself tangled with another's body, warm and comfortable and loved.

My breathing shook with the revelation as I gently extracted my arm from beneath him. He stirred and said something but did not awaken. I was grateful.

Coward.

As innocent as it was, I almost felt I had betrayed Sumner.

Three's quiet, familiar engines purred above, and I realized the sound had awakened me. As the impact of her landing against the hull reverberated through the facility in metallic rumbles, I signaled the hypervigilant Naru to stand down, that this tiny ship did not constitute a threat. The alpha settled the rest of the group with a series of hand signs, and they moved back into watchful poses. The wreckage groaned as it accepted the burden but did not settle.

The noise woke Alecto with a start, and he sat up, blinking. "What is happening?"

"It's all right. Our team is extracting the memory core." I handed him a container of water.

"Thank you." His fingers stayed a moment against my wrist with gentle pressure. His glance connected with mine and away. "Your hand is cool. Do you feel the antibiotics helped?"

"They did help. You're a good medic." I did feel better, despite having slept only an hour or two. The dampness of my skin had as much to do with the humidity as the fact my fever had broken, and my leg felt less warm to the touch. I gulped an entire water ration without fear my stomach would turn inside out. More careful with the nutrient bar after last night's eruption, I broke off tiny pieces at a time to reintroduce my system to the idea of digestion.

"I am so very sorry about last night, Dalí." Alecto finally spoke in the quiet.

"There's no need to apologize." I kept my voice light. "All my friends fight me. Didn't Sumner tell you?"

Alecto's hesitant chuckle was musical. "He did say something to the effect."

"Oh, really? What did he say?"

"That you were as likely to make sexual advances as you were to throw punches, and either would mean I had earned your trust."

Surprise made me choke on a piece of the nutrient bar. "He said that?"

"I do not believe he meant it as an insult."

"No, no. It is … an accurate assessment." I gave an embarrassed laugh, my face burning with the implications. The awkward silence between us stretched out far too long, both of us picking at our nutrient bars. An early riser among the satavi came and sat by my knee, huge green eyes riveted on the food, and I tossed it a tiny piece. They'd earned the treat. The little creature shoved the morsel into its mouth and scampered away.

"What are we going to do?" Alecto asked at last, glancing at the Shontavians. "If they stay here, I cannot see a positive outcome for them."

"Neither can I." My breath rushed out in resignation, steam haunting the chilly, damp air in front of my lips.

"I would like to make a suggestion." Alecto posed the question with careful, measured words. "What if I were to take them into protective custody, and we ask Rion to evacuate them to Zereid?"

Surprised, because my thoughts had been flowing in the same vein, I regarded him a moment. He finally met my stare, his jaw set in determination.

"I think that's a damned fine idea." I crumpled the wrapper of the nutrient bar and stowed it in the bag. "But we'll be ignoring the queen's wishes, breaking half a dozen Remoliad statutes, and fuck knows how many Ursetu laws. If we do this, political enemies like Prinoya will use it against you. I'm willing to stand in the fallout because I have nothing to lose. Are you?"

"After what Naru and the others did last night?" He shook his head. "They are a culture of their own. I would be a coward not to do whatever it takes to save them. They are no more mindless killers than any other mercenary soldier, and neither I nor anyone else who followed the unethical command of an officer without voicing objection can judge them."

"Let's find out what they think."

Naru and the Shontavians still sat nearby, their weapons stacked out of reach from last night's gentle rain under the shelter of the facility. Naru was wide awake, scanning the dark, tree-lined streets and the aftermath of the battle. I grabbed my discarded fatigue blouse and eased myself down beside the alpha.

"Anything out there?" I asked in Ursetu.

A negation sounded deep in its chest, but it did not look at me. "Naru, I would like to talk with you." I shrugged back into the long-sleeved shirt against damp chill. "If we can take you away from Urset, to a place where you and the others can live without war, will you go with us?"

"We are war, peacemaker." One hand made a fist and bumped its chest. "War lives in us. In here, too, even in peace-makers." Naru's talon brushed the center of its broad gray forehead. "No way to live without. Proof." Its expansive gesture took in the battlefield. In the strange light of cloud-shine, Darizh's dismembered body still lay where she had fallen. None of the Shontavians had touched her afterward, as if she were contaminated in some way.

"We all live with war inside us. It is something we must learn to control and discover who we are without it, if possi-ble." I drew up my injured leg and winced as the muscle stretched in a new way. "But there are some who do not carry violence inside them. You remember my brother, Gor. His people have lived without war on their planet for thousands of years. They would offer sanctuary until we find the right place for you." Though I knew this to be true, I couldn't subdue the thought of what might happen on tranquil Zereid if Naru and the others could not suppress the violence bottled inside them.

"Not safe. You know." Naru grunted, catching my doubt. "Better to live among stars."

"You don't have to die. There has to be another way." Even as I said it, the literal truth of the alpha's words began to germinate an idea. "What if you actually did live among the stars in a ship?"

Naru stayed silent for a long moment. "With guards, like this place? No."

"I don't mean that. No guards, no crew. Just you and the others in your own ship, equipped with food synthesizers and water and a view of the stars. We can program the navigation system to travel the galaxy forever without coming close to inhabited planets. It would take time to arrange, but you would be safe on Zereid until we can procure a vessel." Black eyes regarded me with shrewd consideration. The alpha's interest in this solution glowed like an ember, gaining light and heat as it thought about it. The Shontavians were alert now as the shared thoughts passed between them, signing to each other. Naru glanced at them, made a series of signs, and they all responded with a single, simultaneous gesture: the closed fist, then digits spread in a burst of hope for the first time.

"Objective accepted," Naru rumbled. "We travel the stars."

I walked back to Alecto. "What did they say?" he queried, his brow creased with concern.

"We reached an accord." I tapped my implant. "Ozzie?"

"I'm here, Dalí." His voice came instantly. "What's up?"

"We need to talk about an evacuation. Get the team on the com. Sumner probably isn't going to like this."

———

"A quarantined ship." Sumner repeated slowly, his speech still slurred. Even with him in orbit on *Thunder Child*, I could see the raised eyebrows evoked by his thoughtful voice over my implant.

"Yes. It's the only way I can think of where they will be safe and still pose no threat. We have to get them out of here fast without anyone catching wind of the plan or it could be the most hunted plague ship in the galaxy. They're the last Shontavians that will ever be created. The black-market price would be enormous."

"We can only violate Ursetu airspace in an undeclared vessel so many times before we're caught," Ozzie warned. "The survivors aren't going to be quiet about what happened yesterday. *Three* is small enough to fly under the radar."

"We have the memory core and are ready to leave. *Three* is too small to carry a Shontavian. It is crowded already with Ra'sho and me and the core. It must be *Thunder Child*," Melos said grimly.

"One really fast trip then. Life support can provide heat and oxygen in the cargo bay. How will you explain your absence, Dalí?" Ziggy's voice conveyed his dubiousness. "I assume you're coming on board with them since you've managed to create a bond."

"No. I'll stay and deal with the consequences." I glanced at Alecto, who followed the one-sided conversation with laser focus. "Minister Sim is going to shoulder the responsibility of our refugees for the duration, and he will go with you. The Remoliad probably isn't going to like the way we're doing this either."

"In light of your other discoveries, I think the Remoliad will look the other way," Ka'pth interjected.

"You counting on Rhix to take it easy on you?" Sumner asked roughly.

"He's not Rhix here. He's Prince Nazhir, and I've never met him. I don't know how he will react, or what his relationship with the queen is like." I ran my hands through my wild hair, irritated Sumner would play that card. "Best case scenario, Queen Xahria throws me off the planet. Worst case, Lord Khus throws me off the wall of the ziggurat, and the

Remoliad loses any chance of gaining it as a permanent member. We don't have the luxury of debating this forever. The time of the goddess ends at sunup. Horizon's getting brighter by the second."

"Damn it, Dalí," Sumner began irritably, and then stopped. "How do we feed them en route? Zereid is forty-eight hours away. We can't be sure they'll be prepared by the time we arrive."

"They just ate." I avoided looking at the battlefield. "I don't think it will be a problem with their slow metabolism. They will eventually need food, so make sure the Zereid are prepared with high protein content, preferably meat. Their dietary specifics should be in the memory core."

"My priority is the safety of my ship and crew. If the Shontavians threaten either of those, I flush the cargo hold." Sumner's quiet pronouncement sent a chill through me, but I knew he wouldn't do it unless there was no other choice.

"I trust your judgment, Commander."

"We'll be there as soon as Melos gets back. Thirty minutes. Make sure they understand they could be in transit a little longer than two days. We've got work to do. Sumner out."

Three departed in near silence, a dark shape against the clouds.

I tapped off my implant. "Here we go."

"He agreed." Alecto's relief whispered in a cool touch against my mind.

"More or less. There isn't another option."

"The Remoliad will send aid to ensure you and the others are released. I will see to it personally once I am on board." The warmth of his admiration was something I could bask in, but a frost-feather of his worry chilled the heady effervescence. "Are you truly so selfless, Dalí, or do you simply not care whether you live or die?"

I deflected the question and stood. "Let's go tell Naru their ride is coming."

"I would like an answer." He rose too. "If I must console Rion and your mother for your loss, it will be difficult, for I will grieve as well. Not only for their sake, but for mine."

A jolt went through me. For a moment, I couldn't put a name to it, but it was a palm-sweating excitement, followed quickly by panic.

"I would like to explore what it means one day." His voice faltered at my shocked expression. "If I am wrong, I am sorry."

"No. You aren't wrong." My voice sounded too rough in my own ears. "I tried not to think about you that way, for Sumner's sake. I wasn't sure if you and he were…"

"Lovers? A stolen moment of happiness in another lifetime, all else of which we would both prefer to forget. We still care for each other. The moment is over." A gentle note of regret traced his words. "I understand humans do not often enter relationships with more than one being at a time. If this encroaches upon what you have with Rion, I apologize. It is not the Tolkish way to cleave to only one partner."

"No, it's my way as well." I blinked, trying to process. "Rion and I don't share a bed. I'm more a thorn in his side than anything else—an irritation," I explained, when the human metaphor did not translate.

"Oh, my friend, I think you should look again." Alecto laughed softly.

I took his slender hand, marveling at the contrast of our skin in shade and texture, gentle lavender against sand. His long fingers wrapped around mine.

"I would like to explore what it means one day as well," I confessed. "But we should continue this conversation another time and place. I'm … a mess. I don't think I'm ready for it yet."

"When you are," he said, "you know where I can be found."

———

Less than an hour later, the sun burned between cloud and sea, a silver line against the horizon. I shielded my eyes from the gritty wash as *Thunder Child* lifted from the ground and soared away, her volatile but currently peaceful passengers tucked into the cargo hold. The sound of her engines faded as the ship passed through the morning mist.

The sudden quiet created an unsettling atmosphere. It was just me, the satavi, and a score of dead Darizh family troops with the headless Lady herself. I had no idea who might show up next; if Queen Xahria's soldiers would arrive first, or some other rival. The scent of the battlefield hung thick in in my nostrils. I retrieved the last few water rations, shooing away the curious gray creatures who investigated the pack holding the nutrient bars, and found a shady place upwind of the stink to await the arrival of whichever matriarch's army decided to visit today.

The satavi had watched the departure of their enormous genetic cousins from the safety of the trees and the crannies of the derelict facility, and only now emerged from their hiding places. I dug one of the ration bars out and crumbled it, broadcasting the pieces and watching them scramble to snatch up the bits of food. Instead of fighting over them, the satavi shared the crumbs and waited politely for me to scatter more. Their eager, greedy begging for additional snacks tickled against my empathic nets and made me smile despite my growing apprehension. They got another nutrient bar.

I looked up at a skyward whine of engines: a small, unmarked ship made a slow recon circle over the palace grounds. The pilot made several passes over the area before veering away, and the sound of heavy motors became evident at ground level. I hoped they were friendly. Until I had line of sight, it was impossible to know.

I took cover in the crash site to watch their approach. Weapons discarded in the Shontavians' hasty exodus were stacked within the shade of the wreckage, but I didn't arm myself yet. I'd sent the other guns back with my team. If I had a weapon in my hands, they might shoot first and identify later.

The first heavy vehicle turned into view. Armored soldiers leaked out of every turret and dripped from the ladders. I breathed a sigh of relief to see it followed by the reinforced limousine we arrived in before everything went to hell. I emerged from shelter and limped my way down the street, my hands open, arms wide to show I held no weapon.

Queen Xahria's black-armored guards poured into the road. Khus dismounted from the vehicle and glared at me through the open visor of his helmet. His expression was puckered and even more sour than usual, a pulse rifle held close against his body. Moments later, the armored transport opened, and a golden flash spilled out the door. Lam Tiri's excitement sent crackles of electricity racing ahead of him and triggered a wide smile of my own. Not far behind him, Gor unfolded his turquoise-furred self from the vehicle and walked at a more sedate pace, his mind touching mine with love and relief.

"Dalí!" I suddenly had a double armful of fuzzy Ferian diplomat. I staggered back on my gimpy leg, wincing with a laugh and a hiss through my teeth.

"Whoa! Not up to getting tackled at the moment. I am glad to see you too."

"You are injured?" Tiri pulled back and went stiff with dread, his gaze searching the abandoned wreck. "Where are Commander Sumner and Minister Sim?"

"Safe," I reassured him. Then Gor was with me, and our breath and minds mingled as he rested his forehead against mine. The tension which had knotted my muscles for two days drained from my body and left me almost dizzy with relief. Rescued—more or less.

"This is the result of your lauded negotiation skills?" Khus accused me, his suspicion lobbing darts at my empathic nets. "What happened here?"

It was all I could do not to punch him in the face. Anger leapt in a blaze that burned through the leash of diplomatic restraint I held on my tongue. "Before or after you abandoned us, Lord Khus?"

Khus's countenance darkened with my furious jab.

"Steady, my friend. There are things you do not yet know," Gor murmured, his mental plea for caution damping the fire in my chest.

"Prince Razaxha's safety was my primary concern," Khus answered stiffly. "Had I allowed the queen's heir to be kidnapped or killed, my life would have been the price." He smiled at me without warmth, bared teeth glinting in the sunlight. "Forgive me, but your life does not hold the same value."

Asshole. I glared at him until Gor's gentle nudge against my mind reminded me to breathe.

"Briefly, what happened is this: my security officer was taken hostage and seriously injured by Lady Darizh and her troops with the ransom demand we turn the Shontavians over to her as the rightful Queen of Urset." I gestured at the battlefield. "They said no."

"Queen of Urset?" Something faltered in his righteous fury, but it surged back. "You lie. The Shontavians had no weapons capable of inflicting such damage." He stabbed an accusing finger at the now-defunct missile battery. "Where are they?"

"I managed to get a message out from the communications system in the wreckage before the power died. A Remoliad vessel came to our rescue when Lady Darizh's troops attacked. We took the surviving Shontavians into protective custody. The ship reentered the atmosphere a little more than an hour ago and evacuated everyone else."

"You are babbling, Ambassador. A teller of tales." Skepticism glinted in the red aura of wrath as his stare came to rest on what remained of Lady Darizh, and I sensed a cool splash of what had to be relief. He returned that cold, glittering regard to me. "You spoke to someone yesterday, and they were not from the Remoliad." He invaded my personal space for a menacing whisper. "I knew his voice. Tell me who it was."

"I have no idea. They heard my broadcast and answered." My answer encompassed a glib lie, but the implication of Khus's question pissed me off. "You received my distress call, and you did not respond?" Bastard. What game was he playing?

"Who was it?" he demanded, ignoring my accusation. "For whom are you working?"

"Shall I ask you the same question, Lord Khus?" Angry, starving, filthy, and tired of Khus's shit, I had no more fucks to give. "You don't seem surprised about any of this."

I chose the wrong time to be flippant. His knowing sneer matched the crest of dark, satisfied triumph in his empathic broadcast.

"I warned Queen Xahria the Remoliad would seek to gain their own advantage." He leaned in close, his breath hot in my face. "I know with whom you spoke, and who taught you *haya* fighting. You planned all along to betray us to the traitor Nazhir, and you gave him the Shontavians."

"I did not—" A backhanded blow from his armored hand rattled my teeth and sent me stumbling backward against Gor's furry bulk. The coppery taste of blood filled my mouth and catalyzed an explosion of white-hot rage. I was in half a stance, ready to take Khus on even with my bad leg until Gor's hands enveloped my shoulders and pulled me back, his mind touching mine and pleading for calm as soldiers leveled guns at us.

"I will not listen to your lies. You will be held accountable for these actions." Khus swept me with a withering glare. "You will be judged for espionage and acts of hostility against Ursetu sovereignty." He motioned sharply to his men. "Take the ambassador back to the queen's estate."

Armed warrior caste troops surrounded us, faceless and threatening.

"Ambassador Tamareia will go quietly," Gor promised. He lifted me into his arms and carried me to the transport. Tiri's emotional broadcast held fear and confusion as he loped beside us in our ring of guards. "You must remain calm, Dalí," my crechemate whispered. The fluting Zereid language echoed the reproach in Gor's mental touch.

"I'm not hurt enough to be carried," I snapped.

"I wish to ensure you do not provoke him further."

He knew me too well. Gor placed me inside the armored limo. Despite being pissed as hell, I slid gratefully into the cool paradise of the windowless battle limousine, dim to my light-dazzled eyes. I lay my head back against the cushions and uttered a heartfelt prayer of thanks to the gods of air-conditioning as Tiri and Gor took their places beside me. An armed, visored soldier climbed inside, taking the rearmost, shadowed seat and holding a weapon ready across their lap, attention riveted on us with cold concentration.

"All right, what the hell is going on?" I asked wearily. All I wanted was a bath, food, and sleep in no particular order. It seemed fairly certain I wasn't going to get them.

"A full-scale civil war has broken out on the mainland, and yesterday morning, the queen was attacked in her own chambers by one of her guards," Lam Tiri said gravely.

"What?" Shock coursed through me. "Is she all right?"

"She is. The guard Rhani was wounded defending her, but she will recover." Gor paused. "Lord Khus declared martial law as head of the warrior caste. The queen and Prince Razaxha are all but under house arrest by his orders, ostensibly for their protection, but one has to wonder."

"You're fucking kidding me. How is Razaxha taking this?"

"He is angry and alarmed, as are we," Lam Tiri said bitterly. "Razaxha is receptive to diplomatic solutions, and he has his own mind about how things should be done. He is being ignored. Khus claims he is contaminated by the Remoliad." A wave of worry followed Lam Tiri's bleak statement. "I fear for them."

I let loose with a string of bitter curse words in three languages, each one questioning Khus's parentage. "Queen Xahria told me there is no loyalty in him."

"On the contrary. There is ardent devotion to his caste," Gor corrected me. "He sees Queen Xahria's consideration of Remoliad membership as an extremist view, a threat almost as dire as the uprising on the mainland. He will do desperate things to preserve this way of life. I sensed he was not entirely surprised to see Lady Darizh here but relieved to see her dead."

"Darizh had a long-term plan to take the throne, but Lord Khus didn't strike me as a plotter, just a prick," I muttered, glad to hear Gor's reading of the encounter matched mine. "Prince Nazhir hasn't been on the planet for at least four years, so why is Khus convinced he is behind the revolt on the mainland?"

"Can you say with certainty he is not? You do not know him." Gor's eyes elongated into narrow ovals, the Zereid version of a cautioning finger to the lips, and his mental touch reinforced the notion. The guard's attention was focused on our conversation.

"You're right. I don't," I said at last. The exiled prince was already here, somewhere. It was none of my business what he was up to.

My mission had been completed. Now we had to get off the planet in one piece.

Trusting in normal channels to provide a means of escape seemed a long shot. This was Urset. I had technically committed more than one crime, and I doubted Khus would consider diplomatic immunity.

I might have to come up with another way to get my friends out of here. A messier, less civil way.

CHAPTER
TWENTY-SEVEN

SOLDIERS RINGED us in a halo of guns as we were marched into the ziggurat. To my surprise, we weren't immediately confined. Khus stalked directly to the queen's council chamber. Sentries stood watch outside and glanced at each other, uncertain what to do as their erstwhile leader charged ahead. He ignored them and did not wait for permission, the door slammed wide by his forceful entry.

Seated at the head of the table, Queen Xahria sharply raised her head, a bewildered Prince Razaxha standing to the right of her chair. Lady Aneszai spun around, startled, her hand going to the knife at her waist.

"What is this, Lord Khus?" the queen asked. Her voice held a crackle of warning.

"I warned you against placing your trust in the Remoliad. They are bent on our assimilation into their control disguised as peace." Khus slammed his open hand on the table. "Ambassador Tamareia has committed acts of espionage, murder, and conspired to betray Urset. The Shontavians were removed from the planet this morning."

"Murder? What happened?" Xahria's calm surprised me, though perhaps it shouldn't have. This was Urset, after all.

"Lady Darizh is dead," Khus spat. "A battle took place yesterday while we were dealing with the insurrection here."

"Is it true?" Razaxha lifted his head.

"Lady Darizh was killed by the Shontavians." I stepped in front of Gor and Lam Tiri, a shield between them and Khus. This was my mess, and if I had any say at all, my friends would not suffer for it. "Queen Xahria, did you receive a message from me?"

Her brief smile told me what I wanted to know. "Just this morning. Thank you for the messenger," she said, but her expression cooled. "My intentions did not change. I am opposed to off-planet relocation." She rose and came to stand before me. "Am I to understand you disregarded my last instructions regarding the Shontavians?"

"I did. Minister Sim and I felt it necessary to take them into protective custody and ensure their safety."

"Why?" The ring of demand informed me no matter how grateful Queen Xahria was, she was not happy with my actions.

"We discovered they were subjected to experimentation and ongoing torture by Lady Darizh and the Pilean drug cartel. Illegal compounds were manufactured on board the facility and tested on the Shontavians." I paused. "The alpha told us Lady Darizh conditioned them for the objective of your death. She engineered the crash scenario which they purposely failed to carry out."

A fluid curse of disbelief from Lady Aneszai punctuated the revelation. I provided a summary of Darizh's assault on our negotiations and her subsequent execution before I knelt clumsily before the queen, stifling a gasp as my injury shrieked a complaint against the new stretch. "Full responsibility for these actions should fall on me. If there are consequences which must be faced under Ursetu law, I surrender myself to your judgment and respectfully request Brother Gor and Lam Tiri be allowed to return to the Remoliad. They had no part in this." My voice strained against the hot iron searing my thigh. Xahria noted my distress.

"You are in pain, Ambassador. Be seated."

The trick was standing again. I wasn't sure I could do it without swearing in front of her. Gor, unasked, helped me rise. Easing into the chair once occupied by Lady Darizh, I appreciated the irony.

The queen returned to her throne. "Lord Khus, what proof have you against Ambassador Tamareia in your charge of espionage?"

Khus straightened. "Our orbital monitors detected three unauthorized ships invading island airspace over the last day, none of which displayed a Remoliad identification code. One of those ships participated in the battle at the crash site. The ambassador stated they contacted a Remoliad vessel from the facility, but I intercepted that communication. They spoke to no member of the Remoliad. It was Prince Nazhir." He drew himself up in arrogant conviction. "I know he has been supplying the casteless on the mainland with weapons to rise against us. I believe they turned the Shontavians over to him, my Queen."

"Really?" The deep, amused voice sounded from the Queen's inner chamber. "Where are they, Khus? In my pocket?"

It was not Rhix who emerged from the other room. Prince Nazhir stalked into the chamber.

He wore his hair longer than when I last saw him on the Market ship, tight black curls hiding the spiral recesses of his aural canals. Black-on-black embroidery glistened on his tunic, geometric patterns chasing each other around the cuffs, collar, and hem. His full lips were set in a cold, familiar smile, his muscular body taut with coiled energy. In his alter ego, he would have sent the Simish aboard the Market ship scurrying in anticipation of bloodstain removal.

"You dared to come back," Khus growled.

"I returned at the request of my Queen," Nazhir countered, a dark warning in his tone. "Ambassador Tamareia was charged to find and communicate with me. Not an easy task, as I did not wish to be found." His bronze gaze flickered over me and away. "They made a distress call as I arrived, which I answered and relayed."

"I am in your debt, Prince Nazhir." I said quietly. "Your message to that ship saved our lives."

His voice took on the familiar princely arrogance I remembered. "When we spoke, you did not mention stealing the Shontavians as part of your plan."

"We did not steal them, Prince Nazhir. We offered asylum, and they accepted." I folded my hands on the table in front of me in a plea for clemency and directed my speech to the queen. "During the time we spent with them, Minister Sim and I came to realize these Shontavians are unique in both their genetic makeup and their social constructs. They have a spontaneous aspect of culture which was not instilled by the simulations, and a reverence for the stars, which holds spiritual meaning for them. These are fully sentient, functioning beings who suffered trauma. They deserved to choose their own fate."

The queen listened attentively, her head cocked, and Razaxha's eyes grew round with wonder. Xahria considered my words, her hands steepled at her lips.

"Your dilemma was understandable." Her disappointment lay heavy against my senses. "But they were my responsibility, and you did not give me the opportunity to make it right."

"I am sorry, Queen Xahria." I hoped the words conveyed my sincerity. "We did what we felt necessary to ensure their safety."

"You have proof of your accusations against Lady Darizh?" Prince Nazhir asked. There was nothing from him against my empathic nets except a wall of icy calm.

"Minister Sim has a holographic recording of the evidence, which includes Lady Darizh declaring herself queen. We also took the memory core from the laboratory." I mentally kicked myself in the ass for not thinking that part through. "The ship will be in dark space by now. Copies of the data can be transmitted as soon as we are able to contact the ship."

"Where are they bound?"

"Forgive me, Prince Nazhir. For their protection, I decline to reveal their destination."

A bright burst of anger sparked and died against my senses when I refused to tell him. His emotional broadcast returned to a controlled, careful state, giving nothing else away.

"You realize all concrete evidence to prove your accusation is conveniently on board a vessel bound for a location you will not disclose." His eyes met mine in challenge. "You are in jeopardy. Justice is swift on Urset. It may not wait for truth."

I had no hint of his intentions. My knowledge of where he had been for the last few years might be something he wished to keep secret. An execution might work for him.

"There is still physical evidence in the wreckage," I corrected. "Someone could search the sixth level. Minister Sim discovered cases of drug vials, preserved organs, the dead Pileans, perhaps other pertinent clues he did not see. We did not have enough power to investigate the conditioning programs, and that memory core should be intact."

Only the two of us existed in the room, our gazes locked. All else faded into the periphery as we engaged in a silent battle between my need for him to believe me and our mutual knowledge I was, indeed, a proven liar.

He turned away from me at last. "Your judgment, my queen?"

Xahria's cool regard measured me. "Insufficient proof

exists for espionage. Disobeying my command and removing the Shontavians from our planet carries its own penalty. Under the circumstances, I will classify it as a crime of conscience. You will be expelled from Urset."

An unexpected wash of relief showed me how vague I had been about the consequences, but it was temporary. She continued, "However, until we receive copies of your evidence, you are confined under guard. The murder of a ruling caste matriarch carries a penalty of death, Ambassador. For your sake, I hope the evidence is as clear as you state it is."

"I understand, Queen Xahria." I knew the evidence would exonerate me, but not having it at my fingertips was a nerve-wracking prospect.

"As representatives of the Remoliad, Brother Gor and Lam Tiri may stay to facilitate your defense. In these uncertain times on our planet, I will not require them to remain with us afterward."

"If he is willing, I would ask Tiri to stay." Razaxha glanced hopefully at the Ferian. "His counsel will be invaluable as we try to heal the rifts on the mainland."

"I will resign from my appointment in his favor, if it is his wish and yours, Queen Xahria," I said, glancing at Tiri. "He will serve you and the Remoliad with honor."

Tiri's pride flowed in sunny rivulets, clouded by his fear for me. The Ferian bowed his golden head to one foreleg in a formal obeisance.

"It would be my pleasure to stay, Prince Razaxha." His tawny eyes glinted with purpose.

"I will remain until the ambassador is cleared of the charges," Gor said. "Someone has to keep Dalí out of trouble."

I fought to keep an appropriately somber countenance. The queen began to say something more, but before she could speak, Khus exploded.

"My queen, I cannot serve you if you refuse to heed my warnings about the Remoliad and Prince Nazhir."

"Easily solved." Nazhir moved to stand behind the Queen's throne. "The queen asked I take my place as regent head of the warrior caste. And so, I shall."

Khus's rage burned with the white fire of a star, so intense Gor and I both flinched when he spoke. "You left your rank behind when you abandoned Urset. I will not relinquish the role to a casteless traitor. I challenge you, Nazhir."

Nazhir's face went dark and still, the room silent with shock as Khus continued, "I know you purchased weapons aboard the Shontavian Market for those mutinous animals on the mainland. I think the Ambassador was also on board and met you there when they faced the Shontavians." His perceived triumph spilled out in flecks of spittle, landing like acid upon the tabletop. "I demand contest by *haya*. Death will determine who leads the warrior caste."

"Do not do this, Khus," the queen whispered.

"It is our way." His desperation clawed against my empathic nets, near panic at the thought of an altered world.

"Am I to stand here and watch my uncles try to kill each other?" Razaxha interjected, his young voice strained with emotion. "I will not allow it."

"You cannot stop it, Razaxha. It is my right by tradition and caste." Khus drew the dagger at his waist. "Come, Nazhir. Let us see who the goddess truly favors."

My familiarity with his moods and the flaring heat of his emotional broadcast showed Nazhir on the edge of a decision based on anger. He struggled against it, fists clenched tight against his sides. The odds were slightly in Khus's favor: he still wore battle armor, where Nazhir did not. If I assessed the risk, he certainly was calculating the same things.

"I seek no fight with you, Khus."

"Coward." Khus's breath hissed a reptile warning, and

Nazhir yielded to anger, the overflow of red-hot magma against stone. He glanced at his mother.

"My queen?" It was almost an apology.

"Do what you must." A flicker of her fear brushed my mind.

Nazhir stripped off the constricting tunic, now bare to his waist. He had more scars than I remembered, the umber planes and valleys of his torso corded and powerful.

"Take my weapon, Prince Nazhir," Lady Aneszai said and drew the blade, holding it out hilt first. The prince took it from her with a brusque nod of thanks and flipped the knife from hand to hand, testing its sharpness and balance.

Gor's dismay grew thick in my mind as the guards hastily ushered them out of the open space where only days ago, the queen's own challenge had happened. We exchanged a glance as he and Tiri came to stand beside my chair, his unblinking, quicksilver eyes large and luminous with concern. My peaceful brother's heart ached for both Ursetu, bound by tradition to violence. Lam Tiri's golden features held trepidation, but he displayed a resigned gravity. The Remoliad had no place in this argument, no matter how deadly.

The two combatants faced each other. Khus raised his dagger. Light ran in near-liquid drops along the honed edge, and with teeth bared, he beckoned Nazhir to make the first move.

Nazhir struck with the coiled ferocity of a snake. Khus blocked the blow with an armored forearm, deflecting the test strike and sweeping away. The combatants circled each other for the span of a breath and Khus struck at Nazhir's chest. Nazhir parried, caught the other Ursetu's wrist in his free hand and delivered a punch to the face with the fist wrapped around the knife's hilt. Khus stumbled backward. Righting himself, he spat blood on the floor, glaring at his opponent. They scribed an arc of blades, testing defenses, and I heard the sharp intake of Nazhir's breath as Khus's dagger swept against his naked forearm.

A jab at Khus's upper leg; he trapped the blade only millimeters from where his thigh plate gapped at the groin, and they panted over each other's crossed forearms as Nazhir twisted Khus's wrist backward until he roared. He swung the prince away from him. Nazhir rolled over his shoulder and came back up in a lithe, sinuous movement.

Blood dripped from his forearm as he took a defensive stance, his attention never straying from Khus. The older Ursetu came at him, enraged, his blade darting in and nearly evading Nazhir's skillful blocks. Another stalemate as each tried to overcome the other's strength, the room silent except for the sound of their contest. Blades shifted back and forth until Nazhir suddenly went to one knee. The abrupt change of position sent Khus off-balance. Nazhir twisted his body and rolled Khus to the floor, ending up on top of him in a move that was not from the Ursetu playbook.

It was *zezjna*.

Gor's wonder echoed mine as Nazhir disarmed his opponent and tossed the dagger away, the edge of his blade at Khus's throat. "Yield," he demanded.

"I will not," Khus rasped. "Do not leave me alive, or I will haunt your shadow until you pay in blood for your treason."

"You would rather die than change your ways?" Nazhir panted.

"There is no other way for me," Khus said hoarsely. "Quickly, my prince."

Nazhir looked to the queen, who nodded once. Gor turned away, his sorrow poignant as the dagger did its work. Lam Tiri snarled, his distaste for the act at odds with his understanding.

Khus's resentment against a changing world crumpled, slid down my empathic nets, and died with him.

CHAPTER
TWENTY-EIGHT

CONFINED to my room under guard, the queen allowed me to send an urgent request for proverbial bail money to Sumner on *Thunder Child* and an official mission report to the security council. By now, Alecto must have notified them of what we'd done, but he had no knowledge of the charges I faced. I informed the Remoliad of my Ursetu *persona non grata* status, the murder charge, and the transfer of the ambassadorial position to my junior attaché, Lam Tiri of Feria. Delegate Prinoya was going to love that part.

I didn't have official permission from anybody to tell Mom about the stolen human DNA or how the Pileans used those experiments to tailor illegal chemicals aimed at human consumption. I told her anyway. Unless the Pilean representative got paid by the cartels to look the other way, the Remoliad's war on drugs had a new front in Sol Fed.

Afterward, the guards took away my personal devices and the subspace gear. The latter they gave to Lam Tiri, his by right now.

House arrest was still more fun than the detox procedure, but not by much. A Simish doctor arrived to care for my leg. She cleaned out the wound and packed it with antibiotic gel to keep an abscess from forming. After another dose of meds to ward off the bacteria still circulating in my bloodstream, she pronounced me fit for space travel. The guards permitted me to walk outside in the courtyard once a day, but only because the doctor insisted on it.

Lam Tiri and Gor were allowed to visit me each day in an official capacity and assured me they were working through diplomatic channels to procure my release, but after four days, Tiri still had not received any files or messages from the team. I started to worry something had happened to Sumner and Alecto aboard *Thunder Child* and wondered how long it would be before the sand ran out of my hourglass.

I didn't want to die. That development gave me a macabre fit of the giggles.

Near sunset on the fifth day, I lay on the bed, stared at the ceiling in contemplation of jailbreak, and wondered if I could incite a satavi mass riot as a diversion with only the power of my mind. Four of the little beasts sat on my windowsill and gazed in with mournful eyes, begging for snacks.

A firm knock on the door startled all of us. The satavi scattered, and I sat up. "Yes?"

"Ambassador." The rich tones of Nazhir's voice sounded from outside. "I would speak with you."

My pulse surged with nervous energy as I stood. I'd both dreaded this moment and hoped for it, a stressful dichotomy of emotion. "Of course, Prince Nazhir. Please come in."

He stepped into the room, the vigilant guard close behind. He considered the Razeha tapestry for a long moment and spoke at last in a wondering tone. "It has been five years since I was in this room. I am not accustomed to asking permission to enter my own chamber."

"This is your room?" The group-sized bed should have given it away.

"My suite," he said mildly, and crossed to the window. "I took other lodgings until your departure."

"I'm sorry. I am willing to move."

"It is of no consequence. Your presence here is appropriate." There were layers to the statement, but they could not be unpacked under watchful eyes. Nazhir gestured to the door. "Walk with me, Ambassador." A dagger lay strapped against his thigh. I got no sense he planned to use it against me, but the idea this might be a final walk flitted through my head, a remnant of one of those ancient gangster movies with the Cthash siblings. To the guard, he said, "I will take responsibility for the ambassador's supervision."

"Yes, my prince." The guard straightened to attention as we exited the room. Nazhir led me through a second room and down one of the stone staircases into the courtyard. We walked in silence for a few moments.

"You are healing well?" he asked.

"Yes. Thank you."

"Have you been down to the sea since you arrived?" His manner remained stiff and formal.

"No. There hasn't been an opportunity."

"Then we shall walk there." He signaled to the guards atop the tower. The inner courtyard had another flight of stairs set into the lowest level of the ziggurat, our footsteps echoing loudly as we descended the dark tunnel of volcanic rock. We emerged into the face of sunset, Urset's white star descending into the embrace of the gray ocean.

Guards detached themselves from their posts and paced a dozen meters parallel to us on either side as we walked down the sloping, forested hill. The night creatures of the rain forest called out to each other from the treetops and added an eerie counterpoint to the symphony of wind and sea. The location was a good choice, unlikely our conversation would be discernible over the noise.

The ground beneath our feet changed from vegetation, to stone, to a crescent-shaped beach of black sand. We stood at the edge of the water, the tide foaming just centimeters away from our boots. The sentries took up posts atop the rocks which sheltered the cove.

"You left on your own terms." I veiled the statement out of caution.

"Did you fear I had died?" Sarcasm rode the wind, sharp like the cold sea spray.

"Yes, if you want the truth."

He fell silent a moment and then said, "Three things altered me in ways I could no longer ignore. First, I rediscovered the value of loyalty. I chose my own successor."

"Please tell me you picked Simish."

He laughed quietly, his eyes on the sea. "The power behind the title, yes. The face who wears it, no. There are certain appearances which must be upheld, or chaos will ensue. For instance, if word were to spread the dreaded Lord of the Shontavian Market made philanthropic art donations to reputable galactic museums simply so he can see the pieces again, I believe it will be the end of his fearsome reputation."

I grinned as he went on. "But the Market will continue to thrive as it is. The darkness behind galactic civilization continues to grow, and I can no longer take part in that which destroys.

"My second discovery was despite my efforts against it, I somehow managed to develop a conscience. It is inconvenient." He turned his fierce scowl on me. "I will answer for too much when I walk with the goddess. I cannot continue to add to the transgressions I already bear."

"What made you decide to return home?"

"Information runs ahead of shadows. Things are happening here upon which my new conscience demanded I act. When I learned of Arzalat's death, I was already prepared to return."

"Khus believes you are supplying the casteless with weapons."

"Lord Rhix is. Perhaps he mistook me for him. I heard we bear resemblance to one another."

Startled by the blunt admission, I gave him a sharp glance. He watched me with inscrutable eyes, one brow lifted in challenge.

"What was your third discovery?" The wind dragged a wild tendril of hair across my face. Nazhir's hand reached up to smooth it back before he corrected himself in perplexed irritation.

"You changed me." The words were an accusation flung at me like a blade. "For good or ill, I am not the same as I was before I knew you." His jaw tightened. "I do not know whether I should thank you for it. It has been a painful process, and I am still angry. But I think, one day, I would like to know the real Dalí Tamareia." His expression grew thoughtful as he watched the sun sink into the sea. "They seem to be a great deal like someone to whom I owe a life debt."

"You owe nothing. It was repaid twice over."

"You do not understand. It is never repaid." His attention returned to me, countenance fierce with gratitude. "Each time I draw breath, it is one I would not have taken, save for you. I will remember."

Chemistry surged between us, as wild and uncontrollable as ever. Change hormones threatened to erupt in ways which, had the guards not been watching, would have had him pinned beneath me on the sand in a glorious tangle of naked limbs. Damn it.

"I was wrong," he said, his gaze searching mine.

"About what?" My voice cracked against the effort of keeping my impulses at bay.

"Your eyes. They are not the color of smoke and ashes, but of the sea at dusk."

He turned quickly back to the mountain, now blanketed in twilight, and we walked back toward the ziggurat. "Ambassador Tiri received the files and recordings an hour ago," he said. "You are absolved of the charge of murder. A transport will arrive before dawn to convey you and Brother Gor to a Remoliad vessel and then back to the hub."

"Thank you." I cleared my throat, but no more words would come.

In silence, we climbed the dark stairs back to the courtyard. My guard waited there, watching vigilantly for our return, and fell in a dozen paces behind us as we retraced our steps to the door of my room. The weight of so many things I could not say was a stone in my chest.

"Until we meet again, Ambassador." Nazhir bowed his head to me at last. I returned the gesture. His gaze held mine a moment longer before he turned away.

CHAPTER
TWENTY-NINE

KICKED off the planet in my first official capacity as an ambassador. Under the circumstances, I called it a win.

We were bundled into the ship without ceremony the next morning before daylight. None of the royal family attended to say goodbye, but the queen's personal Simish served as a witness to me getting my ass off their planet.

Lam Tiri came to bid us farewell. He stood on his hind legs to touch his forehead to Gor's as they murmured good-byes. I returned his vigorous cheek rub, and Tiri's warm, furry temple rested against mine in a moment of gratitude.

"Thank you for this opportunity, Dalí. I will do my best to perform the office as efficiently as you would have done."

I laughed softly. "I have no doubt you will do better, Tiri. I never intended to make this a permanent appointment, but I can see that in your future. You and Razaxha have a bond. He needs someone who will work in Ursetu's best interests as well as the Remoliad's." I paused and added, "For what it's worth, I know you can trust Prince Nazhir."

"Yes, I think so." Tiri's golden eyes crinkled at the edges. "He told me your recommendation was enough for me to earn his confidence. You did not say you had met Prince Nazhir before."

"I hadn't." I smiled at Tiri's quizzical head cock and put my hand on his shoulder. "The stars are yours, Tiri. Good luck."

With my data device back in possession, I pulled up my personal search engine as soon as we rose from the surface. A quick scan of the news for any mention of Alecto or our mission brought up nothing. That was a good thing. The Shontavians would be much safer without leaks to the media. The holo shifted to other bytes gleaned from galactic news sources, and I skipped over things that didn't interest me. Then, without intro, dark eyes lined in cosmetic enhancement and brilliant white teeth bared in a ratings-winning smile: the one and only Kiran Singh beamed at me from the display on the briefing file. I groaned aloud.

"The dramatic rescue from the Shontavian Market of Dru Goldstein and Kai Anderson captured the attention of Sol Fed last year. The identity of the mysterious "Gresh," the third-gender operative who infiltrated the Market to liberate them, remains a mystery." He leaned forward, flashing a conspiratorial smile. "And in case you're listening, we need to talk. I have something you definitely want to hear."

"Yeah, fuck you," I muttered and flicked the file off my screen. Singh's popularity had only been increased when I sent him my evidence files against Batterson Robotics, one of the financial giants funding the New Puritan Movement's more militant arm. Singh brought down the former president with the truth of his family's crimes. But I had learned the NPM was every bit as evil as Kiran claimed it to be. All he said had been correct.

Shit. I might actually have to contact him.

My crechemate and I were in constant companionship for the trip back to the Zereid hub. He would return to the mountains and his students while I went on to the Remoliad for debriefing (read: ass chewing). It would be some time before Gor and I saw each other again, and I didn't want to waste a moment. For once, we didn't talk about my problems. We reminisced about our childhood in the temple school and laughed about the trouble we caused together. Gor had grown into serenity, whereas I was still … not. But my heart was lighter, and inevitably, he noticed.

"It is good to see you laugh again, my friend."

"I think the antidepressant nanos Dr. Muus added to the detox cocktail are working." I waved it away, but he persisted.

"No, it is something else. For the first time since Gresh and Rasida died, I see hope alight in you once more." His hand stroked my head.

I bit my lip and debated telling Gor about the small flutter of excitement I got in my stomach every time I thought about Alecto. Different from the all-consuming sexual chemistry Nazhir and I had, it was more like the feeling after my first date with Gresh. A sense of …

Possibility. A future.

And, confusingly, the same thing happened when I thought about Rion.

I decided to keep those revelations to myself and offered Gor a smile instead. "Yes, I have hope."

He drew me into an embrace, and I relaxed against him, reveling in the close affection of chosen family, Zereid style.

I tried not to think too much about what awaited me at the Remoliad. I didn't look forward to the debriefing with the security council. The possibility I tarnished my mother's reputation by virtue of our relationship was the only regret I carried. She'd sent me a quick message via Tiri before we left:

• • •

You did the right thing. Glad to hear you still have all your appendages. Give Alecto my regards, and hug Rion for me. I am camping out on Delegate Lapahslo's doorstep until I get answers from him about the Pilean situation. I love you.

An hour before our arrival at the Zereid hub, I put on a diplomatic uniform for the last time—again. A sudden flashback engulfed me, back to the day I dressed to leave Gresh and Rasida at Luna Station. The sensation of her fingers as she fastened the clasps on my tunic. Gresh's hands resting on my shoulders as we met each other's gazes in the mirror. The sharp, detailed memory was like a benediction, a promise all would be well.

They would never leave me.

"My friend?" Gor sensed something, his voice a breath of wonder.

"I'm fine. It's all good." The tears cleansed instead of burned.

Not long before we docked at the Zereid hub, an enormous Burkani officer in Remoliad grays lumbered up to me. "Ambassador Tamareia?" he grunted, a wet spray emanating from his upturned nostrils.

"Yes, Lieutenant?"

"Your orders have changed. You are to disembark here and report to Commander Rion Sumner." He stomped away as abruptly as he'd come.

"So, you are off once more." Gor's musical sigh was melodramatic, but his mind brushed mine with playful humor.

"I guess so." My relief I wouldn't have to face the proverbial firing squad was mixed with trepidation.

The minute we stepped off the transport, my implant alerted me to an incoming communication. Sumner's voice sounded in my head. "Sorry to cut your goodbyes to Gor short, but we need to talk." His voice held a strange note. "Meet me in the bar on level one."

"Acknowledged," I said, my brow furrowed.

Gor touched his forehead to mine, mingling breath and affection. "Safe journey, my beloved friend. Visit me soon."

"Until we meet again, brother, my love goes with you."

Reluctant to let him go, I clung to him a little longer, breathing in the earthy scent of his fur. Gor didn't pull away until I did.

I found the bar, an anonymous alcove frequented more by ships' crews than travelers. Garishly colored holographic advertisements touted manufactured alcoholic beverages. Sumner waited for me at a secluded table, his expression grim. His face still bore the green and yellow shadows of bruising, a half-healed laceration above his right eye. He watched my approach, the stiffness in his posture betraying anger. My first thought was *What did I do now*?

"Sumner?" I wasn't certain I wanted to know what he had to say.

"Sit down."

I hefted my bag into the chair and sat. Sumner had already ordered two glasses of synthetic whiskey from the robotic bartender. He slid me one of the drinks.

"You're going to need it," he said roughly.

"What the fuck is going on?" I had a sudden sense of fear. "What happened?"

"We got played." Sumner toyed with the drink in front of him until he finally met my concerned regard. The pain in Rion's blue-green eyes hit me in the chest. "Alecto."

"What?" Confused disbelief crowded out my other emotions. "What are you saying?"

"He's gone. Vanished. So have the Shontavians."

My mouth made shapes without sound until a strangled "How?" forced its way between my lips.

"The Zereid contacted us this morning. He acted as

liaison between the Shontavians and their government. Yesterday, he flew to the remote area where they were being kept isolated until we could prepare a ship, saying he was going to check on them. He didn't come back." Sumner knocked down a slug of whiskey. "The Zereid went to investigate and recovered his short-range skiff, but no Alecto, no Shontavians. They found signs a large craft landed there and evidence the Shontavians were forcibly removed. Subsequent investigation showed an unauthorized vessel made entry in tandem with his ship. Once they left the atmosphere, they went FTL. There's no way of knowing where they are now."

Denial still beat a steady drum in my head. "You're sure he hasn't been taken prisoner?" I swallowed heavily. "Or killed and consumed?"

"Oh, yeah. I'm sure." Sumner reached into his jacket and pulled out a PDD, tossing it on the table between us. "They sent us a message." He threw back the rest of his drink and stood, taking my bag with him. "We're on dock six. As soon as you're on board, we're leaving." He stalked away, paused, and said over his shoulder, "We can get drunk once we're underway. I think there is just enough whiskey left for both of us."

The device waited. I did not want to touch it, as if the PDD were something dead and putrefying. I dragged it toward me and toggled the screen.

Alecto's visage looked out from the display, calm and achingly beautiful. He appeared to be on a ship, dim figures moving behind him among blinking lights and consoles. "Hello, Rion. I could not leave without a goodbye to you and Dalí. I am sorry. I know this will come as a shock. I promise Naru and the others are in the best of care.

"It is strange, but if circumstances had been different, I might have found a home with you in the Penumbra. Like you both, I possess a gift for playing roles. Well enough to pass as a mercenary captain fifteen years ago and more recently, to infiltrate the Remoliad as an idealistic politician."

He tapped the band on his forehead. "It is easy to fool even Zereid telepaths with a little help from my *riesh*. They respect the mind's privacy and do not push. The *dreshmalahar*, alas, is all too real. There is only so far I can run from what I did on Amanosk, and it will never be enough to outrace the memories. I think you both understand the harm we do to ourselves in the course of duty. When my *riesh* sustained damage, I feared you would see through me, Dalí. I had come up with a way to distract you by feigning attraction. But in the wreckage, I found I am truly moved by you and no longer needed to pretend. I am sorry. Waking in your arms that night was unexpected and lovely. I know we spoke of exploring what it meant, but I will be more difficult to find now.

"I wouldn't hold up under Brother Gor's scrutiny without the *riesh*, but I managed to leave the planet before I saw him again. Ra'sho kindly repaired the broken connections before we reached Zereid.

"The horror is part of me now, but I was fortunate to meet someone who helped me find beauty in the chaos. It is no small wonder I fell in love with her, Rion. She is much like you in many ways."

He leaned back and a woman sat in his lap. Pale skin, white blonde hair, eyes like ice-blue diamonds. At first, I thought she was a Nos.

"Hello, brother dear."

Cold fire raced through my gut, the taste of metal in my mouth.

Miriam Skadi spoke in Sol Standard, her accent graced with the faint drawl of the Europan colony. "It seems a little incestuous now that I think about it. But Alecto tells me you've moved on, so I hope you don't mind." She waved into the camera. "Dalí, hi. Kaisa sends her love and says thank you for the warning. The drug cartel is starting to get on our employer's nerves. You just did us a favor, and it worked out so much better than we could have hoped."

Fuck.

"If you ever get tired of the whole galactic love fest, we could use somebody like you. I was there for the emergency session at the Remoliad. It would have been a great time to make a statement, but I got so caught up in things I forgot. Oh."

She leaned in closer to the camera and solemnly whispered, "I'm sorry about your family."

The screen went dark. I shoved the PDD in my pocket and sat there, stunned.

I missed being numb, sometimes. What coursed through me now threatened to consume me from the inside, acid eating away at my heart, my nerves, my brain.

I'm sorry about your family.

A taunt? Or a threat?

She had been at the Remoliad. Alecto knew my mother.

I was up and running for dock six before I allowed the thought to fully form, pushing my way through disgruntled travelers, blind to everything but the thought of getting to the ship. I pounded down the gangway docking *Thunder Child* to the hub, past the startled eyes of my crewmates, and straight to Sumner's ready room. He looked up, alarmed, at my wide-eyed panic.

"My parents—"

"Damn, Dalí, I didn't think." He quickly stood and came around the desk. "They're safe. The minute we heard the message, we contacted the Remoliad. They swept the station for threats and tightened security."

Tremors wracked my body. Sumner put his hands on my shoulders, and I sagged against him, my breath coming in short gasps. Fucking panic attack wouldn't let go, my upper body muscles shifting and sliding beneath the skin in a hormone cascade.

"It's all right. They're safe," he murmured. His arms went around me and held me tightly. "I'm so sorry. I didn't think."

I clung to him as if he kept me anchored in zero gravity. Gradually, my trembling subsided. My breathing slowed, and the change hormones ebbed from full boil to simmer. "How soon can we get drunk?" I managed.

"After we go FTL, we get shitfaced." His voice rumbled against my ear.

Now I was calmer, the fact he hadn't released me yet began to sink in. So did my awareness of his muscular body under the shirt. My head rested against the beat of his heart, a little too fast and too like the rhythm of mine. Change hormones still raced through my bloodstream, and my body responded to his nearness. Parts of him began to react, too, our bodies too close together for either of us not to notice.

"Dalí," he began.

"Okay, are we ready to … " Ozzie entered the doorway. As Sumner and I both looked up, Ozzie's eyestalks swiveled. "Whoa. Sorry." He pivoted and walked back the way he came, muttering, "About time."

Sumner released me and stepped back. "You okay?" he asked brusquely. His color was high, flushed all the way to his hairline.

"Yeah. Good." I swiped my eyes. "See you at oh-drunk-thirty, Commander. Where are we headed?"

"Ka'pth and Ra'sho completed their analysis of the new drug. It contains commensal bacteria tailored to the human neuroendocrine system."

"What does that mean, exactly?" It didn't sound good.

"It means the Pileans found a way to spread addiction like a disease. Theoretically, it can be passed on to human offspring."

I stared at him, aghast.

He paused. "We're going back to Sol Fed."

The information absorbed slowly. We were going back to

our native system. Both Sumner and I had renounced our citizenship for our own private reasons. It was where I'd experienced my greatest happiness and my darkest moments.

"We have to know if the new drug has found its way there and then cut the head off the cartel's supply line. Any idea where we should start?"

"Rosetta Station. The Labyrinth." I took a deep breath. "And I might know just the asshole who can help us."

GLOSSARY

Glossary of Terms

Third-gender
An intersex human being, usually with a dominant set of male or female reproductive organs.

Changeling Third-gender
A genetic mutation within the third-gender population, these individuals possess neither male nor female gonads and are incapable of reproduction. Their anatomy has specialized hormonal glands, which allow them to assume at will the secondary sexual characteristics of a male or female. They possess a vaginal-like organ without a cervix or uterus, and spongy, nerve-filled tissue in the mons, or pubic area, which can become internally or externally engorged. When externally erect the mons can serve the sexual function of male genitalia.

The Penumbra
A covert agency attached to the Remoliad, responsible for

gathering intelligence and investigating violations of galactic law.

The Remoliad Alliance

A local galactic coalition similar to the United Nations, which facilitates trade, diplomacy, and aid to the member planets. It also enforces galactic laws.

Shontavian Market

A black market on board a starship which remains in constant motion through the galaxy to avoid authorities. Dealing in illegal weapons for sale and trade, the Market derived its name from the sale the genetically engineered creatures called Shontavians, bred solely for fighting wars.

Sol Federation "Sol Fed"

The united colonies within the solar system that originated from Earth's survivors: Luna, Mars, and Jupiter's moon, Europa. Each colony has its own militia and governor. The citizens of the solar system elect Senators and a President to determine federal law.

Zezjna

A philosophy of peace through empathy developed by the Zereid, a highly empathic/telepathic species. The term is also used to encompass a non-lethal defensive martial arts style that relies on empathic senses as well as physical skills.

Enemies and Allies

All the races depicted here are bipedal unless otherwise noted, humanoid, and oxygen breathing.

Andari

A diminutive, ichthyoid species. They live in groups led by a female alpha. Members of the Remoliad.

Cthash

A reptilian species from an arid planet system. The Cthash are born in trios. Each set of siblings is comprised of a male, a female, and an *ix*. The *ix* gender is required for mating purposes and produces an enzyme that allows the hard-shelled eggs of the female to become temporarily porous for fertilization.

Members of the Remoliad.

Ferians

The collective tribes of a feline-like race, covered in short fur. They walk on two or four limbs. Remoliad members.

Kadrelians

An oxygen-breathing species with multiple tentacles used for walking and manipulation. One of the original members of the Remoliad.

Nos Conglomerate

A starfaring race that has plundered less developed civilizations for thousands of years. Opportunistic pirates and mercenaries. Genetically, they are closely related to the human race and are nearly identical in physiology. They are not allied and take advantage of any other system not affiliated with the Remoliad.

Shontavians

A bioengineered race created by the Ursetu solely for fighting wars. Physically resistant to small arms fire, they possess four arms of equal dexterity. Though only the "alpha" line speaks, they are highly intelligent and possess strong telepathic abilities.

Simish

Both a species name and a designation, all members of this Ursetu-engineered species are called "Simish". They serve the Ursetu ruling caste and are well educated in medicine, aesthetics, business, and culinary skills. They are no more than 1.5 meters tall.

Pileans

An insectoid species. Family groups of the same brood share identical forehead crests and tend to engage in the same enterprises. Members of the Remoliad.

Ursetu

Another race similar to humanity in appearance and genetic traits, the Ursetu possess a strictly divided social hierarchy: the ruling caste, the warrior caste, and the casteless. Their planet created and sold genetically engineered creatures for servitude and battle for thousands of years. Newly allied with the Remoliad.

Tolkish

Lavender-skinned humanoids, one of the original members of the Remoliad Alliance. Prone to physical beauty due to the symmetry of their features and slow, graceful movements.

Zereid

A highly empathic/telepathic race. The species is bipedal and covered in short blue fur. They are skilled in diplomacy due to their ability to sense emotion. Primarily pacifist in nature, they have developed a non-lethal martial arts form for personal defense and all serve time in their military, which defends when necessary, but primarily offers compassionate aid to other planets. Members of the Remoliad.

Glossary of Characters

Alecto Sim
Minister of the Remoliad Security Council, from Tolkis. A member of the diplomatic team sent to Urset.

Lady Aneszai
Councilor to Queen Xahria, High Matriarch of Urset.

Princess Arzalat
Crown Princess of Urset, now deceased. Mother of Prince Razaxha.

Dalí Tamareia

Former Ambassador turned undercover operative. A third-gender changeling.

Lady Darizh
Head of the Shontavian engineering program and councilor to Queen Xahria.

Gor
Dalí's Zereid creche mate (blood brother). A large bipedal humanoid from Zereid.

Gresh—Andrew Gresham
Dalí's late husband. A human rights solicitor.

Kaisa
Overseer of an illegal mining operation on Bariish.

Lord Khus
Regent head of the warrior caste and councilor to the Ursetu Queen.

Ambassador Marina Urquhart
Dalí's mother. Former ambassador to Zereid, now Sol Fed Delegate to the Remoliad. Ambassador Urquhart is a female-dominant third-gender human.

Naru
Alpha Shontavian with whom Dalí is sent to negotiate.

Prince Nazhir
Exiled son of Queen Xahria, whom Dalí knows as Lord Rhix.

Captain Paul Tamareia
Dalí's father. Former commanding officer of Rosetta Space Station, retired.

Lord Rhix
An Ursetu mercenary, head of the Shontavian Market.

Rion Sumner
Commander of the *Thunder Child* and its team of undercover operatives. Dalí's C.O., he is a human/Nos hybrid.

Sida—Rasida Gresham Tamareia
Dalí's late wife, pregnant with a child who possessed genetic material from both Dalí and Gresh when she was killed. A genetic research scientist.

Simish
A small humanoid, genetically engineered for servitude.

Skadi
Miriam Skadi, a galactic terrorist Dalí believes responsible for the bombing which killed their family. Sumner's half-sister, a human/Nos hybrid.

The Crew of the *Thunder Child*

Ossixiani clan Sustrix – "Ozzie" – a Cthash pilot, second in command. Male reptilian. One of three siblings.

Tommizax clan Sustrix- "Tommi" – a Cthash medic and communications officer. Female reptilian. One of three siblings.

Zigoxanian clan Sustrix- "Ziggy" – a Cthash weapons officer and engineer. Ziggy is *"ix"* – a Cthash third gender which provides an enzyme critical to allowing a male and female to fertilize eggs for reproduction. One of three siblings.

Ka'pth and Ra'sho – a mated pair of Andari. Intelligence officers.

Melos- a Nos engineer and navigations officer.

Lam Tiri

A Ferian interspecies negotiator and a member of Dalí's diplomatic team.

Queen Xahria

High Matriarch of Urset, head of the ruling caste.

ABOUT THE AUTHOR

E.M. (Elisabeth) Hamill writes adult science fiction and fantasy somewhere in the wilds of eastern suburban Kansas. A nurse by day, wordsmith by night, she is happy to give her geeky imagination free rein and has sworn never to grow up and get boring.

Frequently under the influence of caffeinated beverages, she also writes as Elisabeth Hamill for young adult readers in fantasy with the award-winning Songmaker series.

She lives with her family, where they fend off flying monkey attacks and prep for the zombie apocalypse.

E.M. Hamill: Words that Bridge Worlds

facebook.com/EMHamill
twitter.com/songmagick

ALSO BY E. M. HAMILL

The Dalí Tamareia Missions

Dalí

Peacemaker

Third Front

Nectar and Ambrosia: An Amaranthine Inheritance Novel

Writing as Elisabeth Hamill:

The Songmaker Series

Song Magick

Truthsong